Missionary, Mercenary, Mystic, Misfit

J.

Evil Genius Publishing, LLC.

Evil Genius Publishing, LLC.
Copyright © 2013 by J. All rights reserved.

ISBN: 978-0-9893659-1-8

No part of this publication may be reproduced, distributed, or transmitted in any form or by any means, including photocopying, recording, or other electronic or mechanical methods, without the prior written permission of the publisher, except in the case of brief quotations embodied in critical reviews and certain other noncommercial uses permitted by copyright law. For permission requests, or other inquiries, contact the publisher at **evilgenius.pub@gmail.com**.

Cover photograph by the author in Bur Amina, Ethiopia, 2012.

Missionary, Mercenary, Mystic, Misfit

Special Thanks & Acknowledgements

To Fiona for once again enabling my writing addiction and putting up with my aid work habit. Or maybe it's the other way around.

To Shotgun Shack for being such a good friend and blogging partner, and for so graciously allowing me to continue to reap the benefits of being part of *Stuff Expat Aid Workers Like* while essentially taking a break from life to write this book.

To Bethany, Melody, and Dean for their generous assistance with editing and formatting, and for generally keeping me honest.

To my awesome beta readers: Amy Ellis, Amy Knorr, Carly Sheehan, Christina Milner, Erica, F. Zehra Rizvi, Faith, Francisca Vigaud-Walsh, Janine, Johanna, Kathleen McDonald, Kristen Straw, Lady Amelia, Linda Raftree, Lindsey Talerico, Maria Lopez, Monica Curca, Naveen Srivatsav, Teresa Plana, @ximenacontla, and The Clandestine Literary Chicks of Kampuchea (CLICK).

Thank you for your encouragement, suggestions, and honest critique, even when it was (sometimes) painful to read. This book is far better because of you, and I will always be grateful.

To aid workers of all stripes everywhere for providing so much awesome novel-fodder.

Obligatory Disclaimer: *Missionary, Mercenary, Mystic, Misfit* is a work of fiction. All characters and situations portrayed in this story are fictitious. Any similarity between any of the characters in this story and real-life people, or between situations in this story and real-life situations, is entirely coincidental and unintended.

"A persistent and exclusive focus on the 'other' obstructs more open and necessary debates on the role of aid workers. Such academic invisibility allows popular and misleading stereotypes of aid workers to flourish; more pertinently, it hinders honest appraisals of the experiences of aid work and its challenges."

– Anne-Meike Fechter

"Because if there is one law that all vampires hold sacred it is that you do not tell mortals about us."

– Anne Rice

"In Africa a thing is true at first light, and a lie by noon."

– Ernest Hemingway

Chapter 1

The first lone donkey of the night brayed abjectly in darkness somewhere in the general direction of Somalia as Mary-Anne eased the white World Aid Corps (WAC) Land Cruiser to a stop in front of the Oxfam car park just outside Dolo Ado, Ethiopia.

It had been a long, difficult day, and she was dying for a lukewarm shower and maybe an equally lukewarm bottle of St. George before retreating for the night to the solitude of her tent. Maybe she'd get lucky and be able to sponge a few minutes of Wi-Fi from the WFP V-SAT in the adjacent compound for a scratchy Skype call to Jean-Philippe in Nairobi. Trying to sleep would be pointless. Between the oppressive heat, the donkeys that brayed all night long, and general stress, Mary-Anne knew that no matter how many hours her eyes were actually closed, she'd wake up the next morning feeling exactly the same: exhausted, un-refreshed, her mind unable to focus.

And so, while the thought of another meeting was annoying in general principle, in the grand scheme of her life right then, another thirty-to-forty minutes with the relief director of Oxfam America before heading "home" to her tent a few compounds away was not that big a deal. Mary-Anne showed her ID badge to the uniformed guard at the gate, drove through, and parked next to a massive pile of green plastic jerry cans. Oxfam's office—a large, square tent—was easy to pick out, and she walked quickly toward it through the gathering darkness.

Her thoughts were fraught as she shuffled through the dusty car park. Most of all she thought of Jean-Philippe, a logistical world away in Nairobi. He'd followed her there from Haiti so that they could "be together." But the aid world, and the life which inevitably accompanies it, was taking its toll. After eight months of living in the same flat, they'd barely spent as many weeks simultaneously at home. Now here she was, not even six months into what would almost certainly be a year-long assignment in Dolo Ado.

Tomorrow Jean-Philippe would be off to somewhere else. Western Kenya, maybe. Or Khartoum. Or a life-saving workshop in Zanzibar.

And here *she* was, going to a work-related meeting that in any "normal" profession would be well after hours, rather than talking to the love of her life for the last time before he went off-grid for the next two weeks.

"Hello!" she called from the dangling canvas door to the Oxfam office tent. "It's Mary-Anne from World Aid Corps, here to meet with Jonathon Langstrom." Her voice was tinged with a hint of affected annoyance.

"Come in! Come in!" boomed a voice from inside. "I've been expecting you."

The air inside the tent smelled of canvas and Jumbo Mat mosquito repellant, and in the green flickering light she could make out several small desks littered with In/Out baskets, laptop computers, and small fans. A large camel spider scrambled over a jumble of power cables at her feet. A small air conditioner rattled pitiably in a side window. And deep in the far right corner, his face illuminated only by the pale light of the monitor facing him, sat Jonathon Langstrom.

"Jon. Jon Langstrom…" he extended his hand as he stepped around the small desk and over a LAN cable. His grasp was as warm, his eyes as piercing as Jean-Philippe's had been *that night* back in Haiti at the Port-au-Prince logsbase. But there was no sardonic sneer or growling French. Jonathon Langstrom spoke perfect American.

"Nice to meet you, Mary-Anne. Please, sit down. I know it's late—thank you so much for coming at this hour. I promise not to keep you long."

He motioned her toward a wobbly desk chair before sitting down himself.

"I'd offer you a beer, but it seems we're all out." He nodded ruefully in the direction of a small mini-fridge in the corner. "I promise to make it up to you at Billy-Bob's before I leave town. You know how it is with relief workers. *Impossible* to keep beer in the fridge." A smile tugged at the corners of his mouth.

As she sat, Mary-Anne could see that he was not large or rugged. 5'8", *maybe* 5'9", medium build, neatly dressed in faded jeans, a button-down shirt, and plain brown loafers. Neatly cropped brown hair and oval wire spectacles framed a chiseled jawline and deep brown eyes. On the dance floor at Jet Set, Jonathon Langstrom would have faded into the background, overshadowed by younger, trendier, rakishly good-looking aid workers. But here in the dim light and sweltering heat he was handsome and—she felt herself flush—even magnetic in a quiet, unassuming way.

The bashful young girl with the Samaritan's Purse rucksack outside Store Blue seemed a world away. Without even the hint of a stammer, Mary-Anne returned his firm handshake. This had to be one hundred percent business.

"What can I do for you this evening, Mr. Langstrom?"

"Jon. Please call me Jon." He sat down opposite her, his right foot balanced casually on his left knee.

"As you know, I'm one of the new guys in town. Just got into Addis two days ago, landed here just this morning. And for now I'm trying to meet all the players and get the lay of the land as quickly as possible. Some guy from GOAL just left. Before him it was dinner with someone from UNICEF."

Another donkey brayed, this time in the general direction of town.

Jon Langstrom continued, "And now here I am with you, but no beer in the fridge. My staff tell me that you're the one worth talking to over at World Aid Corps. I'll be sitting in coordination meetings with your chief of party soon enough. Maybe even tomorrow. But if you're okay with it, I'd like to get the skinny directly from someone who by all accounts is a little closer to the real action."

His dark, intense eyes twinkled slightly. "So here's your big chance. Bequeath some wisdom. What do I need to know about the interagency relief operation here in Dolo Ado?"

Her mind wandered briefly back over the previous four (or was it five?) months, and she suddenly found herself wishing she had a Cedric Menthol. Not to smoke, necessarily, but simply to have something to fiddle with.

The refugee crisis response thus far was not exactly been stellar, but not for any particular reason. Sure, there were the usual problems with funding. For all of the platitudes coming out of the upper echelons of the UN and for all of the furrowed-brow coverage on CNN, BBC, and even Al Jazeera, there was, comparatively speaking, precious little flowing toward the Horn of Africa in the way of resources needed for the relief response. 100,000 or so refugees was a lot and there was clearly a need, but even so, spread out as the Dolo Ado complex was over five current camps, it all lacked the visual impact of a single massive squalid camp, like Dadaab. As a result it was exceptionally difficult get Dolo Ado on anyone's radar screen, let alone keep it there for very long.

As if resource scarcity wasn't enough, there was the problem of finding *people*. Competent, experienced, *not clueless* people to run projects, write reports or grants. In short, staff who knew what they were doing *and* who would stick around.

The sticking around was the hard part. There was nothing even remotely interesting or pretty about Dolo Ado. It was just a barren, grimy border town with nothing in it to do, and where madness, if not actual death, from sheer boredom loomed an omnipresent and very distinct possibility. Local Ethiopians as well as expats would spend a short time and then try to get transferred to somewhere, *any*where else, as soon as humanly possible. The local government was not particularly obstructive, but then again they weren't particularly helpful either.

Even so, the scared, too-skinny, intense, chocolate-colored Somali refugees were *still* crossing the border into Dolo Ado, Ethiopia at the rate of something like seventy-five people per day.

It was the classic humanitarian nightmare. More specifically, it was a brewing chronic crisis with no foreseeable end, marginal media visibility, and almost zero fundraising potential beyond a few token, guilty government grants from the predictable cast of characters: USAID, ECHO, maybe AusAID, *may*be JICA. The government of Ethiopia, led primarily by ARRA (Administration for Refugee and Returnee Affairs), would grudgingly support a response. The international community would probably not intervene in the crises in Somalia beyond minor, also token, one-off incursions, and even that only *maybe*.

These people—the refugees in Ethiopia— Mary-Anne knew, were basically screwed.

Jon's voice forcibly jerked Mary-Anne back to the reality of the moment.

"… And what's going on with that fifth camp, Bur Amina? Is ARRA going to actually open it, or not?"

Chapter 2

Mulu Alem gave the pile of coarse, limp papers on his desk a last good shuffle, checked his cell phone (no new messages), pushed back from his rickety wooden desk, and stood up.

He sighed heavily. It had been a long day for him, too. He had seen the predictable steady straggle of haggard, un-ironed NGO expats, the slightly less wrinkled UN expats, and their translators—usually too energetic, too well-coiffed, barely-out-of-university Addis Ababans. They all wanted more or less the same thing: permission for something, a visa for someone, a stamp of approval on a strategy, a sign-off on a proposal, more help from ARRA.

He sighed again, dejectedly.

Dolo Ado was a *total dump*, the edge of the universe for someone like Mulu Alem. Two hundred and thirty-seven days, thirteen hours, and more or less ten minutes into his assignment, and he was already dying for his next trip back to Addis (fifty or so minutes, eleven hours, and another eight long days into the future). Annoying, over-indulged Somalis were flooding across the border in seemingly endless supply, only to sit around in one of the four existing refugee camps, texting relatives back across the border, and getting fat (it was all relative) on WFP rice, camel milk, and/or smuggled pasta.

Mulu Alem hadn't attended four excruciating years of graduate school, learned English, and indefinitely put on hold an engagement with the lovely, willowy, ebony, doe-eyed Aster for *this*.

A large flying insect was trying its best to knock itself silly on the single flickering fluorescent tube mounted high on the wall as Mulu Alem checked his phone one last time purely out of habit (still no messages), turned off the light, and stepped into the short, grimy hallway.

The train of expat humanitarian workers was only part of it. Mulu Alem's real task at the moment was to report back to Addis on the feasibility of opening yet *another* refugee camp. Bur Amina. It annoyed him that this was even part of his job. Allow the refugees or don't allow them. This was a decision for someone much, much further up the hierarchy. And if the decision was to allow them, then live with the consequences of an inexhaustible stream. That was the natural order of things. It wasn't like Somalia was ever going to say, "Okay, Ethiopia—we've given you enough." It wasn't like the drought was going to end any time soon, or Al Shabaab was going to relent. Refugees were going to keep coming as long as the border was open. Everyone knew it as surely as no one wanted it.

Mulu Alem was in the impossible position of having to "make the decision" that everyone knew was *fait accompli*, but that everyone also knew was a career death sentence once made. No one in Addis wanted more Somalis in Dolo Ado, just as everyone knew that Ethiopia would play the "good Samaritan" in the eyes of the international community. Internally, though, it would be turn into a "slay the messenger" scenario.

And Mulu Alem knew that *he* was to be the messenger.

* * *

Brandon smiled to himself as he ordered his second 50 CL "blonde" at the Beer Garden Inn.

He was drinking German beer (beer and cars should always be German) in Ethiopia. He'd managed to get the last seat on the last UNHAS flight from Dolo Ado to Addis, it was only 7:00 p.m. on a Friday night, and his first work-related appointment wasn't until 10:00 a.m. on Monday.

His WAC computer and cell phone were locked safely in his room just a few hundred feet away at Hotel Kaleb, his wallet was full of Ethiopian birr and U.S. dollars, and sixty or so hours before he had to be anywhere. A weekend's worth of possibilities stretched out ahead of him.

Sure, Addis Ababa wasn't exactly Bangkok. Heck, it wasn't even San Salvador. But still, there were far, *far* worse places to go "down periscope" for the weekend. And for the evening, at least, everything Brandon needed was in the large copper vats visible behind the bar.

He lifted the tall glass to his lips and inhaled the malty aroma before taking a long, deep drink. No point in sipping.

This was the life.

Brandon was so engrossed in his beer that he hardly noticed the lithe young woman slide onto the barstool next to him. He turned in surprise when she spoke.

"What are you drinking?"

Brandon chuckled in the silence of his own head. Anyone could see that he was drinking beer. She was obviously chatting him up. It was a maneuver he'd seen in more local bars in more countries than he could specifically recall.

"I'm having the blonde," he smiled pleasantly. The buzz of round one was starting to take effect.

"Blonde?" The shapely young woman wrinkled her nose theatrically.

"Yeah, blonde," Brandon replied. "Blonde *beer*. They have two kinds here. Blonde and brown. I'm having the blonde." And then without even thinking, he added, "But I love *brown*, too." He gave her an exaggerated wink.

The young woman was getting hotter by the second (part of the effect of round one). She put her hand to her mouth and laughed. Her beautiful, dark eyes danced. "You're very funny. Where are you from?" She laughed again.

Either she really thinks I'm funny, or she's better at faking it than most.

Brandon swiveled on the barstool to face her directly and took another pull from the glass in his hand. Only about one-third left. The sun was totally set by now, and it was dark outside. The restaurant was beginning to fill up, but he and the pretty young woman were the only ones at the bar. The ambience—the din of the room, the warm lights, and the rich dark wood—were cozy and comforting. His beer buzz was intensifying, but Brandon knew that if worse came to worse he'd simply stumble back to Hotel Kaleb.

He also knew that the by now smoking hot young woman was trying to pick him up. But tonight he didn't care. He couldn't remember the last time he'd sat and actually had a conversation about something other than humanitarian work with an attractive woman who was not a humanitarian worker. All he'd do was talk. The words came out of his mouth, almost on their own.

"Let me buy you a drink, and I'll tell you all about where I'm from."

Chapter 3

Angie Langstrom was tired. *Very tired*. Against her better judgment, she'd attended the neighborhood moms' weekly coffee—an excruciatingly unenlightened two hours during which she'd feigned interest in conversation about second grade lacrosse, "special" dance, and PTA drama. Apparently being head mom on the PTA was an achievement of some distinction and importance in the eyes of the neighborhood moms, but Angie couldn't really bring herself to engage.

She'd done the aid worker thing right out of grad school, and then the aid worker accompanying *spouse* thing, and then the expat mom thing, and eventually the angry about schlepping around the world while being the only parent truly in the picture thing. And now she was doing the angry spouse essentially single parenting at home in North America while her professional aid worker husband wandered the hell holes of the planet for weeks or months on end thing.

Angie sighed. She *always* seemed to be tired. For as much as she'd longed for the normalcy, safety, and convenience of suburban North American life while living in Phnom Penh or Dakar or Pristina, the truth was that now that she was here, it wore her down. It bored her and wore her down all at the same time. The endless prattling about after-school activities with fleshy white soccer moms, the pointless angst about play dates and Halloween costumes, and the *weeks* of evenings of homework and baths and explaining why "Daddy"—Jon—wasn't there.

Angie let out a long breath as she poured a small glass of Petit Syrah.

"Daddy" was gone again. Ethiopia, this time, or was it Somalia? Not like it mattered, she thought bitterly. What was the difference, but an arbitrary, imaginary line through the dirt in a monotonous, godforsaken desert? Years ago Angie would have indignantly confronted anyone uttering such insensitive generalization, but tonight she thought the words with unabashed anger.

The Petit Syrah tasted smooth and dry.

1:00 a.m. Jon was probably at work. She thought about calling or texting to see how he was, but decided against it. Chloe, their only child was asleep. Morning and the inevitable accompanying tiresome whirlwind that was being the parent of a thirteen-year-old girl was a mere six hours away.

Mary-Anne woke with a start.

It was already bright outside, and the air inside her tent was already hot and stifling. She could hear the indistinct clatter of breakfast in the kitchen and the sounds of the World Aid Corps compound coming to life.

As she lay in the intensifying heat trying to summon the energy to climb out of bed and engage with the world, Mary-Anne mentally reviewed her to-do list for the day. It was pretty straightforward:

- 9:00 AM—general coordination meeting at the ARRA office. (It would be an hour of boredom, laboriously co-presided by Mulu Alem, the ARRA representative for Dolo Ado and whichever senior-ish UNHCR official was in town and hadn't strategically double-booked another "urgent" engagement.)
- 10:00 AM—endure a monotonous three-hour Land Cruiser ride to the Kobe camp where she'd monitor the progress of WAC's livelihoods project. (She'd spend six hours—three hours each way—either trying to make painfully difficult conversation with Mesfin the driver or Tekflu the site coordinator, or feeling guilty for listening to her iPod, to then spend just two hours of arduously translated conversation with beneficiaries.)
- 6:00 PM—Go to "Billy-Bob's"—the unofficial name of the official expat bar in Dolo Ado—and have a few room-temperature beers and maybe a cigarette with the WFP loggies.
- 7:00 PM—Curfew. Go back to the WAC compound. Maybe eat some actual food. Do email, maybe Skype with Jean-Philippe until…
- 11:00 PM—Fall fitfully asleep to the sound of donkeys braying soulfully in the distance.

Mary-Anne sat up, swung her feet around and onto the ground, stood up, arched her back, and stretched her arms as high as her tent would accommodate.

Small children across the Horn of Africa urgently needed her to attend the coordination meeting at ARRA.
Time to save some lives.

* * *

Jon Langstrom's pointer hovered briefly over the "sign in" button. He hesitated, then closed the window.

Why bother checking personal email? There wouldn't be anything, really, except perhaps a few messages from Angie. They'd be terse, cranky messages. Messages about issues that were totally not urgent. Message about issues they'd been over, and—at least in *his* mind—resolved. Or else issues he couldn't possibly address, at least not in any meaningful, concrete way, from Dolo Ado.

So why even bother? It wasn't that he didn't care. Truly. *He cared.* But caring in the abstract sense and making it through the day ahead in the concrete sense were two worlds apart. For the sake of simply getting through a difficult day of meetings and negotiations with competitors masquerading as partners, or a completely unmotivated host government, it was far better to *not* know exactly what was on Angie's mind. *At least for now.* Better to just say, "Sorry, honey. The V-Sat's been down....," or make some excuse about the time difference.

Engaging emotionally with Angie's anger at his absence, or Chloe's teenaged angst, or what*ever* else might be going wrong at home without him *this* time would not in any fathomable way help him get through the day.

And right now, more than anything else, what Jon needed was very simply to get through the day.

Getting through the day was what would keep Mark, his self-important blowhard boss, off his back for a little while. Getting through the day, by definition, would be a success for him, for the organization, and, if one was to be very imaginative, for the hungry Somalis coming across the border to Dolo Ado at the rate of one hundred per day. Or, if nothing else, getting through the day was what would keep his salary flowing, and the bills being paid.

And for all of her bitching and moaning about him being "gone all the time," even Angie could see the value in *that*.

Better to just not check email.

Jon sighed heavily and then stood up. He'd missed breakfast but he

didn't care, wasn't hungry.
    Time for the coordination meeting at ARRA.

Chapter 4

The air was hot and stuffy inside the large container that passed as the meeting room in the small ARRA compound on the outskirts of Dolo Ado. It was only 9:00 a.m. and already the heat was intense, the air conditioners were rattling, and the aid workers were sweating.

Mulu Alem cleared his throat importantly and called the coordination meeting to order.

He began with the obligatory introductions of new attendees: the bright young Ethiopian sitting in for the country director of GOAL; Mary-Anne representing WAC (Brandon—the chief of party was in Addis for meetings); a few new faces from some of the UN agencies. Otherwise it was the usual crowd of Plan, Save, IRC, and a new senior relief director from Oxfam America—Jonathon something.

After introductions, the discussion moved on to the updates: The Norwegian Refugee Council had struck rock digging latrines in Hilaweyn Camp. Cash for work was no longer an option, as refugees couldn't very well dig latrine pits through rock. Save the Children and World Vision were working together on something about uniforms for school children. WFP was continuing to make rice available despite refugees' clear and obvious preference for pasta. The majority of those in attendance remained silent. Nothing of real importance had changed in the last two weeks. The real reason people had come at all, Mulu Alem knew, was to hear the decision of ARRA on the possible new camp at Bur Amina.

The usual formalities, introductions, and updates were out of the way and the floor was once again Mulu Alem's. He adjusted his spectacles for effect and checked his cell phone for messages (no new messages) out of habit before standing up. He could feel the eyes of everyone in the room on him.

"Ladies and gents, as you know, refugees continue to come across the border from Somalia to the processing center here in Dolo Ado continuously. Last week alone nearly 1,000 came across and so far, this week, already more than 300 have come."

The room was totally focused on him. He adjusted his spectacles and fought the urge to check his cell phone for messages.

"And as you all know, the four camps we have now are insufficient. I tell you this truthfully. We cannot squeeze anymore into the camps we have. You cannot achieve your Sphere standards if we do this, and the Government of Ethiopia cannot look into the eyes of the world knowing we *could* have done more to ease human suffering but did not…"

The woman from GOAL coughed loudly. The young Canadian from Danish Refugee Council sitting next to her wrote furiously in his note pad. Mulu Alem glared at the woman from GOAL and then continued.

"Many of you have been involved in our participatory process for identifying the location of a new camp, and for this the people of Ethiopia will be forever indebted. Today it is my utmost pleasure to announce to you that we will open a wonderful new camp at Bur Amina to accommodate another 15,000 Somali refugees…"

The silent focus of the room began to give way to a low muddled murmur of expat aid worker voices and shuffling papers. He cleared his throat loudly.

"Ladies and gents, if you *please*…"

The murmur subsided slightly.

"We will open Bur Amina camp within two months. Let me know within one month if your organization is interested in being cluster lead, and for which sector in the new camp.. Any questions?"

The room erupted into open discussion as several hands shot up. Mulu Alem checked his cell phone once more, slowly, deliberately, this time for effect. No messages. He looked around the room slowly, enjoying the fervor his announcement had clearly caused before nodding at the pretty young program officer from CARE.

"Yes. Your question, please?"

*

Mary-Anne could see that the program officer from CARE was asking a question, and she could see that the ARRA rep was answering. But her mind was elsewhere. Another camp at Bur Amina would mean more work. It would mean establishing a presence in a new place, vying for sectors and zones. There would be the predictable onslaught of BINGO (Big International NGO) competitors snapping up sector lead roles and staking out their claims in the prime real estate of the new camp. It would literally be a fight over poor people.

And all of the smaller, lesser-known, poorer organizations like hers would be left fighting for the leftovers. Mary-Anne and many other aid workers like her would be left "filling in the gaps" or "serving niche markets," or a myriad other cleverly wordsmithed ways that meant picking up the scraps left behind by the larger, better-funded aid machines.

Chapter 5

One thing that Mark absolutely did not deal well with was ambiguity. He prided himself on being straightforward, straight up, no bullshit. Everything was, or *should* be, cut-and-dried in Mark's world. Most people, especially *aid workers* (for reasons he never really understood) made things far more complicated than they needed to be—more complicated than they actually were. No wonder the aid industry was in such disarray.

He grunted disapprovingly at the screen of his 13-inch MacBook Pro.

Mark had made his fortune in the delivery business. He'd started in college, charging his suitemates to move their stuff in his Toyota pickup. Through word of mouth, he'd acquired more business, and by the spring of his junior year, he hired a crew of five and rented a second truck. By the time he graduated a year later, he *owned* a second truck and had a crew of seven non-student full-time employees.

He scowled at the screen again. What was Jon Langstrom's problem?

Ten years, a Harvard MBA, a 2,000-employee delivery business that included a fleet of 150 semis and spanned three states, and a summer home in the Hamptons later, Mark had made enough to retire. He sold the business and moved to Boston to live a "simple life" with his wife (they had no children) in a quaint brownstone in Beacon Hill.

It only took about three weeks of early retirement for Mark to go certifiably crazy from the boredom. One could only play so many rounds of golf or detail one's Ferrari so many times or have so many martinis aboard one's yacht before one needed to actually *do* something. Mark was and always had been a *do*er. He needed a new challenge. And that was when his wife Catherine suggested he volunteer for a local charity. "Do something meaningful with your talents, honey. Give something back… *make a difference*," she'd said.

He started as a volunteer at a local homeless shelter, where it took all of about two months for him to work his way to the top, take over the operation, balance the shoestring budget, cut the "dead wood," properly train the staff and put in place a *real* charter before feeling bored again. Too easy. Mark still needed a challenge, but by now, he'd mastered the "give something back, make a difference, make the world better" parlance of a seasoned do-gooder.

Through a random series of connections at a hoity-toity Boston fundraising gala, Mark met the president of Oxfam America and worked his self-confident networking magic to the hilt. He might not know the details and nuances of global hunger or foreign politics, but there was no managerial, administrative or leadership challenge that he couldn't handle. He was a self-made man, the very picture of the American Dream. Business was business, the rest only details. If Oxfam America was looking for someone to actually *do* things, he was their man.

Another two months and he gave more or less the same speech to an executive search committee. Three days after that, they offered him the job of Chief Operating Officer of Oxfam America. The GB office took all the glory. People just *assumed* that all things Oxfam were *British*. There were wars and famine raging around the world, enough need to go around, and Oxfam America needed to make itself felt within the larger international confederation. Mark was the guy who would make all of that happen.

Which brought him to today, reading another melancholy email message from Jon Langstrom.

He'd sent Jon to Ethiopia with a simple task: Get the lay of the land in Dolo Ado, then find a place for Oxfam America to make its presence felt. Jon already had US $300,000 to work with. Yeah, yeah, play nice with Oxfam GB and the other NGOs, but basically *figure it out*. Mark was not going to let the Horn of Africa crisis come and go without planting a red, white, blue, and lime green Oxfam America flag somewhere in the vicinity. Puntland was out—no need getting abducted by pirates. Dadaab on the Somali-Kenya border sounded like a total nightmare, overrun by the UN and the comms teams of the other large U.S. charities.

But Dolo Ado was low-hanging fruit. Obvious need. Obvious gaps. How in the world was that ever complicated?

C'mon Jon. Don't make this harder than it has to be. Get in there and get it done.

Chapter 6

Most NGOs working the refugee camp circuit in Dolo Ado adhere to the 7:00 p.m. universal in-town curfew. In a place with high Ethiopian military presence, absolutely nothing for aid workers to do except drink in the evenings, a large refugee population, and the border of Somalia largely unmarked a mere two or so kilometers away, a 7:00 p.m. curfew just keeps things simpler all around.

Billy-Bob's was the official expat hangout in Dolo Ado because it was one of a very few (two at last count) establishments in town that would actually serve alcohol to foreigners. The place had a name in Amharic that no one ever bothered to learn once an IMC staffer dubbed it "Billy-Bob's" after the proprietor's large, outgoing male goat.

Billy-Bob the goat (almost certainly not his real name, although no one ever bothered to confirm that either) was famous for habitually making the rounds, greeting every patron with a head-butt before retreating to the branches of a tree in the courtyard. From that high vantage point, Billy-Bob would watch the UN and NGO expats drink tepid St. George beer and smoke Nyala or Rothams cigarettes (or maybe Duty-Free Marlboros if someone was just back from leave and felt generous), occasionally bleating or climbing down for a minute or two to greet newcomers, until curfew.

But beyond Billy-Bob and the fact that one could order St. George, Billy-Bob's (the restaurant) was unremarkable: A short walk through a dimly lit, low-ceiling dining room led to a grimy, fly-infested courtyard where cigarette butts and bits of beef gristle littered the bare dirt between tired plastic chairs and low, greasy tables—and, of course, the tree in the corner that Billy-Bob would climb, once he'd greeted all the expats.

That evening, as Mary-Anne walked through the dark dining room into the inner sanctum of Billy-Bob's she could see that it was more crowded than usual. Fifteen—maybe twenty—expats crowded around three tables chatting loudly. The aging American UNHCR registration coordinator was off in the corner as usual, casually smoking while holding an outdated cell phone to his ear, speaking in loud, broken French to his "girlfriend." The chunky, Serbian WFP warehouse manager, eyes already red, was slurring his way through one of his famous stories about Bosnia back in the day. The sweat-stained young Belgian from Save the Children was trying his best to chat up the pretty young program officer from CARE (the same one from the coordination meeting at ARRA). And the British guy running logistics for the Norwegian Refugee Council was busy teaching inappropriate English slang to two small local children with matted hair and clutching sachets of Plumpy'Nut.

Mary-Anne ordered a St. George from the young waiter and then looked around for a place to sit.
The only empty chair, she saw in a moment, was at of the farthest table, right next to Jon Langstrom.

"May I sit here?" She motioned to the chair as she approached the table.

As Jon looked up a look of genuine pleasure replaced his initial look of surprise. "Of course!" He had to speak loudly—almost shout—over the din of conversation. "Please, sit!"

He reached over and moved the chair slightly for her in a gesture that was more symbolic than practical. "Here, I've been saving the last chair just for you," His eyes twinkled, and Mary-Anne felt the same at-ease-while-simultaneously-slightly-weak-kneed pulse she'd felt when she'd first met him at the Oxfam compound.

Jon Langstrom continued, "And I'm pretty sure I owe you at least *one* beer."

Mary-Anne sighed and brushed a stray strand of dirty-blond hair from her face as she sat down next to Jon. It had been a long day of straining to catch every word, of trying to make sense of what she was hearing, of trying to understand and be understood. It had been a day of trudging from one hot tent or T-shelter to another, asking the same questions to too-thin, jet-black Somali women with scared eyes and crying babies. A day of hearing the same stories of hunger, fear, and uncertainty over and over.
It had been a day of looking obvious, objective human suffering squarely in the face and, at the same time, knowing that the most she could possibly offer was still a drop in the bucket.

She'd thought of Jean-Philippe for most of the three-hour ride back to Dolo Ado. Mesfin the WAC driver tried to chat her up about American movies, but eventually grown silent. Mary-Anne felt guilty for not engaging Mesfin in conversation, but at the same time grateful for the silence. It was a welcome opportunity to let her thoughts wander and watch the monotonous landscape out the window as the WAC Land Cruiser bumped along.

Jean-Philippe was somewhere—she didn't know where, exactly—on a consultancy with MSF. Maybe Juba. Maybe Kampala. He'd told her but she couldn't remember. She loved him, she knew, with every ounce of the intensity and passion she'd felt their *first* time at Dreams Punta Cana, or the night they'd listened from the shadows as the dance band played fast calypso at Mickey Martelli's inaugural party in Port-au-Prince. No, nothing had faded or diminished, Mary-Anne knew, but still, something was different.

She couldn't put her finger on it, but she knew that it wasn't him—it was *her*.

Jon's voice pulled her back to the moment. "Better take a sip of that beer soon. I see Billy-Bob eyeing it." He tilted his head in the direction of the large goat looking down at them from the tree in the corner. "Cheers!"

She clinked bottles with Jon and took a long pull. Then another. And another. The St. George was just okay. Better than Prestige. Not quite as good as Tusker. A fly buzzed around her forehead and she swatted it away.

"Tell me about yourself, Jon."

Asking someone to talk about him or herself was Mary-Anne's strategy for engaging without engaging. Almost everyone liked to be asked to talk about themselves. Get them going and Mary-Anne could socially coast for the rest of the evening.

"What do you want to know?" Jon's voice was pleasant.

"Oh, you know, what exactly do you do for Oxfam, where are you from, got a family? The usual."

She took another long pull of St. George. The bottle was almost empty, and Mary-Anne motioned to the young waiter.

"Well, let's see. I'm the relief director for Oxfam America. It's a mix of this—" He made an expansive gesture toward the darkening courtyard. "—front line stuff, you know, supporting ops, monitoring this and that. Then there's the strategic stuff—lots of urgent meetings in places like Singapore or Panama City. And, of course the usual soul-sucking spreadsheets and meetings of HQ." Jon took a long pull from the bottle in his hand, fumbled in his pocket briefly before pulling out a nearly empty soft pack of Marlboro Lights.

He looked apologetically at Mary-Anne. "Do you mind?" And

quickly added, "Deployment smoker."

Mary-Anne fumbled in her own pocket for her lighter and handed it over. "Obviously I don't mind." She laughed out loud without meaning to, straightened her hair (also without meaning to), and felt herself flush ever so slightly.

He held the pack out to her before laying it on the grimy table, deftly lit his cigarette, took a long puff, and continued speaking.

"I've been in the business, let's see, about twenty-nine, thirty years, the last ten with Oxfam. Before that a mix of other NGOs; some big, some small. I've lived in a few places—mostly Asia, but also bits and pieces in the Balkans during the '90s."

Another pull on the bottle, and a brief, troubling look that Mary-Anne couldn't quite identify before his face returned to normal, to the present.

"So, family. Got a wife and daughter. My wife was an aid worker when we got married. We met in a workshop in Mumbai. I was based in southern Laos; she was weighing babies for some UNICEF study in Nepal. We hit it off. Swapped R&R in each other's countries, and then started living together in the mid-1990s. We did Kosovo together, starting at more or less the same time that NATO stopped dropping bombs. You know, same house, different agencies. That was quite a time…" His voice trailed off for a moment. "We spent about two-and-a-half years in Kosovo together before moving to Dushanbe. We lasted about nine months there before deciding to return home to try out the traditional American Dream thing. That would've been in about 2003."

He drained the bottle of St. George and took a long drag from the smoldering cigarette in his hand.

"Since then, except for an eight month stint in eastern Sri Lanka immediately after the tsunami, I've mainly made the rounds of U.S.-based Headquarters roles and all that goes along with that."

The sun had fully set and the only light was from a few fluorescent tubes strung up at intervals around the inner courtyard of Billy-Bob's. Mary-Anne wasn't positive, but for a split second in the near total darkness, she thought she saw deep sadness in Jon Langstrom's face.

"But, anyway, here I am. Taking a brief vacation from reality in Dolo Ado. Wife and daughter at home in Boston. My daughter is thirteen." He paused. "I can't believe I have a teenaged daughter. There's justice in the universe, I guess." He chuckled self-deprecatingly, snuffed out his cigarette, and held the pack toward Mary-Anne once more.

"Enough about me. How'd *you* end up here?"

Chapter 7

Mary-Anne could feel the St. George beginning to take effect. It felt good after the day she'd had. She hesitated for a moment before accepting the cigarette from Jon.

"Deployment smoker? Is that what you call it?" For reasons she couldn't quite articulate Mary-Anne felt comfortable and safe sharing her story with Jon Langstrom.

"How'd I get here?" She paused to think. "I guess, when you come down to it, my story is not all that different from yours." She took a long drag and exhaled slowly. "I grew up in an uber-Christian, uber-conservative family in an uber-conservative town in southern Kentucky. Nearly married the pastor's son, then bailed at the last second."

Now it was Mary-Anne's turn to feel sadness on her face. Or maybe guilt. Or regret? Sometimes it was hard to tell the difference.

"Yeah, I was literally on a plane to Haiti the morning after the evening I broke off our engagement. He was a good man, you know? There was nothing wrong with him. But I guess that life, being the wife of a pastor, even a really *nice guy* pastor just wasn't the life I wanted."

Two more bottles of St. George magically appeared on the table, and Jon held one out to her. "Here. Cheers. Go on. So, how was Haiti for you?"

Mary-Anne took a sip before continuing.

"Six months ago, I would have spent an hour going into the detail of all the trauma and drama of Haiti. Beneficiaries rioting at distributions, the crappy conditions, the giardia, the stress. But now... I dunno. It's all kind of fading into the background of Dolo Ado. Haiti was Haiti. I spent a year and two months there with Samaritan's Purse. Some of it was great. Some of it plain sucked. *All* of it was hard. I still have nightmares of Haiti."

"Yeah, I've heard that The Haiti was tough."

Mary-Anne placed the cigarette in her hand between her lips and leaned forward toward the flame Jon held out for her.

"So... I don't mean to pry. The pastor's son didn't work out. What's the picture like for you now?"

Mary-Anne thought of Jean-Philippe, somewhere in eastern Africa, doing what? With whom? And suddenly it occurred to her that she didn't even know how to refer to him. *Fiancé?* They'd never discussed marriage. "Boyfriend" hardly seemed to do their relationship justice.

"Partner" seemed to fit about as well as anything. "I met my partner in Haiti. He was with MSF then, long-time MSF-er. Haiti took a bit out of him, though, and now he's sort of taking things slower, doing a bit of freelancing in the aid sector." She thought wistfully of their cute little flat in Westlands. The one they'd spent hardly two months in together before she'd shipped off to Dolo Ado.

"We live together in Nairobi," She chuckled, almost to herself. "That is, we share the rent on a flat in Nairobi, and occasionally we're there at the same time." She glanced at her watch. Almost 7:00, almost curfew. "I took a regional position with WAC for the Horn of Africa last April and then shipped in here about four or five months ago. We normally do three-month deployments, but I'm officially here 'indefinitely.'"

Maybe it was the cumulative effect of two (or was it three?) St. Georges, the fact that Jon Langstrom put her at ease more than almost anyone else she knew, or just the fatigue of the last two months that weakened Mary-Anne's resolve to stay reserved—to neither pry into the lives of others nor share details of her own life. But there in the darkness, under the benevolent gaze of Billy-Bob she heard the words come out as if on their own; words she'd scarcely thought, let alone spoken to someone who was all but a stranger. But as she heard her own voice speaking, apparently of its own volition, what she heard rang true.

"*That's* what I want—the family, the kids the house. And yet everything I see about this life makes it all seem so impossible."

* * *

Officer Endeshaw was tired and cranky. It was late. Too late. And the one thing he very much did not want to deal with just before his shift ended at 3:00 a.m. on a Saturday was another delirious, incoherent white guy.

The incoherent white guy had been brought in by two other officers, found wandering in a traffic circle, wearing only boxer briefs, carrying no ID or cash, and unable to remember his own name. As the senior officer on duty at the Addis Ababa central police station, it was Endeshaw's responsibility to deal with it. The white man was outfitted with a (gently) used prison jumpsuit and placed (gently) in a cell with a bottle of water. They'd wait for him to wake up, then maybe they'd figure out who the guy was and what to do with him.

Having done his duty to the best and fullest of his ability, Officer Endeshaw clocked out and headed for home and bed a mere forty-five minutes past 3:00 a.m.

It would be another three days before the incoherent, anonymous white man would come to.

Chapter 8

Mark had lived his entire life in preparation for a time such as this. The opportunity to show the world, or at least his little corner of it, that a good old work ethic and American values could make the world better. If there was a higher purpose in all of this it was for him to show those wishy-washy, Birkenstock-wearing, tree-hugging, liberal aid workers that, *no*, actually—it *wasn't* all that deep. Sure, global hunger was the result of complicated circumstance and all that, but the remedy—at least in the immediate term—was pretty straightforward.

If people are hungry, give them food.

Enough with the in-house road blocks. He was going to show that annoying wet-blanket Jon Langstrom what it took to make things happen.

He leafed quickly through the papers in his leather trim folio one last time. Printouts of the emails from Jon detailing the challenges—*all the negativity*—with scaling up Oxfam's food security and WASH programming in the Dolo Ado camps; projections from Marketing on fundraising potential, broken down by donor category; and quick analysis (thanks to his executive assistant) of Oxfam America's competitive advantage in the Horn of Africa.

It wasn't a particularly rosy picture. Oxfam was not as well-known as some of the other large competitors for its relief response capability, and protracted, complex humanitarian emergencies were all the more challenging. Moreover, Oxfam America struggled within the larger Oxfam international confederated network to remain viable and relevant operationally. The rest of the network, particularly Oxfam Great Britain, increasingly chose to view and treat Oxfam America as a primarily *fundraising* office. Milk the U.S. public for what amounted to chump change, plaster major U.S. airports with posters of brown-eyed children or slogans about how much difference a chicken makes, and recruit perfumed young staff, otherwise known as "charity muggers" (or sometimes "chuggers"), to hand out flyers in shopping malls during the holiday season. This was what the mighty Oxfam network expected of

Mark?!?

Please.

If a bunch of stuffy Brits wanted to sit around Oxford sipping tea, nibbling biscuits and publishing self-righteous papers on the sorry state of the humanitarian system, let them have at it. But Mark was about getting things done. He knew *how* to get things done.

There was *opportunity* in Dolo Ado. A new camp was being opened at Bur Amina, and if the flow of refugees from Somalia continued (as it almost certainly would), another one after that. Were the Swedes going to step up and take on more? Doubtful. CARE? World Vision? GOAL? Mercy Corps? They'd all be in the mix, of course, but none of them could do it all. There was space for Oxfam America. He just needed Jon to get in there and pee on a few bushes.

Mark ran quickly down the list of key facts and numbers one last time. The board of directors was waiting.

* * *

The global headquarters of World Aid Corps occupied a cramped third-floor space near the corner of N and 23rd in Washington, DC's trendy, happening Northwest quarter. It wasn't as close to a Metro stop as she'd have preferred, but the even trendier DuPont Circle area was but a few short blocks away—easy walking distance when the weather was decent. Sadly, today, the weather was *not* decent. And Jillian was correspondingly cranky as she watched the steady, gray drizzle streak her office window overlooking the 2100 block of N St. NW.

She knew her mood would pass. There was plenty to be happy about, actually. In only six short years World Aid Corps had grown from a small, startup, beltway-bandit sub-contractor into a full-fledged humanitarian NGO in its own right. Yes, with an annual global program budget of $200 million, operational presence in more than twenty countries, some 5,000 staff worldwide, and negotiations underway to open a European office (probably in Brussels), there was plenty for Jillian to feel happy about, even proud of. Her dream of starting her own successful international NGO was starting to come true.

If she was totally honest, though, it wasn't just the rain that annoyed Jillian that day. She turned away from the window and looked back at the open message on her computer screen.

USAID had called a Dolo Ado partners' meeting and had not invited WAC.

It was a simple enough mistake. Until now WAC had not been a significant player in the Horn of Africa. Yes, they'd been in Dolo Ado from the very beginning, but not as a top-tier player. They'd done small bits here and there only: distribute a few MT of rice for WFP in Melkadido; provide materials and labor for the NRC (Norwegian Refugee Council) in Hilaweyn; contribute warm bodies to an interagency assessment led by UNOCHA; help Save with some uniforms for school children in Kobe. Bits and pieces. All good, all making a difference, nothing to be ashamed of. But still bits and pieces, and nothing substantial for WAC to claim as their own. Nothing substantial for Jillian to claim as *her* own.

She knew that Brandon, her—WAC's—chief of party in Dolo Ado would be attending the USAID Mission partners meeting on Monday, forty-eight hours from now, give or take. That was good. At least USAID in Ethiopia recognized WAC. But still, it irked her that USAID Washington was dissing her—Or worse, wasn't even aware of her, of WAC. If there was going to be new OFDA funding for the Horn of Africa, Jillian wanted in on it. She was hungry for a win.

All for the sake of the poor, suffering Somalis, of course.

Chapter 9

Jon Langstrom stared with a combination of annoyance and disbelief at the message from Mark.

Jon,

Board meeting over the weekend. We're good to go full-bore on Dolo Ado, especially the new camp at Bur Amina. We're in the game for real. Lots of U.S. funding potential, but need a project we can sell.

I need you to get in there and carve out some space for Oxfam America. Go bare-knuckles with our European brothers if you need to. Stay until you have something we can sell on this end. Just stake out a claim for us. Make it happen.

Expect this is clear. Email Doris if you have questions.
Mark

It wasn't that simple. Not even nearly that simple. He couldn't just wander into Dolo Ado or the Oxfam compound and declare that Oxfam America was here to claim territory. This sort of thing needed to be negotiated. They weren't the UN. Or some contractor. They had to *coordinate*. You had to meet with the other players, agree on who would do what. It was never as simple as just waltzing in and saying what Oxfam America would do. Why was that so difficult for Mark to get? And what was this about "something to sell"?

Jon began to have a sinking feeling deep in the pit of his stomach. He'd been given a directive by a senior executive to stay in Dolo Ado—indefinitely, basically—until he'd established a programmatic presence, but at the same time he'd been given no parameters. Not sector parameters, no geographic guidance other than "the new camp", not even a round-number dollar figure. "Impossible" might be over stating things, but it was definitely an illogical assignment under the circumstances.

The next message didn't make him feel any better. It was from Angie. She'd copied his work email address—code for, "I'm really serious, and probably mad, too, because I suspect that you're ignoring me." And although it was just dispassionate text on a white screen, he knew Angie well enough to feel her anger, as much from what she didn't say as what she did:

Jonathon,

Just a reminder that Chloe's dance recital is in ten days. Two Tuesdays from now. 7:00 p.m. Remember your promise. Your own daughter is important, too.

Expect to see you then.

She hadn't even signed her own name.

The sinking feeling in his stomach was now an actual knot, and suddenly Jon really, *really* wanted another St. George. Or, like, three. Suddenly he felt angry, too. Angry at Mark and his cock-sure, know-it-all, "I've worked in the for-profit sector and so I can show you aid workers a thing or two" arrogance. Angry at Chloe for taking dance so damn seriously (she was never going to be a professional dancer—she'd started a full ten years too late. Let it *go* already.). Angry at Angie's endless bitchiness at his job and the requirements of that job—requirements that twenty or so years later should come as no surprise; and perhaps, more to the point, requirements she knew perfectly well he couldn't control.

Twenty years ago, the fact that he was about to leave to spend weeks on end on the front line of a complex humanitarian emergency without a break made her horny; now it made her sullen. Back *then*, with all of her amorous attention, he'd barely make it to the plane, rumpled, bags under his eyes, smelling distinctly of her. And back then, *after* the deployment, she'd meet him at the airport with a husky voice and a hungry look in her eyes, and he'd spend more or less the next week practically tied to the bed. Not *literally*, of course (although he wouldn't have minded if it *had* been literal). In any case, he'd struggle into the office after a few days of "comp time", bleary-eyed and gaunt as much from Angie's love and affection as much as from the jet-lag.

These days, if she was even home when his taxi arrived at their Boston townhouse, he'd be met at the door with a stiff A-frame embrace and a "honey do" list; eight or ten things that would have taken Angie all of fifteen minutes to accomplish on her own, but which she very clearly wanted Jon to do out of some sense of principle or need for control. Some days, he wasn't entirely sure which.

Now when he got home, there was tense, resentful silence, or worse, insinuations, sideways comments, thinly veiled accusations that anyone in their social circle would have missed. Now it was Angie's backhanded suggestion that Jon was somehow delinquent as a husband and sub-standard as a father by virtue of having chosen his profession. The evening news on television seemed to delight in endlessly covering stories of local deadbeats whose families lived in hovels and grew paradoxically fat on cheap packaged food. But Jon was a bad person because he missed a dance recital.

Whiskey. Tango. Foxtrot.

He loved Angie and Chloe. *He really did.*

But some days, there was just no pleasing Angie.

Some days, there was just not enough St. George in all of Ethiopia to drown out the noise from the other side of the world.

Some days, he just wanted to ride deep into Somalia, run food distributions for the most oppressed, and let Al Shabaab come and do their worst. *Bring it, bitches.*

Jon Langstrom turned off his computer, switched off the light and half lay, half fell on to the spongy bed. Despite the slow trickle of cool night air coming through the open window his tiny room was stifling hot. He pulled the mosquito net down, tucked it around the corners of the mattress and closed his eyes.

And without intending or wanting it, Jon found his thoughts gravitating toward the young aid worker from WAC.

Mary-Anne.

* * *

"How did you get here?"

Mary-Anne replayed Jon Langstrom's question in her head as she lay in the silent darkness of her tent. How *had* she gotten here? Her mind wandered back to the first flight to Haiti, her first step into the world of international relief. It seemed so long ago, so far away—and not just in time and distance, but in the ways she'd changed.

Some days in Dolo Ado, she still felt like the same "girl" who'd climbed down from the Beechcraft King Air onto the cracked, sweltering tarmac in Port-au-Prince. The thrill of the exotic, the enticing possibility of adventure and romance called to her in Dolo Ado just as they had in Haiti. And, as in Haiti, some days, the volume of work threatened to overwhelm her, just as the gravity of her task there was almost paralyzing.

She'd joined the Samaritan's Purse relief team and gone to Haiti, as much as anything else, for the simple fact that it wasn't Kentucky. Haiti was a socially acceptable excuse, a cover story for getting away from the prying questions and whispering of the small evangelical church she'd attended. Although in retrospect it all seemed inevitable enough, at the time, she could never have anticipated the ways in which the whole experience would affect her. The Haiti earthquake may have been an awful tragedy for millions of Haitians, but for Mary-Anne it had been pure serendipity.

As if in response to an invisible celestial cue card, a lone donkey brayed plaintively in the night somewhere in the general direction of Puntland.

But Dolo Ado? Haiti may have accidentally launched the start of her career in the humanitarian world, but there had been nothing even remotely accidental about her ending up here. Her job as a regional program coordinator with WAC in Nairobi was one that she'd sought and pursued intentionally as a career move. Her deployment to Dolo Ado, while very difficult and hardly exciting or fun, was also something she'd pursued: she'd written directly to the CEO of WAC, Jillian Scott, to ask for it.

But it was all more than just career development. Although it felt odd to say out loud, inside her own head she knew that she felt deep sympathy for the thin, frightened Somalis straggling across the border every day, just as her heart went out to the dazed, traumatized Haitians in the displacement camps around Port-au-Prince two years ago.

Even more, although she struggled to articulate her own thoughts on the matter, Mary-Anne had the growing sense, almost like a slow, dreamy awakening, that she'd found her space. Humanitarian aid felt like where she belonged. Maybe it was a "calling" or a "life mission." Knowing one's place in the universe is already difficult, and even more difficult to be able to put it all into words once you think you know. For humanitarians, there almost always remains the additional challenge of balancing the reality of one's own purpose with what the Entire Rest Of The World wants to read into it.

Mary-Anne felt this tension acutely. When friends and acquaintances from back home, like ghosts from a past life, would write gushing messages on her Facebook wall, it made her sheepish. "You're such a wonderful person!" Or "What sacrifices you're making, Mary-Anne. Kudos to you!" She knew she wasn't wonderful. She knew that some days it was all she could do to drag herself from her tent and get in the car to go to Kobe. Some days, after hours of getting the run-around from refugees who seemed, against all logic, utterly bent on misleading her, she cursed them in her heart. Some days, it was all she could do to deal with Tekflu, the distinguished, soft-spoken Ethiopian attorney turned university lecturer turned humanitarian who worked as the WAC site coordinator for Kobe. As much as Mary-Anne truly loved what she did, some days her job was nothing at all about helping people in need but everything about serving the hierarchy of WAC.

Yet when a critical article or blogpost circulated around the Internet, accusing aid for having lost its way, or perhaps questioning the motivations of foreign aid workers because they lived in secure compounds and drove around in white Land Cruisers, Mary-Anne would feel the heat of righteous indignation rise in her breast.

I have to sleep, she thought to herself. Tomorrow was Saturday, but Mary-Anne had mountains of back paperwork to get done, plus a monitoring visit to Kobe on Sunday.

As she lay on her uncomfortable cot, the liminal state between sleep and wakefulness slowly giving way to sleep, Mary-Anne found her thoughts turning to Jon Langstrom. He'd been around, been in the game for a while. He seemed to have some seniority in a real NGO. He managed to have it all—or so it seemed: field cred, the comfortable job where he could make a difference, a house in a suburb, a family. And he was his own person. In so many ways, Jon Langstrom had exactly what Mary-Anne thought she wanted in life.

Yet there was a sadness about him, a hint of melancholy or perhaps a wall, buried deep, that she couldn't quite put her finger on.

Mary-Anne wasn't attracted to Jon—not like *that*. Not romantically or sexually. Sure, he was fit, articulate, casually self-confident without even a hint of arrogance. He was attractive enough—but that wasn't what kept Mary-Anne awake. He'd been *magnetic* that evening at Billy-Bob's, and she'd not wanted to leave when curfew rolled around.

The last thing Mary-Anne remembered as she faded finally to sleep was thinking that for the first time in what felt like a very long time, she actually *looked forward* to seeing someone.

Jon Langstrom.

Chapter 10

It was Sunday morning, and perhaps as a subconscious means of procrastination, Mary-Anne allowed herself a few extra moments in bed. As she lay there, slowing waking up, she thought back to *before*, and how very different the aid world is in reality, compared with what she thought it would be.

In her daydreams of becoming a humanitarian worker, long before she'd gone on her first mission to Haiti, Mary-Anne had never seriously contemplated the possibility of spending days doing nothing at all but paperwork.

Bono, Sean Penn, Sam Childers—fashionably casual, attractively earnest, and crazed-but-for-a-good-cause, respectively—never write reports, or so she'd naïvely believed at the time. And it suddenly occurred to her that the protagonists of failed American television serial dramas like ABC's *Off the Map*, or NBC's *The Philanthropist* rarely wasted any valuable time hunched over a laptop computer in the sweltering heat, pounding out a sit-rep for a needy cubicle rat at HQ or double-checking the spreadsheet formulas in next year's annual budget *either*.

No, Mary-Anne thought ruefully to herself. Most would-be humanitarians, like their prime-time and/or celebrity inspiration, planned to spend their days becoming one with The Bottom Billion, delivering babies by candlelight in the dead of night in a tent out on the border between Nowhere and Off The Grid, braving crocodiles and hippos to get hygiene kits into the hands of adolescent girls, or enduring days without a proper toilet for the sake of ensuring the provision of a gravity-fed water system which (if properly installed by foreigners) will enable the grateful yet simultaneously empowered villagers to break the cycle of poverty for sustainable perpetuity. That's what *she'd* envisioned before the reality of a real aid job had taken hold.

She remembered, too, what Jean-Philippe used to say about a certain affected loftiness among what he derisively termed "the amateur humanitarian dreamer class." They loved proclaiming that they were about *implementing*, about getting things done, about cutting through the "red tape," and—most importantly of all—about providing aid directly to those who need it most. In a sarcastic voice (and surprisingly good impression of a Midwest American accent), he'd mimic them talking about how they learn more in ten minutes walking around a Third World marketplace than they do in a year behind a desk, or how they wanted everyone to know that *they* were practical, results-oriented people with no patience for politics or agendas, or the artificial complexity that so many professional humanitarians were known for imposing on what otherwise seemed to be black and white situations (at least to the amateurs).

Then he'd do the French mouth-fart ("*pfffffi*"), make a dismissive shrugging motion and point out the obvious fallacy in the logic of amateur humanitarians who rail against the industry for not being "accountable," yet at the same time scoff at those who waste time with coordination, bureaucracy or documentation (basic accountability and quality assurance measures) or anything else that could be considered dealing with the "mucky muck" of an Aid Industry tasked with managing the delivery of some $17-$20 billion USD worth of aid globally, annually.

She knew Jean-Philippe was right. And, no, it wasn't particularly fun or exciting. It wasn't even interesting, but it *was* important. Mary-Anne knew as she rolled out of bed, now fully awake, that she'd spend that Saturday in the open-air, thatched-roofed Internet kiosk in the WRC compound, doing the unsexy grunt labor that keeps the Aid Industry's fuel tank full and bearings properly lubricated.

First, there were the innumerable emails that needed responses: emails from program support staff in Nairobi who needed supply-chain data; and emails from marketing and fundraising staff in Washington, DC, who needed photographs of beneficiaries and stories; emails from cluster leads needing information about past and future planned NFI distributions, hygiene promotion trainings, and monitoring visits.

Then there was an email message from Rick, the USAID/OFDA technical advisor based in Addis. The message was to Brandon, WRC's operations director in Dolo Ado (and Mary-Anne's supervisor), but Mary-Anne had been copied. It read:

Brandon,

Looking forward to lunch today. How's 13:00 at the Top View Restaurant in Megenaga?

Text me if you can't make it.

See you there.

Rick.

Good. Brandon was doing his job, schmoozing Rick. Word on the street was that OFDA would have funding available for Bur Amina when and if ARRA ever got around to opening it. As expected, ARRA had announced the opening of Bur Amina at the coordination meeting yesterday. Which meant that every 501(c)3 US PVO with any on-the-ground capacity in Ethiopia would be scrambling for a piece of the pie. The partners' meeting was on Monday, and everyone knew that a formal announcement of available funding was coming. Brandon was having lunch with Rick, the main OFDA decision-maker, today.

Good move, Brandon.

For the next few hours, Mary-Anne answered other emails, worked on a month-end NFI report, and started drafting a strategy for WAC to move into Bur Amina. Brandon would have to approve it eventually, but he'd be in Addis for the next few days and it couldn't hurt to get a few thoughts on paper now.

The more Mary-Anne thought about it, the more she became convinced that the most effective way for WAC to get a foothold in Bur Amina would be to focus on emergency food and transitional shelter. They were already participating in the food and shelter clusters, had good relationships with the other members (IRC, World Vision, Oxfam, Save the Children), and enough decent experience in other parts of WAC's global network to make a convincing case for "capacity," possibly winning a few good grants.

The World Food Programme was always looking for partners and, for the moment, Bur Amina was wide open. That would sort out the emergency food portion of Mary-Anne's strategy. Shelter would be harder. There were some strong shelter sector players in Dolo Ado—Norwegian Refugee Council, Danish Refugee Council, even GOAL—but with OFDA bringing in new funding, WAC could possibly sneak in under the radar with a U.S. Government relief grant. It was a gamble in the sense that going for an OFDA grant would be a lot of work, both in preparing the proposal and negotiating the award, with no guarantee of funding. Even if funding was won, it would be a lot of work to implement—OFDA was among the more high maintenance of the government aid donors out there. Longer term, if WAC did poorly, it could reflect badly and hurt its reputation as a competent aid provider. But if they did well…

Mary-Anne looked at her watch. Almost 1:00 p.m. Brandon should just about be getting to the Top View Restaurant. She sent a text message to Brandon to call her before he started talking business with Rick, and then moved on to a quarterly progress report for ARRA.

*

Three hours later, Mary-Anne reached an acceptable stopping place. Tomorrow was Sunday. She'd have to leave for Kobe by 7:00 a.m. If she went to sleep now, she'd be able to sleep in until 6:00 and still have time to search her hard drive for photographs of goats to satisfy the demands of someone in the DC office who needed to respond to a donor who'd purchased a goat for a Somali refugee family through WAC's "Gift Catalog."

As her pointer hovered above the "Facebook" link in her bookmarks bar, Mary-Anne suddenly realize that *Brandon still hadn't checked in*. Out of habit, she refreshed her work email inbox. It made no sense—Brandon wouldn't be sending email from Addis in the middle of the day on Saturday. But there was a message from Rick, like the first, sent to Brandon and copied to Mary-Anne:

Brandon,

Sorry to miss you at Top View. I stayed until 3:00 but didn't see you.
Hope everything's okay. You owe me a bottle of cheap Merlot.

Call me.

Rick

Call it women's intuition. Call it aid worker's paranoia. Or call it general ESP.
Although she couldn't explain why, Mary-Anne felt an uncomfortable knot begin to form in the pit of her stomach.

* * *

After twenty, almost twenty-one years of marriage and thirteen years of parenthood, Angie Langstrom knew exactly what she had to do. She had to set boundaries.

She thought wistfully back to the days when she and Jon were young. She'd first met him at a workshop in Mumbai in 1986, at a training workshop on the importance of and methods for involving the community in need assessments.

She chuckled to herself. It was laughable now, really, that anyone at all would be in need of such a conference. The world had changed, and the aid world right along with it.

And *that* was exactly why it was time to set boundaries.

She'd given already too many years of knowing her husband could be called away at any time; of knowing that huddled masses of humanity yearning to breathe free on the other side of the world would invariably trump her own human need for security and stability, her maternal desire to raise a balanced child in a balanced family. Families ate together, went to movies, wandered shopping malls, went camping, or sat at home and played Scrabble. But those things never seemed to happen for her, for them.

Yes, a lot had changed since 1986. The Berlin wall was history. Vietnam had normalized relations with the U.S. Libya, and Iraq had gone off the chain. The great Rwanda genocide and Goma humanitarian debacle (the *first* one) had shown the way to humanitarian accountability. The Balkans crises (too many to recount specifically) brought "complex humanitarian emergencies" and "fragile states" to the forefront of everyone's thinking. The Tsunamis and Hurricane Katrina had shown everyone that even the most prepared places are still not prepared enough. And Haiti had shown everyone just how bad it can get, whether they were talking about the unpreparedness of the country or the incompetence of the humanitarian system to respond in a cohesive, coordinated way.

Humanitarianism was *cause du jour*. People were lining up, even scrapping over hardship deployments. Name the war zone: Darfur, Iraq, Gaza, Mali… and you couldn't get a seat on the plane, thanks to scores of aid workers on their way to make the world more equitable. There weren't enough aid jobs in all of Afghanistan—but one all too easy example—to accommodate the hordes of white, Western women determined, against all reason, to endure sickness, abduction, rape, and torture, all for a chance to claim the status of having helped their blue-*burqa*-clad sisters.

All of which begged a central question for Angie Langstrom: Why did *Jon* always have to be gone? Surely there were others he could send. It wasn't like he was the only one out there. Disasters and crises were nothing new. They came and went all the time. If you miss out on Goma, don't panic. Another crisis in Sudan is right around the corner. Not called to the Haiti earthquake response? Sit tight—a flood and simultaneous meltdown in Pakistan will happen in a few short months. Besides, by the time the humanitarian community got itself together and deployed to the scene it wasn't like things were exactly urgent. Bad or serious? Yeah, sure. But *urgent?* Not so much.

All the more reason, Angie thought to herself, to not have to put up with another twenty years, or even another five years of Jon missing what felt like every event of importance to her, to their family. It was time for him to make the choice to put family first. Time for him to decide that his own wife and daughter were as important as an endless supply of nameless disaster survivors, Angie thought bitterly. She'd been there. She knew what it was like to work as a professional humanitarian, to feel the urge to help, to feel the sense of responsibility. She, as much as anyone else, wanted the world to be safer and nicer and better. Perhaps because of all of this, Angie Langstrom also felt it was both reasonable and within her rights to demand that her husband and the father of their daughter *be* a husband and a father.

* * *

The mid-morning Sunday sun beat down on Sector 3-C in Kobe Camp as the WAC Land Cruiser ground to a halt. Mary-Anne was already tired and hot as she opened the front passenger door and stepped down in to the dust. Mesfin, the driver, turned his head and spoke to Tekflu, sitting in the back seat, in quick, clipped Amharic. His voice trailed off as he caught Mary-Anne watching him.

She didn't speak more than a word or two of Amharic. About a third of WAC's Dolo Ado team was foreign: Danish, Tanzanian, Somali, Bulgarian, German. Her—American. The actual beneficiaries—the Somali refugees—rarely spoke Amharic. When she needed to talk to refugees, Mary-Anne spoke through Tekflu, and he used mostly Arabic. Beyond that, the bulk of Mary-Anne's work was in English: the coordination meeting, the calls from HQ, occasional media interviews, the never-ending stream of email demanding this or that—all in English.

So with the exception of basic traveler survival phrases for trips to Addis or pleasantries with Ethiopian staff, there was not only no real need, but also no real opportunity for Mary-Anne to learn Amharic. Mesfin could speak to Tekflu in Amharic with complete confidence that Mary-Anne could never eavesdrop, even if she was standing right there.

Months ago she'd given up caring what Mesfin discussed with Tekflu. She'd passed more hours than she could remember bouncing down the rocky road between Kobe and Dolo Ado, staring out the window, her mind wandering as Mesfin shouted over the road noise to Tekflu in the back seat. Tekflu's insistence that she ride "shotgun" had been awkward at first. Then it was an annoyance. And then she'd simply given up caring about that, too. Get in the front seat. Hit the road. Get to the meeting on time. Still, somehow right then, it annoyed Mary-Anne that Mesfin still thought he couldn't speak his own language in front of her. She made an annoyed face, and slammed the car door closed a little harder than she'd intended.

As they walked through sector 3-C, she heard Tekflu's voice, low and calm beside her.

"Mesfin is a good man, madame. He's only trying to be respectful. He's also ashamed because he doesn't speak English well."

"Oh…," Mary-Anne felt instantly ashamed herself. "I'm sorry," her voice wavered more than she wanted it to.

"Don't worry, madame." Tekflu was the picture of calm composure. "He forgives you."

Chapter 11

The air inside the large canvas tent with "UNHCR" stenciled on the roof was hot and stale. Fifteen, maybe twenty, Somali women crowded inside. Some sat squished together on folding cots; others squatted or sat cross-legged on the floor. A few nursed small infants. All of them wore long robes and full *hijabs*. And all of them, Mary-Anne couldn't help but notice, were much too thin.

It is one thing to read about the world's poor and disenfranchised, the so-called Bottom Billion, the refugees who flee their homes in the dead of night only to hunker beneath a harsh sun in crowded camps like Kobe. It is one thing to see their images on CNN or Al Jazeera or humanitarian agency websites. It is one thing to hear Richard Engel or Anderson Cooper rhapsodize in concerned tones about their plight. And it is something *altogether different* to meet them in person, to see them up close, close enough to touch. It is altogether different when you are close enough to hear them tell their own stories with their own voices, close enough to tell that water is scarce and be reminded that bathing every day is a luxury and a privilege.

In Mary-Anne's experience, while it might have been possible to become complacent simply seeing them every day on the news or on Alertnet, facing them in person day after day was always a jarring experience. At the same time, she'd grown, or so she felt, to almost *love* them. Five months into the response operation in Dolo Ado, she'd begun to recognize most of the women in the camp sectors where she monitored WAC's interventions through focus groups and key informant interviews. She even knew some of them by name and started to look specifically for their faces as she walked through the camps or drove past water points.

There was Aamino, 23, three children. Her skin was the color of black coffee and her eyes were darker still. Her husband had been killed by Al Shabaab for his camel, and Aamino had taken her three children and fled toward Ethiopia even before her husband's body had grown cold. Halgan was older, maybe 30, Mary-Anne guessed, but she looked much older. She had tired eyes and was bone-thin, but always had fresh henna on her palms and fingers. Mary-Anne had never seen Halgan with any children, and assumed she was alone. Then there was the more matronly, but exotic Aasiya. All of the women of Sector 3-C deferred to Aasiya and she carried herself with an air of confidence and unspoken authority that permeated the air wherever she was. Mary-Anne had come to rely on Aasiya as a confidante and source of information about how things were going in Kobe Camp.

There were several new faces in the focus group today, hanging on the fringes, unsure of what a focus group was all about. Mary-Anne knew without translation that Tekflu was running through the standard litany of questions to the group. After each question, the room erupted into chatter, then Tekflu would carefully translate the responses back while Mary-Anne wrote everything down. Normally Mary-Anne found these conversations fascinating, but today found herself struggling to focus. The combination of stifling heat inside the tent, road-weariness, lack of sleep, and worry about Brandon and USAID all swirled together into a sleep-inducing potion, and Mary-Anne found herself fighting to keep from nodding. Not like it mattered all that much, she thought to herself. The women in today's group were not saying anything new or particularly interesting. Not enough food (there was never enough food); they preferred pasta, not rice or pulses (WFP was providing rice and pulses, so that was that); they preferred to defecate out in the open because it was "cleaner" rather than squatting over the same hole in the same latrine used by everyone else in Sector 3-C. They didn't like walking all the way over to the MSF clinic in Sector 1-A. It was too far, and besides, they preferred their own traditional medicines and healers. A wrinkled older woman with a lavender *hijab* was holding forth on this point. Or maybe they just didn't trust the foreign doctors—the translation was unspecific. The smell of body odor and children with dirty bottoms intensified. Mary-Anne fought to keep from yawning.

After what felt like an eternity later, the focus group ended. Mary-Anne breathed a sigh of relief as she stepped from the crowded tent into the bright sunshine. It was almost unbearably hot, but at least the air was fresh (sort of) and there was some breeze (sort of). Her normal practice was to mingle for a few minutes informally with the women of the focus group. She'd ask their names, inquire after their families (the ones she was acquainted with), hold their babies, or pat their toddlers on the head. Sometimes she'd walk to their tents just to see where they lived and get a sense for how things were. Today, though, Mary-Anne just wanted to get back into the WAC Land Cruiser as soon as possible and head back to Dolo Ado. If they left quickly, they might even make it back before dark.

She was just about to bid farewell to the entire group and start for the Land Cruiser when Tekflu touched her arm. "This woman would like to speak with you, Madame."

Mary-Anne turned and saw a young woman—too young—looking up at her holding a thin—*much* too thin—child in her arms. The woman couldn't have been more than seventeen or eighteen, Mary-Anne could see, and through Tekflu she confirmed that the small, thin child was about two. With a low, frightened voice, the young woman went on to explain that she'd come through the processing center one week ago. Then, three days ago her child had begun to have diarrhea, fever and chills. Now her child—a little girl by the name of Dhuuxo—hardly moved and hardly made noise. The young mother was worried.

Mary-Anne looked again at little Dhuuxo: thin black legs hung limply over her mother's arms, her mouth partially open, jaw slack, and her eyes were starting to roll back up into her head. Maybe malaria, maybe dengue, maybe dysentery.

"Tekflu, tell this woman to take her daughter to the MSF clinic in Sector 1-A *immediately*."

As she heard the translation, the young mother's face became pinched with worry. She spoke, slowly, softly in a voice intense with anxiety. Tekflu translated: "The clinic is far, it's very hot, and her husband is waiting for her to cook…"

Mary-Anne was suddenly annoyed again. The woman's baby was obviously dying. There was no decision to be made. She spoke again, more stridently than she should have. "Your daughter will die today if you do not take her to the clinic. Your husband can wait. Take your child to the clinic now."

Tekflu gave Mary-Anne a strange look, but translated in a low voice. This time, as she heard the translation the young mother simply looked down. When Tekflu finished, her reply was almost a whisper.

"She says 'thank you.'"

*

The drive from Kobe Camp to Dolo Ado took most of the rest of the afternoon. Mesfin put in a mix tape of Amharic music and concentrated on the road ahead. For the first time, Tekflu accepted Mary-Anne's suggestion that he ride in the front passenger seat, and promptly fell asleep for the entire trip, awakening only briefly for a moment or two every time Mesfin bumped into a pothole or over a rock.

Later, as she lay in her cot that night, the heat of the desert slowly waning, Mary-Anne could not push from her mind the image of a too-young Somali woman, eyes downcast, holding a limp, too-thin child in her arms, growing smaller in the distance.

* * *

The call with Mark had gone badly.

It was easy enough, in the silence of 3:00 a.m. wide awake from jet-lag clarity, to persuade himself that he was right and that his perspective made sense. But somehow it all fell apart as soon as Mark came on the line.

"*Damn…,*" he cursed under his breath.

Their conversation replayed itself in Jon's head. Mark had been obviously annoyed to receive a call on Sunday—already a sign that things were headed in an unproductive direction. Then Jon had had the audacity to indirectly question Mark's wisdom.

"I'm not sure that this is one to go it alone on." He'd paused, taken a deep breath, and soldiered ahead. "Oxfam GB actually has a good strategy, good capacity on the ground, and is open to working with us. They'll let us field Oxfam America staff as part of the response, and they'll let us participate in the quarterly regional steering committee meetings in Nairobi." Another deep breath. "If we put our resources behind Oxfam GB we'll be able to truthfully tell our donors that more than ninety percent of their donations are going to programs. It will be far less than that if we try to set up and run our own operation, and I think—"

"Jon, I told you to stake out some territory for Oxfam America," Mark interrupted rudely. "I don't give a damn what Oxfam GB is doing. I want something that is ours. I want to see American flag stickers on things."

Jon could hear Mark cough loudly on the other end of the line before he continued. "I told you this by email already. What part of 'get something I can sell' don't you get? I've got more applications for senior operations roles coming in the door than I know what to do with. I've talented people, go-getters who could be making double *my* salary on Wall Street or maybe even more in dot-coms falling all over themselves for a crap-ass salary and a shot at doing *your* job."

Mark was talking louder now.

"We've got resources. We've got a *clear mandate* from our board. There's obviously humanitarian need. From where I'm sitting it looks an awful lot like the only thing holding up the show right now is *you*."

Jon's mouth was dry and mind was blank. Mark's voice was suddenly quiet and calm—*too* calm. "You figure it out, Jon. You figure out how to get us on the map, there in Dolo Ado or I'll find someone who can."

Jon had visions of himself straddling Mark's torso and holding his head under water until the struggling stopped. "I have non-negotiable family commitments at home in about two weeks—"

"*Figure it out*, Jonathon." Mark cut him off mid-sentence. "You do what you have to do, but *figure it out*. Seems to me that walking into your coordination meetings or whatever and informing people that Oxfam America is starting up a new $300,000 project should take all of ten minutes. I really don't get why you're making this so hard."

Those outside the humanitarian aid industry are frequently critical of professional humanitarian workers for their apparent cynicism. Cynical, snarky aid blogs, gallows humor and what may often appear to outsiders as wanton excess living are held up as proof that the humanitarian system has run amuck, lost its way, and ceased being about "the poor." The critics are perhaps partly right, but for reasons they don't understand. Maybe the cynicism, the snark, the excessive team house drinking *are* at least evidence, if not proof in and of themselves, that the aid system is broken. But where the wide-eyed critics are wrong is in believing that these are what make aid broken.

In fact it's the opposite: Aid is not broken because aid workers are cynical, hedonistic alcoholics. Aid workers are cynical alcoholics because aid is broken, and further, because they have been repeatedly slapped down by their own leaders for trying to make it better. Which is essentially what was happening to Jon right then.

At that moment something broke inside Jon Langstrom. For perhaps the first time, he understood in so many words that he was tired. Jon couldn't remember the number of times he'd had more or less the exact same conversation over the years. The country in question might change or the logo on his namebadge might change, but everything else would be boringly similar. Every NGO he'd ever worked for (seven, altogether) had the exact same issues, his current job with his current employer, and the argument with his current boss were only the most recent in a long line of sameness.

Jon was tired. *Very* tired, after years of trying to fight the system, trying to change the system from the inside, he'd suddenly lost the ability to fight. He just wanted it to all be over.

"Got it. Okay."

Jon was suddenly terse himself. If Mark wanted to go down in history as the COO who had dumped 300 grand on a swirling complex humanitarian emergency with no perceptible plan, vision, or even a general sense for how the money should be used, then suddenly it was all fine with him. *Inshallah*, he'd be long gone from Oxfam America by the time anything came of it. More likely, *nothing* would come of it and no one would be able to say what the impact of the money had been. Either way, totally not his problem.

Jon pushed the red button on the touch screen of his iPhone, angrily sending Mark into oblivion. "User-assisted call failure" was his new favorite term.

The interagency relief effort in Dolo Ado would continue whether or not Oxfam America's $300,000 was well-spent. The absolute worst that would happen would be that $300,000 would disappear undocumented into the pockets of a whole continuum of Ethiopian and Somali middle men, *commercents*, transporters, low-level officials, maybe a few refugee sheikhs. Well, that and some over-indulged east coast philanthropists would be given something other than a truthful explanation for how their donations had been used.

He glanced at the darkening sky, and then his watch. 5:00 PM. Billy-Bob's must be open now.

Chapter 12

The USAID partners' meeting in Addis Ababa Monday morning came off without a hitch. The small uninteresting conference room inside the American embassy was packed with the usual US PVO suspects: CARE, Save, IRC, Samaritan's Purse, Mercy Corps, Plan, World Vision. There would be money available, Rick announced, for an expanded relief effort in Dolo Ado. The size of the pot was unspecified, but OFDA was looking to make several awards in the US $500,000 to $1,000,000 range. Proposals should be for one year. While OFDA anticipated spending the bulk of its relief budget for Dolo Ado on straightforward sectors like WASH, shelter, NFIs, and livelihoods, Rick was (naturally) keen to see innovative approaches—using cell phones for something, or maybe something about "crowdsourcing"—to some of the common crosscutting themes like gender, protection, and environment. No deadline for proposal submission had been set, but the U.S. Government wanted to get live-saving relief flowing to those who needed it most with minimal delays. Anyway, when the money was gone, the money was gone. Get those proposals in ASAP.

The only question came from the deputy operations manager of IRC: Did OFDA have a camp preference in Dolo Ado? Could they propose interventions for *any* of the five camps? "No," Rick had clarified. The initial four camps were saturated with European money. OFDA's funding was only available for the new camp at Bur Amina.

Actually, there *was* one small hitch, Rick noticed as he shuffled his papers into a pile and prepared to leave the conference room: Brandon, his buddy from World Aid Corps, hadn't been there. Probably hung over, Rick chuckled to himself. *Classic.* He'd known Brandon since they'd served in the Peace Corps together in Sri Lanka more than ten years ago. Rick had jumped on the USAID career track, while Brandon had preferred to do the NGO thing, but they'd stayed in touch and met up whenever their work-related travel would allow. Brandon was probably in a crappy hotel right now, nursing a splitting headache and trying to remember the name of a local woman he'd awakened to find next to him in bed. There was strange comfort in knowing that *some* things never change.

Rick glanced at his watch. Still time to drop his peeps at WAC a note about OFDA funding for Bur Amina before lunch. As he turned off the light and closed the door to the conference room, Rick thought to himself that he'd better copy Mary-Anne, Brandon's go-to, just to be sure. He chuckled again. *No telling when Brandon might resurface.*

* * *

Mary-Anne did a double-take at Rick's quick message on her screen:

Brandon,

Too bad you missed my briefing yesterday. Short version: OFDA has cash for relief programming at Bur Amina. Would love to see WAC get in on the action. No deadline, but obviously you'll want to make this happen ASAP.

Send me a note or give me a ring.

P.S. I'm copying Mary-Anne, in case you're unavailable.

Rick Goldings
Technical Officer
USAID/OFDA
U.S. Embassy, Addis Ababa

Where was Brandon? The reason he'd gone to Addis in the first place was to attend the OFDA briefing with Rick. There was USAID money for Dolo Ado and their CEO Jillian had made it crystal clear that she wanted them—Brandon and Mary-Anne—to win some of it for World Aid Corps.

She dialed Brandon's number and let it ring until the call went to voicemail. It wasn't like him to go AWOL.

In the pit of her stomach, Mary-Anne now felt acutely the knot she'd only felt vaguely on Saturday. She had mountains of M&E and reporting work on her plate, now an OFDA proposal, too, and a possible security incident if Brandon couldn't be found.

Mary-Anne checked the world clock on her iPhone. 6:00 a.m., DC

time.
She dialed Jillian's number.
The CEO of World Aid Corps answered on the second ring.

*

Jillian had been supportive but also concise and firm: Pursuing OFDA funding would be a non-negotiable. Mary-Anne was to take the lead in designing the proposal and negotiating whatever needed to be negotiated in order to make it happen. Win the grant. That was the main thing.

Confirming the location and status of Brandon was obviously of urgent priority. Mary-Anne had the authority to commit whatever WAC resources were necessary to that end, but was specifically to task Rolf the security manager with locating him. Rolf should be dispatched to Addis Ababa at once. What would happen once Brandon was located was inconclusive. Just find him and move forward from that point.

And (Jillian made sure to emphasize this point before hanging up) Mary-Anne was the acting chief of party, the decision-maker, the most senior WAC person in Ethiopia *until further notice*.

Deciding what would happen once someone found Brandon could wait. But the relief effort in Dolo Ado had to continue. And, importantly, there was an OFDA grant to win.

Until further notice, Mary-Anne would report directly to Jillian.

*

At almost that exact moment, the mysterious foreign patient in ward 3 at Tzna General Hospital stirred, then opened his eyes. He seemed confused and agitated at first, but became calmer as the doe-eyed nurse Aster held his hand and stroked his arm. The matronly head nurse clucked and smiled knowingly. Aster had that effect on young men. She checked the chart at the foot of the mysterious foreign patient's bed.

The white foreigner had been brought in unconscious by the Addis Ababa police at around 11:00 a.m. on Saturday. Since then he'd done little more than twitch occasionally and soak up IV fluid. They'd begun to wonder if he'd ever wake up.

The matronly head nurse smiled again. *Let Aster hold the foreigner's hand for a while.*

*

Angie had made up her mind.

Time to establish some boundaries. *Time to give Jon an ultimatum.*

There was nothing going on in Dolo Ado, or wherever, that absolutely required his presence, specifically. More to the point, he was the relief director for the U.S. branch of a major global NGO. Oxfam. He had minions. He could send one of *them* to deal with whatever needed dealing with out in the wilds Godforsakenstan. Let someone more junior—a program officer maybe—miss family events and holidays for a while. Jon had put in his time.

Chloe was a full-on teenager who needed a stable, present-in-the-moment man in her life, ideally her own father. For the sake of their daughter, Jon needed to be there.

Chloe's dance recital was less than two weeks away.

Angie knew what she had to do as she turned on her computer and began to draft the message to Jon.

Ten minutes later she clicked "send" and turned her computer off.

Only 7:00 PM, and one glass worth of Syrah left in the bottle.

Chapter 13

The crowd was mercifully small at Billy-Bob's that night. The sullen, dark-skinned youths huddled around a large metal platter of *injera* in the enclosed restaurant ignored her as she walked past, and the WFP logistician holding forth to the three Save/UK ops staff nodded in only brief acknowledgement before settling back into a story about harrowing shenanigans in Tbilisi or Islamabad.

Even Billy-Bob, the namesake goat, seemed distracted and uninterested as Mary-Anne seated herself alone at a corner table in the gathering twilight and ordered her first St. George. If a goat can appear bored—and it is truly amazing how much human emotion a goat can convey via its facial expressions—Billy-Bob surely did as he gently butted Mary-Anne's outstretched hand grudgingly before retreating to solitary rumination in the sanctum of the tree overlooking the courtyard.

As lame as drinking and smoking alone in the darkness at Billy-Bob's might seem to some, Mary-Anne gave a sigh of inner relief as she seated herself at an empty table on the periphery and ordered her first round. A moment later she lifted the bottle in silent toast and then took her first sip of St. George under the benevolent gaze of Billy-Bob.

She fished in her rucksack for the pack of Marlboro Lights she normally kept there, shook one out and lit up. Head back, arms relaxed, she watched the smoke curl lazily upwards.

Deployment smoker. She chuckled softly at the recollection of Jon's lighthearted descriptor.

And as if on cue, Jon Langstrom walked through the door into the outdoor courtyard of Billy Jon's.
Mary-Anne inexplicably felt her pulse accelerate, and that realization made her face flush. She wanted to… *talk* to Jon Langstrom. She wanted to know what made him tick, how he could be so calm and self-assured in the midst of so much uncertainty. Jean-Philippe made her neck hot and her loins ache. Jon Langstrom made her brain tingle.

Their eyes met and Jon motioned questioningly toward the table in front of Mary-Anne. The WFP loggie and Save/UK ops guys, deep in conversation and enshrouded in cigarette smoke, barely looked up. Mary-Anne tried to not seem too eager, but for the first time since she'd last lay naked in Jean-Philippe's arms, she intensely wanted to be near someone. Someone *specific*.

She smiled as coyly as she could and motioned toward the cheap plastic chair next to her. Jon smiled, too, and nodded as he walked toward her.

He sat down with a deep sigh, held up Mary-Anne's partially drunk bottle of St. George and gestured to the waiter with a motion they both assumed meant, "Bring me another." The waiter nodded, and Jon Langstrom reached for the pack of cigarettes on the table.

As he lit up, he looked over at Mary-Anne.

The fading light from the sky above, the flicker of the lighter below, the glow of a half-burnt Marlboro between her fingers, all cast her face into sharp relief. She had amazing hazel eyes, sculpted lips, and a high forehead, framed with an unruly mop of dirty-blond hair. That Mary-Anne was beautiful. Jon felt his pulse accelerate, too. More than anything else, he wanted to… *talk* to her.

"It has been one hell of a week… and it's only Monday," he said in a tired voice.

Jon exhaled a cloud of smoke toward the blue-black sky above and then sipped his beer.

St. George, Jon thought to himself, is a truly unremarkable beer.

It was neither as fragrant as Singha, nor as light as Suprema, nor as tasty as Taybeh. It was better than Murree's Classic Lager, but not by much. But under the right conditions, say, after a hard, hot day in the field, or a lame coordination meeting, or a day of annoying emails, St. George could be as refreshing as a straight answer and as comforting as an old friend. And an old friend, more than anything else in the whole world, was what Jon needed right then.

"Yeah," Mary-Anne agreed, her voice trailing off. She took another long drag, stubbed out her cigarette and pulled one more from the half-empty pack. Before lighting up, she continued, unconvincingly trying to sound somewhat upbeat/ironic.

"The first real working day after the announcement of a new camp at Bur Amina and our operations director, my boss Brandon, is AWOL in a meeting with USAID. Our CEO is cranky, and putting it all on me. I have triple the work on my plate now than I had when the donkey woke me up this morning." She lit the cigarette and puffed once, quickly. "Bur Amina is going to change things for us."

Jon cradled the bottle loosely in his right hand as he listened intently to Mary-Anne.

"It's good. I mean, I *guess* it's good. More help for more refugees. More grant money on the table. It's an opportunity for me to move up the ladder, I suppose. But it feels a bit overwhelming. I know WAC isn't the largest player in Dolo Ado," she looked apologetically at Jon. "But still, I'll be basically leading the response for an entire organization. I *think* I know I can do it. But I don't *know* if I can do it. Does that even make sense?" Mary-Anne arched her eyebrows inquisitively and made eye contact with Jon without turning her head as she drained the last of the St. George.

Jon sipped his beer and then laughed softly. Damn, she was attractive. If he'd been ten years younger. And single. *And... and...*

"Yeah, it makes sense. Moving from program officer to management is a big change. Maybe you don't change desks or sleep in a different cot, but you're supervising people who used to be your peers, you're making decisions you used to advise your bosses on... There's a lot of security in being an employee, and there's a lot of risk involved in being the boss. You have to think differently and take things more seriously. It can be scary."

Another sip from the bottle of St. George. Billy-Bob stirred in the branches above, then was still. The sky was dark now, except for a hint of velvety purple barely visible above the courtyard wall in the general direction of Sudan. Jon Langstrom continued.

"You want my advice, step up. Take this opportunity and run with it." It was Mary-Anne's turn to listen intently. "Battlefield commissions can be the curse of Hades or a gift from the gods. Your CEO picked you. Yeah, maybe she was desperate, she's got her reasons. But still, she picked you. She didn't ask you to hand the phone to someone else."

Jon turned and looked directly at Mary-Anne. "Opportunities like this don't come along every day, and forgive me, but especially for someone your age, with the amount of experience you've got. You want to take this one and run with it. Get in there and meet with ARRA. Go to Addis and meet with USAID, then get it going for WAC in Bur Amina. Don't let the big boys intimidate you," Jon's eyes were twinkling now. "This place is the end of the earth. Everyone's star players are in Afghanistan, or Dakar, maybe Port-au-Prince. You can go up against any response leader or operations director here."

"But what if I blow it?" Mary-Anne tried to keep the anxiety out of her voice.

Jon snorted. "What if you do? In six months, everyone who's here now will have rotated out and been replaced by a bunch of fresh faces who see you as 'senior.' One year from now, all anyone who's here now will really remember will be R&R in Mombasa, maybe a few incidents in the field, and… this place." He nodded at the table surrounded by the guys from WFP and Save/UK while reaching for the bottle on the small, greasy table. *Empty.* He waved once more to the waiter, held up two fingers, and placed the bottle contemplatively back before going on.

"One year from now, you'll be on another response in another country and all that the vast majority of anyone will remember of *you* is how long you lasted. Some will remember what organization you worked for, and if you were really 'close'—that is, if you drank a *lot* of beer together at Billy-Bob's— they might even remember what your position was."

The sky was totally black now. Jon went on, his voice suddenly tired.

"I've seen more people screw up, make idiotic mistakes, be incompetent, cost their employers huge amounts of money, waste resources on programs that didn't help people, melt down their personal lives, and then go on to senior positions with other organizations in other countries. For as rough and mean as the NGO world can be, it can also be too, too nice at times, too. People who should have been bodily removed from the premises under escort by building security get farewell parties and gushing letters of recommendation. Sometimes when you step back and look at it all, it can be almost impossible to see the difference between excellence and full-on dumbassery." He paused while the waiter set two more bottles of St. George in front of them.

"That's not cynicism or jadedness talking, by the way," he looked over at Mary-Anne, his eyes twinkling, once again a half smile tugging at the corners of his mouth. "That's simply the way the NGO world, and I suppose also the real world, works. So take this promotion and run with it. Ride the train as far as it goes. If it's not for you, get off and do something else. But if a career in the aid world is what you want, then recognize this opportunity for what it really is."

Mary-Anne turned Jon Langstrom's words over in her mind as she took a sip of St. George. *"If a career in the aid world is what you want, recognize this opportunity for what it really is."*

Suddenly, as if by divine epiphany, there in the deepening darkness, Mary-Anne knew with absolute certainty that a career—*a life*—in the humanitarian world was *exactly what she wanted*. Any prior uncertainty or reservation was gone. Mary-Anne was unequivocally and irretrievably hooked, infected, addicted. This, this place or a hundred others more or less like it was where she belonged. The coordination meetings, the arduous community assessments, the M&E reports, the late nights hunched over a laptop computer in the sweltering heat, the grimy, smoky expat hangouts. The donkeys braying, plaintively in the desert in the wee hours of the morning. *This* was what she was meant to do.

At that moment, she also understood Jean-Philippe in a way she hadn't before. For the first time, Mary-Anne understood his fear of commitment to her or to any*one* or any*thing* that might compromise his ability to respond to his own personal humanitarian imperative. She understood because she now felt it, too. And just like her realization that "there is no God" more than a year ago in Haiti, the inner acknowledgement of her own personal humanitarian imperative was at once frightening and comforting. Comforting simply because there are few things more comforting than knowing, even if only fleetingly, one's place in the world; and frightening because there are few things more worrisome than suddenly beginning to realize the collateral costs of living out one's life purpose. But beyond even the acute, if still diffuse, fear of what a life of humanitarianism might ultimately cost, there was still something else about Jon Langstrom's words that stuck and bothered her.

His face was barely visible as she turned in the uncomfortable plastic chair to face him more directly. "I hear what you're saying. 'Take this opportunity and run with it.' I get it. But I don't want to build my career on other people's screw-ups." Mary-Anne wrinkled her pretty nose. "I don't want my success to be based on the fact that I simply sucked less than someone else or that… I dunno. I want to do the work well because that is the right thing to do and because 'our beneficiaries' deserve it."

"Yeah, I know," Jon chuckled. "Look. Being excellent at your job, planning and implementing programs that work, that 'make a difference' or that 'help people' or whatever… that's one thing. But managing your career path is something very different. The truth is, you need to do both. Just understand that being an excellent humanitarian worker and having a bright future career-wise are not necessarily linked. Don't assume that by doing the first, you'll get the second automatically. And similarly, don't assume if you manage to achieve the second, that you were successful at the first." Jon could turn from joking to serious as if with the flip of a light switch, and the switch had just been flipped. He was serious. "Make no mistake, neither the logo of a successful household charity on your business card, nor a senior-sounding title in that same household charity make one a humanitarian."

A loud burst of raucous laughter from the WFP/Save table interrupted their conversation. Jon Langstrom took a long pull from the bottle of St. George in his hand, and Billy-Bob the goat bleated loudly in the darkness behind and above them, presumably from the branches of his favorite tree.

Mary-Anne changed the subject. "So how did *you* do it, Jon? I mean, you seem to have it all together. You've got the career, you've been around, you have the beautiful family, a nice job in the U.S. but you get to travel… I'd seriously like to know." Her voice trailed off as she looked at him inquisitively.

Jon could feel the St. George hitting his bloodstream. He'd drunk the first two much too quickly on a nearly empty stomach, and as he took another pull on the third he could feel himself becoming unnaturally talkative. "It's not all as awesome as it looks from the outside," he paused to light another cigarette.

Deployment smoker.

"My wife has been mad at me for most of the last nine or ten years. No matter how far in advance I tell her about my travel and no matter how transparent I might be with her about times and dates, there's always some urgent, last-second reason why I should have booked my ticket to come back one day sooner. No matter how much advance notice there is or how many times I remind her, the fact that I'm traveling always somehow manages to come as a surprise the night before I head out, followed by angry silence as I head for the airport."

Jon sighed heavily.

"My daughter used to be this sweet little girl, but now she's the queen bitch who won't talk to me, really, except to demand permission to use the computer. My boss is a jerk—not stupid, very smart, in fact—but clueless about the humanitarian world, and unwilling to acknowledge that he is. He thinks this is all simple. In his world efficiency is about sharing admin support between departments and buying travel tickets from Travelocity rather than through a conventional travel agent. He's convinced that if I'd just read *Good to Great* I'd somehow be able to run programs better."

Another pull. Jon was on a roll. "On this trip, in fact, I have the pleasure of being stuck between my jerk boss who is insistent that I stay here for 'as long as it takes' to get some new project going, and my wife who is equally insistent that I am back in Boston in—oh, let's see—exactly eight days, now, for a dance recital. Chloe, my daughter, has a dance recital. It's not her first. That was years ago. Nor is it her last. But this is symbolic for my wife. It's not about some damn dance recital. She wants me to cut my deployment short as a matter of principle."

Jon Langstrom peered at the St. George label on the bottle in his hand. The Amharic letters seemed to dance before his eyes. The Save/UK and WFP guys were getting louder. He stubbed out the cigarette in his hand, offered the pack to Mary-Anne (she declined politely), before lighting up again himself. The words tumbled out, now.

"I mean, what does she not get? It's a dance recital. *A middle school dance recital*. People miss those all the time and the world continues to turn. And as much as I dislike him, I can't just blatantly piss off my boss."

"But surely your wife understands," Mary-Anne interjected. "She understands that you can't just blow off your job—"

Jon was suddenly bitter. "She understands and at the same time she doesn't. She thinks that I'm some humanitarian badass who will get snapped up by any NGO the second I put my CV out there. But it's never like that in the aid world. Like I just explained, no matter how good of an aid worker you are, no matter how much 'difference' you make in the lives of beneficiaries or whatever, it is not the same thing as playing the game well. And make no mistake, it *is* a game. The problem is that I've never been very good at playing the game."

Another contemplative sip.

"Which means that I'm forever an employ*ee*. I'm forever at the mercy of those who play the game better."

As she lit up her last cigarette of the evening (seriously, her last), Mary-Anne caught a glimpse of Jon's face looking sadder than she'd ever seen it. Then darkness. Then his voice in the darkness. "I'd walk into live fire for my wife and daughter. I'd endure hardship, deprivation. I'd submit to torture if I thought they needed me to do it."

"Family first, right?" Mary-Anne interjected again.

"Yeah," Jon nodded. "Family first."

Another pull from the bottle. Mary-Anne's face was soft and beautiful in the flicker of the lighter. Almost 7:00, almost curfew. Time to call for the waiter, time to pay the bill. If he stayed any longer he knew he'd say things he'd regret later. He'd already said too much.

"But sometimes 'family first' means you *miss* the dance recital."

* * *

Jean-Philippe's Skype light had been green, but he'd neither answered her instant messages nor accepted when she'd tried to call. As she collapsed onto her cot, too tired to shower, Mary-Anne's final thoughts as she sank into exhausted sleep were of him, wondering where he was, who he might be with.

Chapter 14

Mary-Anne spent the better part of the wee hours of the morning, since long before the first post-daybreak donkey mournfully made his presence known, pondering the *NGO Information Paradox*.

The NGO Information Paradox holds that there is always simultaneously too much information and never enough information. Mary-Anne remembered Brandon explaining after his fourth St. George following a day of doing Jillian's bidding via email. As he'd put it, just consider the volume of email communication produced by a single INGO during the first week of a disaster response operation and the positively massive amount of information it all represented: information about the disaster itself, usually forwarded and re-forwarded; information about internal things—who will deploy, who will support from HQ, fundraising strategies, will we do direct mail? Will we encourage our Twitter followers to text #WACHELP to +123.456.7890 to donate $10 to "disaster victims here and around the world," information about technical things like the Sphere standard for emergency shelter and how it applies to a burgeoning "strategic corporate partnership," or the number of Aquatabs needed to ensure clean water to a displaced population of 60,000; or automatically generated information about who is on vacation in the Caymans and can be reached for emergencies only, and whom to contact for non- or quasi-emergency inquiries in the absence of said Caymans vacationeer and until which date.

Billy-Bob had bleated as he normally did and Brandon had downed the rest of his beer in one long pull.

He'd then gone on to bemoan the fact that, at the same time, if the twice-daily Sit-Rep from the response manager to the executive team is fifteen minutes late, heads roll because, "We're just not getting the information we need." Or by the same token, the exact same response manager can never actually make a decision (or at least not an informed decision) because it is all but impossible to get any kind of information out of the field team: Are we getting 50,000 or *500*,000 MT of CSB from WFP? Is Valerie Amos tweeting live from Schiphol airport *or from our NFI distribution???* Are we partnering with Save the Children or with CARE? Did our warehouse get overrun by rioting beneficiaries on live CNN, or was it just a really poorly run distribution? Are we the cluster lead for WASH or for Livelihoods?

He was slurring by that point, and as Mary-Anne paid the tab and steered him toward the WAC Land Cruiser under the knowing smirks of the UNHAS pilots and UNICEF technical specialists he'd ranted on aloud to anyone and everyone about how NGOs are never-sated, information-hungry monsters. The more information you feed to an NGO, the more is needed. There is no getting out in front of it.

That, Mary-Anne nodded to herself, is the nature of the NGO Information Paradox. She'd taken a few hurried mouthfuls of oily breakfast washed down with another two shots of black Ethiopian coffee, and was now two-thirds of the way through her inbox. It had been mostly the usual—automated Listserv emails from ALNAP and AidJobs, updates from AidSource discussions she was following, routine correspondence from partners, and the minutes of the last coordination meeting at ARRA. There were also two email messages from Jillian. First was a message to WAC's board of directors and senior management group informing them that Brandon was missing, what steps were being taken to locate him, and that Mary-Anne would act as WAC's chief of party in Ethiopia, effective immediately and until further notice.

The second was more measured, copied to a larger group of "normal" employees at HQ and pretty much every employee of WAC in Ethiopia, in which she appointed Mary-Anne WAC's acting chief of party without going into the reasons why, also effective immediately and until further notice. Somehow, seeing it all in writing from Jillian's email address made it seem really real. Then, perforce, a slew of emails demanding information she didn't have and had no idea how to get. She locked her computer. Ten minutes until WAC staff meeting. *Time for one more shot of black coffee.*

Mary-Anne knew that she could only hide behind the normal daily email ritual before taking on her real tasks: lead the WAC response team and make sure they won some of the new OFDA money. It was the moment she'd dreamt of and pictured in her mind's eye for months—moving up to management. But now that it was real and she was really in charge of something, her knees felt weak. She'd sat through more of Brandon's staff meetings than she could remember, but for some reason, the prospect of chairing one herself made her mouth dry. Suddenly the NGO Information Paradox loomed large: She didn't know nearly enough about what was going on in the field to even report to Jillian, let alone make good decisions about it, let alone supervise staff or *lead*. As she jotted down a few agenda points in her WAC logo spiral notebook, it occurred to Mary-Anne that management and leadership are the easiest things in the world *until you actually have to do them.*

The first half-hour of the staff meeting was easy. Listen to the site coordinators and department leads give their updates. As they droned on in a range of different accents, Mary-Anne pondered the fact that even as regional program coordinator, she'd always felt as though she was flying blind for lack of real, usable information. Getting useful information about funding pipelines, donor demands, or conditions in field sites, for example, had always been like pulling teeth. And WAC, like pretty much every other NGO on the planet, seemed to think that the remedy was mandatory staff meetings where everyone went around and said what they were working on (while everyone else in the room daydreamed of R&R). Nine times out of ten, it was a pointless exercise that added virtually zero value.

Once the updates were finished, though, it was game time for Mary-Anne. She took a deep breath and dove in by stating, in as matter-of-fact a voice as she could muster, that Brandon was AWOL and she was now their boss until further notice. As she spoke, Mary-Anne watched the faces of those in the room. Tekflu silently smiled his approval from behind his wire-rimmed spectacles, while the chain-smoking Bulgarian warehouse manager stared at the floor, stone-faced. Rolf, the security manager (he'd worked with MSF and Jean-Philippe in Haiti) nodded broodingly as he heard his assignment: Go to Addis immediately and find Brandon. Do whatever has to be done, but *figure it out*. He would report directly to Mary-Anne. Andrew, "Andy," the wiry, sandy-haired guy from Denmark would step in to replace Mary-Anne as senior program officer in Dolo Ado. He'd jumped ship from Mercy Corps to join the WAC relief team in Dolo Ado—spoke flawless English, very good Amharic, and had excellent rapport with the programs and operations team. Mary-Anne knew Andy would move naturally into the role. The final agenda point was to put together a design team to pursue the new OFDA money.

Mary-Anne would be the design team lead, of course, but Andy would be invaluable on the program design side, and Mercy, the cheerful Tanzanian finance officer, would make sure the budget made sense. Even as she spoke the assignments, Mary-Anne began to feel the weight of responsibility settle on her shoulders like a mantle. As the twenty odd staff filed dutifully out of the WAC meeting room, she knew it was time to do or die. No more skipping by under the protection of mid-management above. She was in charge now. *This was the real thing.*

* * *

Angie knew she'd done the right thing by sending that email to Jon—the one where she'd demanded that he be home in time for Chloe's dance recital, or else. After twenty years, it was time to throw down the gauntlet. Of that she was certain. But seventy-two hours after clicking "send," Angie Langstrom was still second-guessing.

What if Jon didn't make it? After twenty odd years of the ups and downs that invariably accompany the life of a partner of an expat aid worker, after all they'd been through *together* was she *really* ready to call it quits over a *dance recital?*

She looked across the kitchen table at her—*their*—only daughter, Chloe. She had Jon's nose, Angie noticed, as Chloe hunched over her homework. She was a beautiful girl, Angie thought. *A beautiful young lady.* The thought of tearing their family apart almost overcame her. Not that she'd never contemplated it before, but she'd never before been this close.

Chloe looked up, caught her mother watching her and smiled. A sweet, innocent, contented smile, before refocusing on Shakespeare or maybe algebra.

She had Jon's eyes, too.

Angie thought back to a conversation that she and Jon had had many times. He'd be on the phone or on a grainy Skype video. Or maybe he'd be in person as they lay together in the darkness, her head on his shoulder, his hand caressing her face, his voice soft. He'd be confessing his love for her and Chloe, and say, "I'd walk into live fire for my family…"

In the early years, that statement caused tender emotion to well up in her heart and tears to well up in her eyes. But lately it had begun to cause the bitter gall of resentment to well up instead. Promising to walk into live fire sounded sacrificial and gallant, but in the end, it was really nothing. When was *that* ever going to be necessary? Promising to walk into live fire for one's family was like promising to donate to charity one's lottery winnings without having ever bought a lottery ticket. It wasn't that she didn't believe him—she *did* believe him, or at least believed that he was sincere—but she didn't need him to walk into live fire. She just needed him to be home, to be a husband, to be a father.

Angie missed Jon. The *old* Jon. The old *Them*. One part of her longed for the old rush, the romance, the heady days when changing the world for the better while simultaneously keeping true love alive truly seemed like a viable, attainable option. But another part of her bit back hard on the anger pent up and unreleased, now, for more than a decade. Some things from the past simply could never be left totally behind. And in that moment, the anger and the loneliness threatened to overwhelm her and Angie suddenly felt stronger and more resolved than ever before. This *was* the right thing to do. There was no going back. It was time for Jon to choose once and for all.

* * *

Mark had read on the UNHCR website that $500 would provide the shelter, NFI and basic material needs of a refugee family in the Horn of Africa. And so, by his calculation, a fund of $300,000 would allow Oxfam America reasonably claim six hundred families helped as "theirs"—if he could ever get Jon Langstrom on the case, that is.

The more he turned it all over in his mind, the clearer and incontrovertible it all seemed. The main thing lacking in all of it was money. People like Jon went on about local capacity and process, but to Mark those were obstacles posed mainly by lack of money. The only *real* problems facing an impoverished country or disaster zone, or so it seemed to him, were resource deficits. With enough money you can buy capacity. With enough money you can circumvent process and just go straight to the thing you need. Inject enough cash into a context like Dolo Ado and all the problems would go away. The more money, the faster it all gets better.

Mark was growing more agitated by the minute.

He'd given Jon Langstrom $300,000 to "get something going" in Dolo Ado. And then he'd upped it to $500,000. *Half a million.*

Why the foot-dragging and the endless meetings with ARRA or Oxfam GB? Pick a spot—any spot would do (there were four already, plus a fifth about to be built at Bur Amina)—hire some local staff, rent some space, and just do it.

Mark was stressed. He'd promised the board that there would be an identifiable Oxfam America presence in Dolo Ado by the end of the month. He needed Jon to come through. Now.

Chapter 15

Mulu Alem checked his cell phone (no messages) and looked at his day planner. His first appointment of the day was with "Mr. Jonathon" from Oxfam America.

Mulu Alem sighed. The new camp at Bur Amina was nothing but a headache. In the two weeks since he'd announced it at the NGO partners meeting, it had meant nothing but mountains of paperwork and a solid flow (no longer just a steady stream) of NGO staff sucking up his time, scrapping for a piece of the action.

As if that wasn't enough, it would be at least another month before he could take a weekend back in Addis with the willowy, doe-eyed Aster. He hadn't seen her in almost two months already. In the past two weeks, he'd noticed a precipitous decline in the number of email, calls, and text messages from her. She didn't return his calls or his messages. Something was going on, but he had no way of finding out what.

Mulu Alem checked his phone one more time, just to be certain. Sure enough, there were no new messages or missed calls from Aster.

God, he hated Dolo Ado.

There was a knock on the door.

"Yes, come in please."

It was Mr. Jonathon from Oxfam America.

"Hello, Mr. Alem," Jon extended his hand. "Thank you for taking the time to meet with me."

Mulu Alem nodded and shook Jon's hand, then motioned to a rickety wooden chair opposite his desk. "Please have a seat. Do you care for a mocha?"

"Yes, sure. Mocha sounds good. Thank you."

As he seated himself at his desk Mulu Alem looked carefully at Mr. Jonathon of Oxfam America. He was dressed neatly in the classic NGO worker uniform of khaki chinos and a button-down, long-sleeved shirt with the sleeves rolled up just past the wrist. He'd pressed his clothes and shaved, Mulu Alem noticed. Respectful. In the nearly one year Mulu Alem had been in Dolo Ado, he'd pretty much seen it all. He'd had foreign aid workers come into his office wearing everything from tattered cutoffs, flip-flops, and tank tops, to suit jackets and ties. Some were scared of him, others talked down to him, while others had been outright demanding and rude. Some tried to speak to him in broken Amharic, while others spoke to him in first-grade English. He never really knew what was in store each time the door to his office opened and another foreigner from another NGO wandered in.

On first glace, Mr. Jonathon had the demeanor of someone who had been around the NGO world for a while. He was fit, not fat, not thin, casual, but not sloppy, and had an air of confidence without arrogance. Mr. Jonathon looked Mulu Alem directly in the eyes and spoke clear, normal English in a comfortable, measured cadence.

"So what can I do for you today, Mr. Jonathon?" Mulu Alem knew, or thought he knew, but wanted to hear Mr. Jonathon say it.

"Well, first I just wanted to meet you in person and thank you for your support to Oxfam..."

"Yes, it's okay. It's the reason ARRA is here. More or less the *only* reason," Mulu Alem let his impatience show. After almost a year, he was done with the cultural formalities bit.

Mr. Jonathon looked taken aback for a split second, then continued. "I want to discuss with ARRA the possibility of Oxfam America taking on a new initiative in a new sector in Kobe Camp. We know there are unmet needs there, particularly in the food and nutrition sectors. I'd like to hear your thoughts on how we might best work together to cover those gaps." Jon paused for a moment before going on. "Oxfam GB, our parent organization is already there, so I want to make clear that I'm specifically asking for your approval to work there separately as Oxfam AmericaA."

There it was out.

Mulu Alem scratched his chin contemplatively and glanced down at his cell phone (no messages). "Yes, we appreciate the good work that Oxfam is doing in Kobe Camp. Many Somalis benefit from your education program and water provision, and your colleagues are always most keen at the coordination meetings." He paused briefly and peered at Mr. Jonathon over the top of his wire-rimmed spectacles.

"But if you want to work in Kobe Camp, I suggest that you expand your current activities instead of taking on more sectors. There are still gaps in education and water provision, too. You already have the staff trained and the infrastructure. Just expand these. WFP and UNICEF can take care of food and nutrition." Another pause. "Why does Oxfam

America need a separate project? Isn't Oxfam the same Oxfam everywhere?"

It was a good question. It was the question *he* would have asked, had the tables been turned. Truth be told, it had been a bit of a gamble to even ask. Jon had been over the reports, the situation updates, and the minutes of the coordination meetings. Kobe Camp was the one place in the whole Dolo Ado system where existing Oxfam GB presence was sufficient to enable the easy addition of a discreet "U.S." project, and where there was a noticeable gap in coverage in a sector where Oxfam America had "strategic interest"—food and nutrition. And from that perspective Kobe Camp was the low-hanging fruit that Jon Langstrom was looking for: a place where, if he could get ARRA on board, Oxfam America could swoop in and establish presence—"plant the flag," as his annoying boss, Mark, liked to put it. Not only that, but if he could make Kobe happen, everything would be at a stage that he could leave for a few days to get back to Boston and that damned dance recital. Kobe was the shortest distance between where he was right now to making both his boss and his wife happy at the same time. Or, failing that, at least get them both off his back for a little while.

Jon had hoped Mulu Alem would agree. But sadly, it didn't look as if that was going to happen.

"It's important to us, for the sake of our generous donors, to have a specifically American Oxfam project in food and nutrition." He had to at least try. "Of course, Oxfam is one big organization globally, but in this case we're trying to highlight some of the work that we do which is supported by our U.S.-based supporters. They're very keen to see their money go specifically to a food and nutrition project. Kobe Camp seems well-suited because even with WFP and UNICEF there are gaps in food and nutrition coverage."

Maybe it was the heat, already emanating from the cracked pavement and seeping in through the windows. Maybe it was the fact that it had been almost two weeks since he'd had communication of any consequence from the willowy, doe-eyed Aster, doing god-only-knew-what on her own in Addis Ababa. Or maybe Mulu Alem was just tired of INGO politics and game-playing. In the last six months, not one single soul had ever complained about conditions or service coverage in Kobe Camp. Kobe Camp was on no one's radar, but Bur Amina was on practically *everyone's* radar. The media, the UN, his boss, and the entire Ethiopian Ministry of Home Affairs were all down on him—*him*—to make Bur Amina happen and happen well. Let the Americans and the

British figure themselves out someplace else. New resources needed to go to Bur Amina.

"Kobe Camp is a low priority for the interagency response in Dolo Ado right now," Mulu Alem said flatly. "I saw you at the last coordination meeting. You know we have a new camp opening within two months at Bur Amina. If Oxfam wants to expand its current work in Kobe, I'll be happy to approve that, but I—ARRA would strongly prefer that you put new resources into Bur Amina. There will be more than 20,000 new refugees there by the end of the year. We'll need every NGO partner we can leverage to work there." He lowered his chin and peered at Mr. Jonathon over the top of his spectacles again, for effect, before finishing. "I am personally committed to ensuring the maximum possible resource saturation in Bur Amina. If Oxfam America wants to do its own food and nutrition work in Bur Amina I'll approve. Or any other normal sector in Bur Amina, I'll approve, too. But for Kobe... I'm sorry, but I cannot."

*

As he left the ARRA compound and walked toward the Oxfam Land Cruiser, Jon Langstrom could feel his life begin to slip slowly sideways.

Chapter 16

It took Brandon several days to really remember the events of the past weekend, and even then there were gaps. He remembered chatting up the lithe young woman next to him at the bar of Beer Garden Inn. He remembered her suggesting that they "go someplace else." He remember paying the tab and getting into a taxi with her. After that it got fuzzy. There was the vague recollection of loud music, disco lights, another taxi ride and another place, another bar, maybe. There'd been more drinking, and then it all sort of faded into nothingness.

The staff at Tzna General Hospital put together the rest. He'd been drugged and robbed. And drugged *heavily*, by the looks of things. Unconscious for three days, and only partially coherent for another four. Brandon hadn't even known his own name when he first came awake. That was some pretty serious drugging.

By the time he'd been at Tzna General for a week, Brandon had remembered who he was, where he was, and someone from the hospital had been to Hotel Kaleb to retrieve his belongings. On day five, he'd actually called Rolf, the security manager, to check in and let him know what had happened. To his surprise, Rolf was actually in Addis looking for *him*.

Rolf had been furious when he first walked into Brandon's hospital room, but he'd calmed down once the attending physician assured everyone that Brandon was mostly just dehydrated. They'd spent maybe half an hour discussing the state of things with WAC. Mary-Anne had been made chief of party until further notice following Brandon's unexplained disappearance. Rolf had sighed heavily upon sharing this particular news. She was both of their bosses.

Brandon wasn't worried, even despite Rolf's angst. It could be worse. Besides, Mary-Anne's promotion essentially meant that he could immediately stop worrying about going for a new OFDA grant while simultaneously setting up operations in a totally new location—Bur Amina. The doctor had been strict: Take it easy for a week or two, no airplane travel, and drink lots of fluids (non-alcohol fluids) and get those kidneys and ureters working again, all of which meant Brandon would have to endure chillaxing in Addis for a while.

He looked over at the pretty young nurse—the one who'd been so tenderly stroking his hand when he'd awakened for the first time. She was sitting by the bed reading an English book—it looked like a romance novel. As she turned a page, her gaze caught his. She smiled and took hold of his hand. Brandon's heart skipped a beat.

"Mr. Brandon, you're feeling better?" *What an amazing smile, and a figure to die for.* "The doctor says if you're strong enough I can take you to the park for a little while today. Or if not today, maybe tomorrow." Mental images of himself arm-in-arm in the park with nurse Aster were quickly replaced by images of racially mixed children bouncing around the front yard of a tidy ranch house in Colorado. He felt her fingers lightly intertwine with his.

Staying a little longer in Addis would be just fine.

* * *

The battered AK-47 fit naturally into Ali's hands. The solid weight, the cold metal, the texture of the battered wooden stock. The bolt made an impressive snap as it fell into place, chambering a round. He could see that the hammer was in the cocked position, ready to fire. *But no need to fire right now.*

Just holding the gun made him feel stronger, more like a man.

The Arab who'd come to Ali's village last month had given guns to most of the young men, and then taught them how to disassemble, reassemble, clean, and load in the shadowy candlelight of the sheikh's tent. Ali learned faster than most, and within just a few minutes, was helping those around him practice. He'd glowed with pride when the Arab patted him affectionately on the head and called him "younger brother," and then said, "Sleep with your weapons tonight. Tomorrow we practice shooting. I can see that this young *jihadi*," he'd motioned toward Ali, "is destined for greatness."

By the time the Arab left, Ali could hit a Coca-Cola bottle from fifty paces on the first try. "Keep practicing young brother," the Arab said. "And always keep your weapon close. Know it fully, whether in the light of day or the darkness of night."

Now, weeks later, Ali was on his first mission. The *jihad* needed vehicles to move martyrs into position for attacks against the infidels. In the pale moonlight, he could just make out the form of Hamid crouched behind a large bush on the other side of the road. He couldn't see them, but he knew that the others were there, too, some in the ditch behind him, others up on the ridge behind Hamid.

Hamid was waving and pointing. Faintly, in the distance, Ali could hear the sound of a car approaching. His pulse quickened. "Fire into the air at first," the Arab had said. "Try not to damage the vehicles. They almost always stop when the shooting starts. If they don't, then we have to shoot them. But try to not damage the vehicles."

Ali's pulse quickened. *This was for real.* He said a quick prayer for strength and courage. The headlights of the approaching vehicle were visible now, still small in the distance. He pushed the safety lever quietly down to the middle position: *full auto*.

* * *

Mary-Anne awoke with a start. It had been days since she'd really slept. Between the oppressive heat, even at night, the never-ending cacophony of rumbling trucks and lonesome donkeys, and the jarring images that flooded her head every time she closed her eyes, sleep—*real* sleep—seemed forever hopelessly out of reach.

As if on cue a donkey brayed loudly in the semi-darkness.

Mary-Anne looked at her watch. 5:00 AM. She knew it was futile to try to sleep more, tired though she was. Her brain was more awake than asleep now. She swung out of bed and pulled on yesterday's cargo pants. "Depending on how things go today, I can get one, maybe two more days of wear out of these," she thought. She rummaged through the pile of random clothing partially folded on the small plastic table near her bed for a suitable shirt or blouse. The only piece she had that was not full-on field funky was a dark blue WAC logo golf shirt.

Mary-Anne sighed.

She hated wearing NGO-branded clothing. A branded vest or hat was okay. She could wear a hat during the focus group or at the distribution, and then take it off easily enough as she walked into the local restaurant for lunch, or the local expat bar at the end of the day.

But branded *clothing*, she reflected to herself, was asking for trouble. Mary-Anne knew that as long as she was wearing anything branded, other aid workers would totally judge her based on the logo on her shirt or vest or hat. Every aid agency has its reputation and persona, usually negative, grounded in a snarky parody of the organization's acronym or name: CARE=Complete Arrogance Regardless of Experience; World Vision=Blurred Vision; Save the Children=Shave the Children; UNHCR=Unhelpful Children mucking about with Refugees; WFP=Waiting for Payment; IRC=Irk; ARC=Arse; MSF=Men Speaking French, and Mary-Anne's own organization, WAC=Women And Children or Wine And Cheese. Those attributes, reasonable and realistic or not, were always applied to anyone seen wearing the brand.

As if that wasn't enough, non-aid workers totally judge an organization in the worst possible way based on what they see someone, anyone, doing while wearing that organization's T-shirt or cap. If a focus group ended in anger and chaos, and a beneficiary saw her walking for the car? The buzz would be that, "WAC doesn't listen to people's needs..." Or if she got upgraded and was seen sitting in the "Premier Access" lounge? Suddenly it would be all over the interwebs that WAC squanders donor dollars and lets its staff fly business class. Or maybe she'd be spotted in a local restaurant (say, Billy-Bob's) quaffing a lukewarm St. George at 4:30 p.m., WAC staff would then be labeled as a bunch of day time drunks who only come to Dolo Ado to party. Mary-Anne again concluded that wearing branded NGO clothing was more or less the same as being live on CNN for the entire day. It was setting oneself up for an inevitable lose-lose.

She sighed resignedly as she pulled the WAC logo golf shirt on over her head. *Whatever.* She'd spend most of today out in the field anyway.

*

As she quickly gulped down yesterday's re-heated *injera*, greasy scrambled eggs, and a second shot of scalding hot black coffee, Mary-Anne checked her email. The NGO Information Paradox was mercifully not yet in effect for the day. There were only two messages.

The first was from Rick at USAID in Addis. He'd heard from Brandon. Too bad about the unfortunate events of last weekend and he sincerely hoped that WAC would be okay without Brandon's leadership for the foreseeable future. And speaking of the foreseeable future, he also sincerely hoped to see a proposal from WAC very soon. There was money for Bur Amina and Rick was sure that WAC would be a strong applicant. Should Mary-Anne wish to discuss further, she was welcome to call the number in his email signature or swing by the office in Addis, should she be heading that way soon.

The other was from Jillian, the CEO, in DC. Just checking in mostly, and hoping Mary-Anne was doing okay. But *also*, there was to be a meeting in DC, in about a week (exact date not yet confirmed), for all of the OFDA partners in the Horn of Africa. She wanted Mary-Anne to be there.

As Mary-Anne walked toward the car park where Mesfin sat waiting in the idling Land Cruiser, the weight of what rested on her shoulders suddenly felt very real and very heavy. Her mind went instinctively to Jean-Philippe, her mental and emotional go-to when she needed support. Even if she couldn't call or text or talk to him by Skype, just the memory of his piercing green eyes, his unruly mop of almost-black hair, the feel of his lean, muscular frame holding her close were sources of strength and comfort. She tried to recall the sound of his voice repeating her name (*Mehreee-ahhhhn*), but to her surprise and dismay, couldn't. Jean-Philippe's voice in her head had been replaced by the voice of Jon Langstrom. And although she was not ready just then to admit, even to herself, any romantic feelings or attraction to Jon, she was crystal clear on one point: The person she really wanted to talk to was Jon Langstrom. She wanted the reassuring sound of his voice making sense of the humanitarian aid industry for her. She wanted the comforting sense of him in the cheap plastic chair next to her at Billy-Bob's, the warm glance of his hand as he lit her cigarette, the pleasant twinkle in his eye as he held out a bottle of St. George for her.

"Madame, are you ready?" It was Mesfin. He'd opened the front passenger door for her. She could hear his Amharic mix tape playing.

"Sure, let's go." Mary-Anne glanced at her small day planner. "Let's go to Kobe first, then Bur Amina."

Chapter 17

The sun was high in the sky and heat waves were shimmering off the road by the time the WAC Land Cruiser ground to a stop at the entrance to Sector 3-C in Kobe Camp. Tekflu was in good spirits today, and their conversation during the three-hour ride from Dolo Ado had been pleasant. The odd "bad Ethiopia day" or "bad Dolo Ado day" notwithstanding, Mary-Anne really liked Tekflu and Mesfin. She trusted Tekflu, too, and in the time since arriving in Dolo Ado had grown to rely heavily on his advice and judgment. As they stepped down from the Land Cruiser, she asked him, "Tekflu, do you remember the little sick girl we met last time we were here? Her mother brought her, they were the last two people we talked to in Kobe before we left that day."

Tekflu nodded. "I do," he answered evenly. "Shall we try to find her today?" Mary-Anne thought she detected a hint of softness in his voice.

"Yes, I'd like to try to find her. I really…"

Her voice trailed off as they approached the community meeting tent and Aasiya came out to meet them. The focus group participants were ready. Time to go to work.

The focus discussion was lively, the participants animated. But there was really nothing new discussed. The project—or more specifically, the DANIDA-funded portion of WAC's nutrition project—was nearly over. There would not be a follow-on tranche, at least not with DANIDA. The overall stats for Kobe Camp showed it was in that supremely unsexy space between "acute" or "emergency," and "just really poor." The nutrition stats basically said that people were undernourished but not in imminent danger of dying from starvation, making Kobe Camp therefore no longer eligible for most of the common relief donors and relief grant programs that focused solely on "life-saving interventions." At the same time, Kobe Camp was still a refugee camp and, by definition, therefore *not* a "development context."

Worse, there was no sparkling opportunity for an "innovative approach" in Kobe. Short of someone inventing an app that would deliver calories to beneficiaries (preferably adolescent girl beneficiaries) via mobile phone, there was virtually zero opportunity for a game-changing innovation or trendy public-private partnership. It was a simple, absolute calorie deficiency within a population that lacked the means to produce its own. Which meant that the remedy was exceedingly straightforward: distribute food.

Mary-Anne found herself in the soul-sucking position of having to explain all of this to a room full of refugee mothers. The project wasn't totally over just yet. There'd be another two or three Plumpy'Nut distributions in Kobe, followed by another six weeks of growth monitoring and nutritional education at the MSF clinic over in Sector 1-A. The women nodded somberly. They understood.

She did her best to sound confident and reassuring; she would personally do all she could to find funding to continue the nutrition project, even after the DANIDA funds ended, but she knew what would happen. They'd get *maybe* two small distribution's worth of lentils from WFP, and then Kobe Camp would essentially fall through the cracks, at least as far as WAC was concerned. She could already feel the gravitational pull of Bur Amina and the potential for OFDA money. Maybe there'd be a program officer she could put on the Kobe Camp nutrition project, and maybe there were some small funding that could be scraped together. Maybe, if everyone promised to poop in the latrines instead of the bushes they could move some of the WASH funding over to nutrition to keep the Kobe program alive for a little while longer. But in the end it would be the same. WAC would follow the funding, which was very clearly going to Bur Amina. Kobe Camp would muddle along, its inhabitants hungry, but not to the point of death.

Such is the way things work in the humanitarian world. Mary-Anne knew that the women there in the tent knew it, too. She was just the messenger. *Just the messenger*. There was precious little at the field level that she could actually decide, precious little action that she could take. Even as WAC's chief of party, her actual authority was limited. She could, theoretically, go against Jillian, leave the OFDA grant and a toe-hold in Bur Amina on the table for the sake of keeping a live trickle flowing in to Kobe. But if she did that, she wouldn't last long.

Mary-Anne knew that what was needed and what she had to do was not necessarily the same thing. And for the first time since donning the title of 'humanitarian' she began to feel tarnished.

The focus group ended as they all did: The women thanked her and then chatted around the entrance to the tent, eventually wandering off toward their respective T-shelters. As the conversations began to lull,

Mary-Anne approached Aasiya and motioned for Tekflu to come translate.

"Please ask her about the little girl we met last time."

Tekflu translated, and Aasiya furrowed her brow as he spoke. Then she slowly shook her head, spoke a few quick words to Tekflu in Arabic, and gave Mary-Anne a smile that said, *Please don't ask me any hard questions.*

"She remembers the little girl and her mother, but she doesn't know what has happened to them. She hasn't seen them since last week when you were here."

"Can she ask around, maybe find out something?" Mary-Anne bit her lip and tried to keep her voice from sounding too anxious.

Again, Tekflu translated and Aasiya answered, nodding vigorously and smiling broadly at Mary-Anne.

"She will find out. Next time you come, she will know what happened with them."

* * *

The sun was beginning to look large and round as it sank toward the horizon in the general direction of Sudan. As usual, Mary-Anne was tired. She was grateful that the partners' meeting in Bur Amina was her last stop of the day. After that, it would be another hour in the Land Cruiser to Dolo Ado, then Billy-Bob's where she'd put back a few bottles of St. George and—she hoped—see Jon Langstrom.

There were only six people in the meeting: Mulu Alem from ARRA; a middle-aged woman Mary-Anne recognized as the country director for GOAL; a stern-looking older man, very tall and thin, from NRC; and two guys—she guessed about her own age—from Save the Children and World Vision. The sole point of the meeting was to identify the cluster leads for WASH, NFI, and emergency education in Bur Amina once it opened.

The introductions went well enough. Mulu Alem confirmed that the new camp at Bur Amina would accept the first refugees in about six weeks, assuming UNOPS could have the drainage dug and the sectors laid out, and that they could cover key sectors. UNHCR would create a matrix, while UNHABITAT and CHF would cover shelter. UNICEF would lead the health cluster (although MSF would do pretty much all of the clinical work). WFP would take on food, but as usual needed implementing partners. The primary sectors in need of leads, as everyone knew, were WASH, NFI and education. Within five minutes, it was confirmed that World Vision would be the cluster lead for WASH and that Save the Children would take emergency education.

Which left NFIs up for grabs. And naturally, per the aid world norm, it was never simple.

The humorless-looking man from NRC turned out to be the director of programmes, and he insisted that his organization was in the best position to lead the NFIs cluster. After all, NRC had all but been filling that role at three of the other camps. They were in touch with the needs of the refugee population, had established relationships with vendors in Ethiopia as well as throughout the region, and they had an existing supply chain up and running.

He'd begun to read painstakingly through a detailed analysis of NRC's supply chain capacity, including the number of cubic meters of warehouse space in Dolo Ado alone. Halfway through the matronly woman from GOAL rudely interjected that the cluster lead didn't necessarily have to be directly active in the sector of intervention for which it was the lead. In fact, in her opinion, NRC's investment in procurement in logistics might be an argument against considering NRC as the cluster lead because they'd be too busy managing their own supply chain and running their own distributions to really provide leadership to others, or to actively represent the interests of the cluster within the context of the larger interagency response. She went on to opine that, in this instance, GOAL might actually be a better choice as NFI cluster lead because while, *of course*, they had significant global experience and expertise with NFIs, and while they were somewhat active in the NFI sector in the Horn of Africa, they had sufficient bandwidth here in Ethiopia to take the lead, not just in name, but in actual practice.

She started to ramble on about how GOAL was the best choice because they had the winning combination of expertise, capacity, and freedom from conflict of interest: How in the world was it a good idea to have as the cluster lead an organization that was also competing with the members for grants and funding in that same sector? That was hardly fair for the "newer, smaller partners" (she gave Mary-Anne a sympathetically indulgent smile as she said that) and it reduced provider diversity, which ultimately reduced the overall quality of intervention in the sector.

NRC's director of programmes began to flush (difficult to discern at first in the dim fluorescent light of the conference room) and touch the back of his neck. When the woman from GOAL took a breath, he jumped right back in.

"Madame" from GOAL was being ridiculous and insulting. Was she suggesting that NRC would unfairly leverage its status as cluster lead to bully other partners or compete for funding? No, of course not, and it was preposterous to suggest. Really, if that was GOAL's formal perspective on the matter, maybe an email to the CEO in Dublin was in order.

Even in the fluorescent light, the back of his neck was now very obviously as red as a boiled lobster. The two young guys from World Vision and Save sat silently watching the spectacle with bemused expressions. The matronly woman from GOAL shifted angrily in her chair and fiddled with the dangly tribal bracelet on her left wrist.

The programme director from NRC was standing now and shaking his fist. The red flush of anger had spread from his neck to his ears and face. Almost shouting, he accused GOAL of having lost loyalty to true European humanitarianism—the kind that focused on professionalism, attention to detail, and accountability as a means of ensuring sustainable impact at the field level.

Mary-Anne's mind raced. They were *both* right on some points. There was an argument to be made in favor of a smaller NGO as the cluster lead, just as there was validity in the idea of the cluster lead not being heavily operational in that sector in that response... *Maybe WAC could be the NFI cluster lead.*

This was by far the largest disaster response operation ever undertaken by WAC to date, and sure, their total relief budget for Dolo Ado was a fraction of what a Save the Children or an Oxfam would spend just in Bur Amina. But then again, she'd been involved in practically every aspect of NFI procurement, supply chain management, and distribution in Haiti. Where larger organizations tended to pigeonhole people, make them all small cogs in large machines, smaller ones exposed their people to more aspects of a relief response. Between Haiti and now Dolo Ado, she'd already gained a breadth of hands-on frontline experience that many aspiring aid workers would positively kill for. The same was true for much of her team. Maybe WAC as WAC hadn't done a lot of NFI work on the same scale that the heavier hitters had, but then again Bur Amina was only one camp, and it wasn't even the largest one.

Suddenly, Mary-Anne knew what she had to do and, almost without thinking, raised her hand and simultaneously half-shouted over the din of NRC versus GOAL, "World Aid Corps volunteers to serve as NFI cluster lead for Bur Amina."

The programme director from NRC stopped mid-sentence and gaped at Mary-Anne, slack-jawed. The country director from GOAL sat back heavily in her chair and half-sniffed, half-snorted in conspicuous annoyance. The guys from World Vision and Save grinned and nodded in silent approval.

Mary-Anne continued. "We have the capacity and bandwidth to take on the role of cluster lead, and while we have strong interest in operational presence in Bur Amina, our interest in NFIs specifically is limited. And…" she looked pointedly at Mr. NRC and Ms. GOAL, "*we* would seem to be the most neutral of the interested parties here today, which under the circumstances is probably what you want." At this, she made sustained eye contact with Mulu Alem.

Mulu Alem nodded thoughtfully. He was a little disappointed that Oxfam wasn't in the room. He'd seen Oxfam run NFIs in other places and thought they did it well. But oh well. Bur Amina wasn't that big. WAC could probably handle it.

"I agree. I support WAC as NFI cluster lead. I also suggest that you consider working closely with Oxfam. I know they're looking at Bur Amina."

Chapter 18

Mary-Anne's pulse and mind were both still racing as she stepped down from the WAC Land Cruiser in front of Billy-Bob's. She'd just committed her organization to taking on a major coordination and leadership role in a relief response that was high-profile globally. The UN was watching; global mass media were watching. It was prestigious, and in many ways it would be hard to screw up the cluster lead role, Mary-Anne knew. Being the cluster lead for NFIs or any other sector, really, would mostly be a lot of chairing meetings, taking notes, sending notes out, haranguing members to come to meetings, haranguing NGOs doing NFIs in Bur Amina to come to the meetings, to get them all to play nice with each other. Being the cluster lead was as close as an organization could get to coordination ground zero. And it would basically be like herding cats.

The enormity of the task of being cluster lead was not what made Mary-Anne's head reel now. It would not be especially difficult or demanding work. Rather, it was the ease with which someone in her second relief deployment ever, promoted in the field by default to a position she could never have applied for and won, could go in and take over the lead role for an entire sector for an entire camp on the strength of nothing more than simply having the *cojones* to speak up.

As she dusted off her khaki cargo pants, instinctively feeling to see if the half-empty pack of Marlboros was still in the oversized side pocket, and untucked her WAC branded golf shirt (hopefully no haters or judgers would be at Billy-Bob's that night), she grappled with a confluence of emotions: the heady rush of having won a significant gain against the nagging, rising tide of self-doubt that plagues almost every humanitarian worker at such times, overshadowed, as ever, by a longing ache for Jean-Philippe.

*

It was the usual crowd at Billy-Bob's that night. Fifteen or so of the by now familiar NGO and UN expats chatted loudly, crowded around the plastic tables, and the owner of the restaurant had added extra help. At least three dark young men moved quickly among the tables, clearing away empty bottles and bringing full ones to replace them (almost no one ever ordered food at Billy-Bob's). Billy-Bob himself was in fine form, making the rounds and cheerfully—as cheerfully, at least, as a goat can ever be—abutting the flat of his head against the outstretched hands of NGO expats. "Tunnel of Love" by Dire Straits was playing over the small house speakers, and it seemed to Mary-Anne as she walked through the low inner doorway leading to the courtyard, that the song perfectly fit the setting of the traveling carnival troupe that is the expat contingent in international relief responses from the Stans to the Sahel.

She looked around quickly and spotted Jon Langstrom, as usual, seated by himself at a small table in the corner under Billy-Bob's tree. She ordered four bottles of St. George from the waiter before walking toward him. Even if, by some weird coincidence, Jon wasn't drinking, she'd still need all four. He smiled and nodded, as he always did, and motioned for her to sit down in the only other chair near "his" table. As she wound her way through the noisy crowd toward him, it suddenly occurred to her that "they" had a routine, and that thought was comforting. She felt comfortable with him, and that meant a lot. But there was something more that she couldn't quite put her finger on. There was something else, too—a twinge of something, deep in the pit of her stomach. Something strange, yet familiar.

As she sat, the waiter appeared and placed four bottles of St. George on the table. "Tough day, huh?" he asked as he looked at her quizzically.

"I've had two meetings that totaled, maybe ninety minutes between them. But it feels like I've been going all day." She paused to offer a bottle to Jon, took one herself, and half-heartedly raised it in his direction. "Cheers," she said before putting it to her lips and thirstily downing half of the contents.

"It *must* have been a tough day. I'm one down already, but I can see I won't be keeping up with you tonight!" Jon Langstrom laughed. Mary-Anne chuckled, too. It was good to hear his laugh.

"Yeah, I guess. There's a lot going on." She took another pull. Only about a centimeter left in the bottle. "Between an OFDA proposal that I have yet to type even one word of, generally gearing up for Bur Amina, simultaneously closing out all of our residual grants in Kobe, and still trying to come through with something for Kobe after all those grants finish…" Her voice wavered as she thought of the women she'd grown used to seeing in her Kobe focus groups, and it suddenly dawned on her that as a senior program officer, the part of her job she'd enjoyed the most was those focus groups. But as chief of party, she'd have larger, more important tasks to look after and would have to delegate monitoring to someone junior, like a program coordinator or program officer.

Jon's voice pulled her back to the present. "Hmmm… that *is* a lot… a lot to put on one person." He sipped his own beer contemplatively and fished a cigarette out of his breast pocket. "You got a light?" Mary-Anne fished the cheap orange lighter out of her cargo pocket and handed it over. As he lit, up Jon continued.

"Sounds like WAC is running you pretty hard. How's your team here doing with everything? And how much *real* support are you getting from your chain of management?"

It was Mary-Anne's turn to be contemplative. "My team here is solid. Young, some of them, but solid. There's no one I don't trust, really, although my security manager is a bit of a character. But I've got very good programs people and a solid operations team." She downed the dregs of the first bottle of St. George and reached for a second. "Support from my chain of management… well, I suppose it depends on what you mean by 'real' support. I've been given the authority to make strategic and programmatic decisions, to hire and fire, to negotiate on behalf of the agency here in Ethiopia, and I've been given financial authority commensurate with my position as chief of party." As she spoke the words, it all suddenly felt like a lot.

"But in terms of actual supervision, I'm given the broad strokes only. 'Make it happen,' or 'win grants.' That's pretty much it, which I guess is good, right? At least I'm not being micromanaged."

Mary-Anne went on. "I mean, I know the systems and policies. I know what humanitarian accountability and good participatory processes are, I know the Cluster System and I know how donor funding works. But at the same time…"

Dire Straits had given way to Radiohead over the house speakers, and Jon was looking at her intently now.

"… At the same time, it all still feels like I don't really know what I'm doing. So much of it feels so loose and, well, so *random*." Mary-Anne craved a cigarette of her own, now, and she began to fish for the half-pack of Marlboros in her cargo pocket. "So, today, for instance, at the partners meeting for Bur Amina, NRC and GOAL were fighting over the cluster lead for NFIs. And I just waded in and took it. And ARRA just gave it to me... to *us*, to WAC. We're the cluster lead for NFIs in Bur Amina!"

She found a cigarette, began to put it to her mouth (*deployment smoker*), and then paused to continue speaking. "It's like, there's this whole part of what we do that is so... so much not about beneficiaries. I mean, seriously, NRC or GOAL would probably do an equally good job of leading the NFIs cluster. And seriously, WAC? Who's heard of us? We're nobody. And ARRA just put us in charge of somehow ensuring the flow of stuff to 20,000 people. That's *crazy!* That whole meeting was about posturing and positioning and recognition." The surrealism of it all suddenly flooded Mary-Anne's brain in ways that she struggled to put into words. "One minute I'm trying to convince refugees to defecate in a hole in the ground, the next minute I'm cutting a deal with the Government of Ethiopia. It's like there's this whole world within the world of humanitarian aid that's... you know, *nothing at all about humanitarian aid.*"

Jon held the lighter out and Mary-Anne leaned forward, a battered Marlboro between her lips. For a split second, she was back on the terrace at Punta Cana, feeling the warmth of Jean-Philippe's hand on hers, lighting her Cedric Menthol, that night of all nights. She savored the memory as she leaned back and watched the first puff of the evening float toward the black sky above. Then, as if out of total darkness, she heard Jon Langstrom begin to speak.

"So look, here's the thing that you need to understand," his voice was low, calm, and reassuring. "So far as I know, this is not taught in any of the development degree programs. This would be one for the 'things they never tell grad students' folder." A smile tugged at the corners of his mouth for a moment before he went serious again.

"It's important for you to understand that pretty much the only space in the humanitarian industry where your job is really, truly, and completely about achieving quality standards, about helping the poor or survivors of disaster or conflict, about rescuing the human trafficking victims or making sure that the women's savings group gets a reasonable interest rate and relevant non-financial services to go along with their loans is at the *project level*. You move away from the project level, even based in here in 'the field' in Dolo Ado as you are, and it becomes about *resources*. Even on a relief response like this one." He took a long drag on his cigarette and exhaled slowly.

"*Think about it.* Think about what you spend your day doing, and tell me if I've got this wrong. At the project level it's about the humanitarian imperative, and Sphere Standards, and impact, and sustainability. But you get even one increment away from that, it's about money. Plain and simple."

Jon drained the last of the bottle in his hand, and then studied the label for a moment before turning toward Mary-Anne. He leaned forward, toward her, his eyes intense, his voice low. She almost had to strain to hear him over Richard Marx coming through the sound system as he continued.

"I don't think this is cynicism. And besides, cynicism is just truth that someone doesn't want to hear. And that's what *this* is: The *truth*. You move outside of the project space—the space where it is your job to interact with the end-users on a regular basis and where the substance of your interaction shapes what you do daily—you move outside of that space, and your job is no longer about doing, but becomes about enabling those who do the doing."

Another long drag, another slow pull from the bottle of St. George.

"It is important to understand this because everyone wants to claim that what they do in their cubicles or coordination meetings 'makes a difference' or some other self-gratifying descriptor. And hopefully it all *does* make a difference. But the bald reality is that unless you are one of a miniscule and proportionally shrinking privileged few in the aid world who daily interact with beneficiaries as a provider of humanitarian project activities, the truth is that you are an enabler."

Richard Marx faded into REO Speedwagon. Mary-Anne was rapt now. Jon had a way of describing the inner workings of the aid world the way a paleontologist describes the predatory capability of a velociraptor: respect borne of understanding, and perhaps even admiration, despite some brutal realities.

"Most people misunderstand this about the aid industry, even those who work in it now and have worked in it for years. Most people think of the aid industry as 'the field' and 'HQ'—'the field' being any country where beneficiaries live, and 'HQ' as a catch-all, really, for pretty much *any*place else. They think that if you're in 'the field,' some third world country, perhaps, you're somehow out there 'actually doing it' more than someone who's sitting in Brussels or Singapore. But the fact is that the majority of those in 'the field' are doing the same work. They might live in more exotic, more interesting places, but what they're actually doing—the tasks they undertake, the decisions they make—is in most cases no more field work than their counterparts sitting in DC."

Jon took another pull from the last untouched bottle of St. George on the table. Mary-Anne glanced at her watch. 6:15 PM. *Not even close to curfew.* She waved to the waiter and, once she had his attention, held up an empty bottle in one hand while holding up two fingers with the other. The waiter nodded. Jon continued.

"Which means that most of the time, those in the HQs of the world are actually 'doing it' just as much as those in 'the field.' In fact, more and more, the *real* work of the aid industry is in HQs." Jon was starting to slur slightly, but he didn't slow down for even a second.

"We've got it all wrong when it comes to working and surviving in the aid world. The self-appointed aid pundits, the Bill Easterlys and Linda Polmans of the world hammer us for having messed up priorities and no commitment to efficiency. And in response, we run workshops on humanitarian accountability and hold training on Sphere standards."

Jon paused, lit another cigarette, and puffed contemplatively for a moment. As he continued speaking, in the back of his mind he wished REO Speedwagon would finish and the mix tape would move on to something better.

"We've missed the point that at the end of the day, at the *ground* level, doing aid just isn't that complicated. *Difficult*, maybe, but not so complicated. We basically know what to do and how to do it. Anyone with access to Google can figure out in a matter of minutes that the Sphere standard for clean water is fifteen liters per person per day. Or that a feedback mechanism, maybe a complaint box or message board, in every beneficiary community is a basic minimum practice for humanitarian accountability. Or that when you run distributions, you should actually register people beforehand and do some basic community prep so that it's not chaos on site when the truck shows up."

He paused as the waiter set two more bottles of St. George on the table.

"But for as much as we whine and moan about them—and believe me, *I* do it, too—we never address the actual *substance* of what the critics are saying. Because what they're saying, indirectly—and even *they* don't fully get it—is that they're attacking the very structures of the industry that we take for granted as some sort of immutable fact of life. And make no mistake: These structural issues are universal. It's not Oxfam or WAC or Save or CARE. You don't escape this problem by moving to another organization or taking a different job in your current organization, because this is the nature of the aid industry itself."

Billy-Bob the goat shuffled in his tree and bleated softly, but no one could say whether in affirmation of Jon Langstrom's soliloquy, or because he thought Jon was becoming too preachy.

Chapter 19

Mary-Anne shifted uncomfortably in her seat. Jon was cutting closer to the bone than she felt up to dealing with after the day she'd had.

"So how do *you* do it?" she asked, almost impatiently for the second time that week. "You've got the wife and daughter and the cute townhouse in New England, but they're not enough. You've spent time in the field, but now you're saying that's not really the field. You've got a sweet job at HQ where you make strategic decisions, supervise people, have financial authority, and control the flow of resources. But now you tell me that you're only enabling, not actually doing?"

Mary-Anne pulled hard on her cigarette and exhaled forcefully. She felt drawn to Jon, a strong intellectual and emotional pull. He was a tortured soul, she could tell, in ways that resonated strongly with her. But some days, he went deeper than she was up for.

Jon Langstrom chuckled self-deprecatingly. "Yeah, you're right. I'm probably over-thinking it all. Actually, I *know* I over-think it." He was slurring heavily now, his words laborious. As if by magic, one of the dark young men arrived, cleared away the empty bottles and left four new, full ones. Bad Co. had mercifully replaced REO Speedwagon. Jon picked up one of the bottles, studied it for a moment, then took a sip. And suddenly he was back on track, eyes lucid, speech clear.

"Not sure how I do it, to be honest. Most days I believe in it. Some days it's just a job." Another sip. "I think you have to find the space where you spend as many of your days as possible doing tasks that you actually like. Or failing that, doing tasks that you don't hate. But what ruins most of us, and what no one ever bothers to tell the new ones—" Jon nodded exaggeratedly at Mary-Anne, "—is that you have to manage the path."

He was getting serious again, but this time, Mary-Anne was into it.

"Most of us bounced from job to job, country to country because the place or the job sounded interesting. Then we all started taking regional or HQ jobs because they seemed like promotions and getting promotions seemed like the thing we all ought to want to do. It's easier than anyone thinks to accidentally fall into just following the path of least resistance. And before you are even conscious of the passage of time, you've already let ten years slip by."

Jon tipped the bottle of St. George up, nearly vertical and swallowed several times. His roll was still on. "It's as if one day you wake up, stuck in a cubicle, twelve pounds heavier that you should be, no retirement fund, unable to make a move, and taking orders from some corporate tool who decided to 'give something back.' You've basically check-mated yourself."

He looked melancholy for a moment, and then finished, "My advice: Figure out what you want to spend your day doing, and plot a career path that gets you there. Don't worry about the title or the location."

The courtyard of Billy-Bob's seemed to sway and revolve, and Mary-Anne knew she'd drunk more than she should have. She placed the two-thirds full bottle in her hands back on the table. "Nights in White Satin" by the Moody Blues was coming through the speakers now, and for the second time that evening, the words on the mix tape seemed to perfectly reflect what they'd just discussed.

Ten minutes until curfew. Just enough time to pay the tab and drive the two kilometers to NGO street.

* * *

Jillian Scott was in an exceptionally good mood. WAC was about to be featured on Charity Navigator, one of her senior field staff in Nicaragua had just been interviewed (positively) on MSNBC, non-grant revenue was up despite a positively crappy economy, and she'd just been invited to the USAID/OFDA partner's briefing for the Horn of Africa.

That Mary-Anne is doing a bang-up job.

Somehow, between Brandon—before he'd gone AWOL—and Mary-Anne, WAC had gotten the attention of USAID in Addis Ababa. It seemed that a nice, plump award was only a proposal away, and with her team on Dolo Ado on the case, led by Mary-Anne, the proposal would be ready within days. Jillian had prepped her contracts and finance staff to be prepared for a mad push as soon as the draft came in from the field. Even now, they were in their cubicles by the coffee room boning up on 2CFR.228, geo codes (although it wasn't likely they'd need to procure very much stuff from Somalia… or North Korea), and OFDA marking and branding waiver requirements.

As she checked her makeup and smoothed her hair in the washroom, Jillian knew that winning this grant from OFDA was about far more than money. Of course money would be nice, and depending on one's perspective, it was even the point. With that money, they could scale up their relief operation in Dolo Ado, help more people, and all of that.

But for Jillian, it was also more. They'd managed to land a few hundred thousand to deliver the health component of a larger program in western Afghanistan here, tens of thousands for some community mobilization in Indonesia there. But these were all as a sub, with another more established INGO reading WAC budgets, requiring WAC capacity statements, and auditing them. Jillian was tired of being the aid equivalent of a middle school sibling crashing her older brother's high school graduation party.

Winning a significant high-profile OFDA award would put WAC on the map as a player, not just in the desert wilds of Ethiopia/Somalia, the jungles of Southeast Asia, or the bullet-ridden ruins of Afghanistan, but here in DC with the InterAction clique of "private and voluntary cooperating sponsors." For the first time, she'd be able to look the other PVO CEOs in the eye as a true equal. For the first time, her organization—the organization she'd built from the ground up—would be taken seriously by people and organizations with real power. Win this first OFDA grant. Get it right. And next she'd be going after USAID development grants, maybe even Food For Peace. She pictured warehouses stacked to the ceiling with sacks of rice labeled "From the American People," and WAC's logo over the door.

Time to go to the partner's meeting. This one would be easy. Sit there, nod appropriately, figure out who the three most powerful people in the room were, and invite them to a drink right after the meeting. The *real* meeting, the USAID Horn of Africa Roundtable— the one where things might actually get decided—would be next week. Mary-Anne was coming in for that. *Perfect.* A young, extremely attractive, obviously competent young humanitarian worker just starting out in what anyone could see would be a brilliant career. Those good ol' boys at USAID would love her to pieces, and those professional talkers endlessly clogging the conference rooms and bogging down the discussion at InterAction— *they* wouldn't stand a chance.

Chapter 20

Mary-Anne brushed a stray strand of dirty-blond hair away from her face as she squinted at the words on Andy's computer screen. Sweat stung her eyes and she was keenly conscious of her own body odor. Not that it mattered, though. Everyone in the small room was stinking by now. The air conditioner had given out hours ago, but the members of the WAC Ethiopia design team were under the gun to crank out an OFDA proposal. They had four, maybe five days, to get a usable draft saved in MS Word before Mary-Anne left for Washington, DC

It would take her about forty-eight hours to get there, and while in theory the team staying back in Dolo Ado would be able to massage the draft and attachments while she was *en route*, in reality it needed to be basically done before she left.

Mary-Anne would stop in Addis Ababa to discuss WAC's proposal with Rick at USAID. That would suck up one day, but it would be worth it. WAC wouldn't be able to submit their proposal to USAID Washington without the full support of the Mission. That meant that the proposal would need to be mostly done by the time she left for Addis.

Then, she'd spend one night in Nairobi at her apartment—the one she shared with Jean-Philippe. She'd throw something other than cargo pants, combat boots, and WAC logo golf shirts into a small suitcase and head for North America. If the stars aligned, she'd overlap with Jean-Philippe. It had been months since she'd seen him and days since they'd even talked.

The truth was, at this point, Mary-Anne had no concrete idea where Jean-Philippe even was. Their last Skype conversation, if you could even call it that, had been nearly a week ago. His status showed the red "do not disturb" icon, but she'd pinged him anyway. The connection had been poor, and there'd been lots of background noise. Mary-Anne had had to strain to catch even a few words. There'd been a feminine voice in French, low and husky in the background. Then it all sounded like R2D2, right before the line had cut out. At that moment, Mary-Anne had felt the cold chills of suspicion and worry creep up her spine, but between the heat, the donkeys, and the general exhaustion due to a lack of real sleep in weeks, she hadn't had either the time or the emotional energy to engage.

At any rate, she'd arrive in Washington, DC some seventeen hours later, via innumerable inconvenient connections. She'd get off the plane at Reagan International Airport, take the DC metro to a small hotel near Dupont Circle, freshen up, and head straight for the USAID Horn of Africa Roundtable at the Ronald Reagan building with hardly time to put on new makeup and brush her teeth in between.

All of which amounted to the reality that Mary-Anne had no real choice but to continue to hunker in the air conditioner-less office with several other sweaty, stinky aid workers.

Andy had a partial draft of WAC's OFDA proposal for Bur Amina on his computer and wanted Mary-Anne's input on how to achieve the required indicators. It wasn't possible to do an actual assessment in Bur Amina since it wasn't open yet. Everyone knew that ARRA would open it by the end of two months, just as everyone knew that it would eventually be a temporary home to some 20,000 Somali refugees. Everyone also knew that the challenges and problems faced by the 20,000 in Bur Amina would be pretty much the exact same ones faced by the 23,000 in Kobe Camp or the 14,000 in Hilaweyn. But knowing these all intuitively wasn't really a response to the portion of the proposal guidelines that asked for "evidence-based"' rationale for activity selection.

"But how can we assess the needs of a population that, technically speaking, doesn't even exist yet?" Andy was asking. Mary-Anne's brow furrowed. The lone strand of dirty-blonde hair wouldn't behave, and she pushed it back once again.

"Extrapolate," she answered. "Extrapolate based on assessment data from *other* camps. Talk about our experience in Kobe." She flipped through her notebook, found the page she was looking for, and continued. "You can even throw in the last two quarterly reports for our DANIDA WASH grant as evidence. Based on our experience with the population in Kobe, we should be able to make assumptions about what we'll encounter in Bur Amina, even though we're not proposing WASH interventions to OFDA."

Andy nodded in agreement.

"And be sure to say that we'll do a baseline assessment immediately, once the grant actually starts."

Andy was already typing, and Mary-Anne knew that he'd probably spend the night massaging the logframes, wading through the USAID "key words" and "crosscutting themes" regulations. They'd have a solid draft by tomorrow.

As she gathered her things to leave, Mercy came over, laid her hand on Mary-Anne's arm, and in a low voice said, "Ma'am, I need to speak with you, privately."

"Sure," Mary-Anne was surprised at Mercy's intensity. She picked up her laptop computer, a stack of loose papers, her cell phone, and a cheap calculator on top. "Let's step outside."

Outside, in the sparse shade of a scraggly date palm, with wide eyes and a solemn voice, Mercy told her. "I'll have to check some more, but I'm quite certain that someone in the Kobe team is stealing from us."

* * *

Jon Langstrom had spent the past two days trying to get traction on a partnering agreement with someone… *any*one. Plan, PATH, Save, Concern, GOAL, CARE, DRC. No one wanted to partner with Oxfam America and their $500,000. He read the message on his screen one more time:

Dear Mr. Langstrom,

Thank you for your kind offer of partnership on behalf of Oxfam America for Bur Amina, Ethiopia.

However, I regret to inform you that at this time our strategy for Ethiopia remains focused on Bokolmayo and Melkadida. At this time, we have no intention to expand our programming presence into Bur Amina, and so cannot accept your proposal.

With regards,

Roger L. Ward
Senior Operations Director
Caritas Ethiopia

Typical. He grunted in frustration and scrolled back through his inbox. Out of boredom he opened a two-day-old message from Aengus, the Oxfam site manager for Dolo Ado. It was copied to all senior Oxfam staff in Ethiopia and read simply, "WAC leadership transition in Dolo

Ado. Please see below." The message that followed was from Mary-Anne, informing the interagency response from the UN heads to country directors and chiefs of party that she would be replacing Brandon Powers as WAC's chief of party, effective immediately. Of course, none of this was news for Jon, but reading the message and seeing Mary-Anne's name in the automated signature caused an idea to bubble up in the back of his head.

What about partnering with World Aid Corps? They were going to Bur Amina, and they were going for grants.

Jon Langstrom picked up his local mobile phone and dialed Mary-Anne's number. Without him wanting it to, his heart skipped a beat when he heard her voice on the other end.

*

Andy and Mercy unanimously agreed that a partnership with Oxfam America would only make WAC's proposal to OFDA stronger. They could claim all kinds of general "synergy" in the proposal, and, if Jon could be persuaded, co-fund portions of WAC project staff salary with the $500,000 that he was throwing on the table. This would reduce WAC overhead, thereby "deepening impact" at the field level. Also, depending on what could be negotiated, Oxfam America might even let them write part of the $500,000 in as "match" for the OFDA grant, increasing the likelihood that it would be funded by OFDA (nothing donors love more than a match multiplier), as well as scoring a marketing "win" for both Oxfam America and WAC ("For every dollar you donate, we match with *three!*").

Chapter 21

Angie Langstrom checked her Gmail one last time out of habit as much as anything. She didn't seriously expect anything to be there, so it was with a mixture of trepidation and anticipation that she clicked on the new message from Jon. The message was predictably short, almost terse. He'd scheduled his flight back to Boston—he could stay for about a week before returning to Ethiopia. But at least he'd be there for Chloe's dance recital.

Even Angie was sick of thinking about it now.

The damned dance recital.

Twenty years ago, she would never have pictured herself drawing the line in the sand at Jon being at a dance recital, but in the here and now, something had to give. Things could not continue as they were. If he couldn't take control of his professional life enough to be present at an event of importance to the family, then this probably *would* be the straw that broke the camel's back.

Angie sighed heavily. She didn't want to be adversarial with Jon. But she needed him to get it together on the marriage and family front. What she really wanted was for him to get it together because *he* wanted to and not because she'd browbeaten him into it. Yet, knowing Jon as she did after twenty odd years of living with him and putting up with him, she'd also slowly begun to realize that there is sometimes a very fine line between doing what your spouse wants because you really, really want to, and doing what your spouse wants because it is simply the easiest way to make the noise stop. And when you get to that point, Angie thought bitterly, your relationship becomes essentially a game of emotional "chicken."

No, this wasn't what she wanted. Or, rather, this wasn't how she wanted to go about getting what she wanted, but desperate times called for desperate measures. Besides, she told herself, this wasn't about winning a personal victory against Jon. *This was for the family.*

*

Jon snapped his laptop computer shut. *There, it was done.*

He'd be back in time for Chloe's dance recital, so Angie should be happy, although he was fairly certain that Chloe would neither notice nor care one way or the other. He'd booked the ticket and sent the message. That should keep Angie from sending a bossy/complaining/threatening email for at least another twelve hours.

Now all he had to do was nail down a partnership deal with WAC for Bur Amina. A partnership deal was not, strictly speaking, what Mark wanted, but hopefully it would be close enough to pass as having "planted a flag" or "pissed on a few bushes," or whichever other vaguely imperialistic metaphor Mark might be going with at the time.

Seriously. Between Angie and Mark it was a small miracle that he got anything done.

Jon glanced at his watch. Almost 10:00 PM. Far past last call at Billy-Bob's, and too late, even, to text Mary-Anne to see if she wanted to join him for a nightcap of St. George from the Oxfam refrigerator. Anyway, he'd see her tomorrow night at Billy-Bob's, or failing that, later in the week at the next partners meeting in Bur Amina. He looked forward to their chats over beers at Billy-Bob's. But that was all, he assured himself, almost defensively. Sure, she was an attractive woman, and yes, he did look forward to seeing her, now almost every evening. *But that was all it was.*

He felt in his pocket for the partially crushed pack of duty-free Marlboros. A solitary beer and a cigarette under the stars before turning in for the night didn't sound all bad. As Jon stepped out into the night he could see several colleague expats lounging on the veranda of one of the duplex staff housing buildings a few meters away, enshrouded in smoke, a few empty bottles lying on the ground. They waved and motioned for him to join them. Actually, a few beers and a few cigarettes with colleagues before bed sounded even better.

As he walked toward them, a donkey brayed loudly just outside the wall in the general direction of the UNHCR compound.

Chapter 22

It had been three days since Mary-Anne had been able to escape the confines of the WAC compound, and almost a week since her last visit to Kobe Camp. To be sure, there *was* a certain exhilaration in being in charge, in leading her small team. For the first time in her career she was the one to see clearly where a response was headed, to know the steps to take to get there, and *also* the one to make it happen. As each day passed, she felt herself becoming more comfortable in the role of leader and more confident with the title of "Chief of Party." WAC's Dolo Ado team was responding well to her direction, and even the few she'd feared might resent her promotion had come around without incident and seemed to accept her as their boss. It was a great deal of work, and she rarely slept more than five, or if she was lucky, six hours per night. But it was work she found herself loving.

Nevertheless, Mary-Anne felt a familiar quickening as she laced up her combat boots, hung her fake Ray-Ban sunglasses (Jean-Philippe had picked them up for her at the night market in Pattaya) over the top button of her (unbranded) button-down shirt and walked toward the car park where Mesfin was waiting with the white WAC Land Cruiser. As she fastened her seatbelt and adjusted the sun shade Mary-Anne briefly pondered the paradox of being so far from "the field" even while sweltering in the heat of Dolo Ado, hardly four kilometers from Somalia. Yes, it was good—very good —to be getting out of the WAC compound and out to "the field," however one might choose to understand the term, for the day.

"Many days I didn't see you, Madame!" Even Mesfin was cheerful.

"Yes, it's been crazy, but I need to get back out there today." The rising sun was already intense and Mary-Anne put on her fake Ray-Bans. "Where's Tekflu?"

"We take Tekflu in Bur Amina, Madame. I'll call him when we get close, and he'll come out to the road."

An hour later the WAC Land Cruiser ground to a halt outside a nondescript shack by the side of the road, just outside Bur Amina Camp.

Mary-Anne could see Tekflu sitting at a small table just inside the door.

"I will take mocha with Tekflu, Madame. Maybe you join us?"

Two months ago Mary-Anne would have been annoyed by the stop. Thirty minutes spent drinking coffee in a smoky shack by the side of the road meant getting back home to her small dome tent thirty minutes later. Thirty minutes lost drinking coffee in the morning could translate into two fewer rounds of St. George at Billy-Bob's that evening. Every moment was precious. But after three days of sitting in an un-air conditioned conference room, a day in the field stretching out in front of her, the thought of local coffee in a local shop surrounded by local people suddenly sounded very, very good.

"Great. I'd *love* a mocha!"

As she sat there sipping coffee and absently tuning out Mesfin and Tekflu chatting in Amharic, Mary-Anne allowed her mind to wander. Her usual first thoughts were of Jean-Philippe. Where was he? Was he safe? Who was he with? She tried to recall the sound of his voice saying her name ("*Mehrrreeeee Aahhhn*"). It had been weeks since she'd last heard his voice. Lately, though, she'd noticed her thoughts gravitating toward Jon Langstrom.

It was just a field crush, she knew. If even that. And *certainly* nothing more. They happened all the time. You go out to the field, maybe for a year, or maybe for a week. There's someone there you find attractive. Or maybe even not so attractive. At first. But then you hang out with them a bit, and maybe it's the isolation or the loneliness or some vague *je ne sais quoi*, but they start to seem enticing, desirable even. Maybe you fantasize a little, but that's all. It stops there and goes no further, Mary-Anne told herself. Even as she thought the words, though, she also knew that there was more to Jon than just a field crush. Yes, of course he was married, she was with someone—with Jean-Philippe—and even under the most carnally desperate circumstances imaginable, there was no way she wanted to deal with the inevitable and ugly complications such a love quadrangle would bring on. And yet, there was something inexplicably magnetic about him. Three weeks ago, she would never have thought it, let alone admitted it, but right then Mary-Anne knew in her heart that in the hypothetical absence of the aforementioned complicating factors she could picture herself with Jon Langstrom.

Tekflu's voice pulled her back to reality. "Will you finish your mocha, Madame? We should leave soon."

Mary-Anne hurriedly gulped down the last of her coffee and stood up.
"Yes, I'm ready. Let's go!"

*

The visit to Kobe Camp was like re-watching a favorite old movie that she hadn't seen in a very long time. Mary-Anne was re-struck by the poise and dignity with which the Somali refugee women carried themselves, and re-envious of their satiny smooth, almost jet-black skin. The colors, the textures, even the smells were almost comfortingly familiar and yet exotic again, as if she was experiencing it all for the first time. Although she'd seen it many times before, she found herself wanting to photograph the henna markings on people's hands and arms. She intentionally walked slowly enough through sector C-3 so that the barefoot children running behind could keep up, and she didn't mind as they pulled at the light hair on her arm or messed up the settings on her digital watch by pushing all the buttons. While Mary-Anne monitored the Plumpy'Nut distribution and sat in on the hygiene promotion, she saw beneficiaries whose names she'd never learned but whose faces she recognized. In an odd way, it was almost like reconnecting with old acquaintances.

The DANIDA project was winding down well enough. Targets were being met. The activities would be completed on time and within budget. The donor would be pleased, the beneficiaries would be grateful. Success all around.

The sun was starting to dip in the sky as Mary-Anne followed Tekflu and Aasiya back through Sector C-3 toward the WAC Land Cruiser. It had been a good visit, but now she was ready to head back. She looked forward to sitting for a few hours in the air-conditioned comfort of the backseat and zoning out while Mesfin and Tekflu listened to the Amharic mix tape and discussed whatever it was that Ethiopian men liked to discuss. She was ready to get out of sight of Kobe Camp and then slather her arms in hand sanitizer. She was also ready, should they make it back in time, to have a beer or two at Billy-Bob's before curfew.

Her combat boots kicked up little puffs of dust as she shuffled along, and she noticed that the normally omnipresent crowd of small children was curiously absent. They'd seen enough white aid workers traipsing through the camp that Mary-Anne was, apparently, no longer interesting. Up ahead she could see Aasiya slowing, then stopping, speaking briefly to Tekflu, motioning toward Mary-Anne as she spoke. Within a few steps she'd caught up with them. Aasiya was still talking as Tekflu nodded somberly. He turned abruptly and spoke to Mary-Anne.

"Remember the mother with the sick little girl?"

Mary-Anne nodded. "Yes, I remember. Of course. Does she know what happened?"

Tekflu nodded back. "We'll go see her now," He motioned toward a house nearby.

The "house," Mary-Anne could see, was what most people in suburban North America probably think of as a "hovel." It had begun life as a UNHCR tent, but the intervening months had not been kind. There were several tears in the fabric, some clumsily repaired, and others flapping open. A red dirt yard, of sorts, was marked with thorn bushes. In one corner was a blackened fuel-efficient clay stove with a few random plastic and aluminum pots scattered nearby. A few scrawny chickens pecked at the ground and flies buzzed everywhere.

Aasiya called out in Arabic at the entrance to the tent and from inside came a soft feminine reply. She looked at Mary-Anne, nodded, and pulled back the tent flap. As her eyes adjusted to the dim interior Mary-Anne could see the young mother sitting cross-legged on the ground, breastfeeding a baby. Another child, maybe 10 or 11 years old, lay sleeping on a small cot. The inside of the tent smelled intensely of charcoal smoke and body odor.

"What happened to her little girl, the one we met before?" Mary-Anne asked. Tekflu, standing just outside the tent translated and Aasiya asked the question. In a soft, steady voice the young mother answered.

"Her daughter died that same night, after we left," came the translation.

Everything that had been in Mary-Anne's head throughout the day—the exhilaration of being WAC's chief of party, the pursuit of an OFDA grant for Bur Amina, distracting fantasies about Jon Langstrom, the pleasure of a day in the field, her thirst for a St. George—all vanished in a single, terrible instant.

"No!" she heard herself cry out. "Why... *oh, that's awful!*" Against her will hot tears stung her eyes. "Why didn't she take her daughter to the MSF clinic?" She searched Aasiya's face with her eyes.

Tekflu translated again from just outside, followed by a brief exchange in Arabic between Aasiya and the young mother. Then the translation back. "The MSF clinic was so far, almost one kilometer. She was too tired and she had to cook for the family—"

"Why…? Oh dear. Couldn't *anyone* have helped her?" Mary-Anne's tears were flowing freely now.

Aasiya spoke softly to Mary-Anne. Again Tekflu translated.

"Who can help them? There are so many, and they come more every day. Everyone is trying to survive. Everyone has their own problems."

The young mother spoke again. Then, again, she heard Tekflu's voice just outside. "She says it's for the better. They have—*had*—three children, no work, not enough food. It's for the better…"

"But, no!" Mary-Anne interrupted, half-crying, half-shouting. "It's *not* for the better. It's her *daughter*. They could have saved her…" And then, after a brief, miserable pause, "We should have saved her."

The afternoon was waning and Mary-Anne could barely make out the face of the young mother, expressionless, staring at the ground. It was a supremely sad and surreal moment as the young mother spoke, her voice low and soft.

"She says she is very sorry, Madame."

Chapter 23

Mary-Anne lay on her cot in the darkness, physically and emotionally exhausted but unable to sleep. Her eyes were dry—she'd cried her last tears in the backseat of the WAC Land Cruiser between Kobe Camp and Dolo Ado—but her mind played back the images of her last moments in Kobe as if on a continuous loop.

Tekflu had tried to console her.

"Madame, you did nothing wrong," he'd said, but in her heart she knew better. It would have added only a few minutes, fifteen at the most, to simply put the young mother and her sick girl into the Land Cruiser and drive them to the MSF clinic in Sector A-1. Yes, it was against WAC policy to transport beneficiaries in WAC vehicles without specific permission. And yes, she understood the logic: *You take one sick child to the clinic in an agency vehicle, and next thing you know you're operating an ambulance service.* But she was the chief of party. She could have authorized the exception herself.

But she didn't.

And now the little girl was dead.

The image of the young mother, sitting on the dirt floor in the gloomy darkness of a tattered UNHCR tent, apologizing—*apologizing*—in a low, soft voice haunted her.

She'd wept in the backseat as Kobe Camp, once again, grew smaller in the distance. And Tekflu, in his stable, gentle way, had tried to help her feel better.

"We can't save all," he'd said reflectively. "And you can't save any. You didn't make that little girl die." She knew he was right, but it didn't help.

"Don't feel sad, Madame. By leading WAC, you are helping many people." He'd turned around and looked directly at her as he spoke.

"Don't think too much about what else you might have done. I can see from your actions that you are a good person."

Good person. "You are a good person." Tekflu's overly generous words rang in Mary-Anne's ears, even as the memory of a frightfully thin child lying limp in her mother's arms continued to declare otherwise.

* * *

Mark was furious.

It wasn't that Jon Langstrom had been insubordinate outright, and that was part of the problem. In a manner of speaking, depending on what kind of light you cast on the situation, a partnership with WAC was still a project that Oxfam America could brand as its own. No, what galled Mark was the slippery, manipulative, semantic game-playing, Clintonesque way Jon had done what he knew good and well Mark didn't want.

Mark had asked for a project. *A neat, tidy, stand-alone project.* Buy some kitchen kits or put up some T-shelters. Okay, share basic logistics—warehouse space or transportation—as made sense in the context, but otherwise *just do it*. He'd been clear that, at least up to a point, money was no object. How Jon had managed to spend three weeks, now, in Dolo Ado and not only fail to deliver on such an obvious and basic task, but also commit Oxfam America to something almost directly opposite was utterly beyond Mark.

Mark knew the board of directors enough to know that if Jon were to talk to them himself, they'd be eating out of his hand in a matter of minutes. Jon would first lay his twenty-plus years of experience out on the table, then blather on about "complexity" or "coordination," throw in an anecdote about some hair-raising experience, maybe in Kosovo or Sri Lanka, and the board would get all gooey. They'd congratulate Jon on such a wonderful "synergistic partnership." Then, six months later there would be a long, boring report about how one couldn't say, really, whether Oxfam's contribution to the relief effort in the Horn of Africa made any difference.

But Mark didn't want the board all gooey, and he certainly didn't want a long report about the non-impact of his agency's programming. Nor did he want to partner with some tiny no-name outfit that no one but Jon seemed to have ever heard of. He wanted to impose order on chaos and extract simplicity from complexity. No asking permission or approval from the usual gaggle of do-nothing NGOs. No hand-wringing about how complicated the context was. Find out what people need and give them that. Slap on a few Oxfam America stickers. Problem solved. End of story.

No point in even responding to Jon's email, really. Jon would be back in Boston next week for a few days. Mark would give Jon a piece of his mind then.

Chapter 24

Jon had known that it would be only a matter of time before he got sucked into other Oxfam tasks in Dolo Ado. After three weeks and two or three odd days on site, he was honestly surprised it had taken this long for something to fall onto his plate. *That's just how it works*, he told himself. And the truth was he didn't mind. As much as the partnership in Bur Amina had grown imminently more interesting now that Oxfam America was partnering with WAC (and it would, therefore, eventually be his job to work and interact directly with Mary-Anne outside of Billy-Bob's), he needed a break from Mark's incompetent meddling. So when Aengus, the Oxfam site manager in Dolo Ado, had asked if Jon would be willing to monitor some of Oxfam's work in the field, Jon was beyond willing.

A monitoring trip to Kobe to check on Oxfam's emergency education programming was just what he needed.

* * *

Jean-Philippe sounded tired, Mary-Anne thought, as she clicked the "hang up" button in her Skype call window.

Their connection had been surprisingly stable for almost forty minutes, and they'd been able to talk longer and with greater ease than at any time since Mary-Anne had come to Ethiopia. Jean-Philippe had just returned to Nairobi, and more of the conversation than Mary-Anne would have preferred centered on what she thought of as "management issues": agreeing on a few pieces of furniture for their small flat in Westland, deciding whether or not to sublet to a few of Jean-Philippe's friends from UNHCR while he and Mary-Anne were away, or discussing whether to call an exterminator for ants or wait for the landlord to do it.

There'd been time for tenderness, too, and Mary-Anne's heartbeat had accelerated as she'd listened to the sound of his voice as much as to the actual words as he spoke to her as he had during their last days together in Haiti. In those days he'd been passionate, direct, unabashed. "I do love you, Mary-Anne (*Mehhreeeee Aaahn*) ... you know I do."

Tears had come to her eyes when he told her how he missed her during the weeks he'd spent, first in Conakry, then Herat, with a life-saving workshop (#LSW) in Doha sandwiched between the two. She'd been to enough relief zone team houses to know what went on in them, but when Jean-Philippe expounded at great length of his love for her and her alone, and how the memory of her (helped along by a few badly exposed and poorly focused photographs on his iPhone) and the thought that she was waiting faithfully for him were all that kept him going (particularly while in Conakry), Mary-Anne felt herself allowing herself to believe without reservation.

He'd brightened, as much as Jean-Philippe ever brightened, when she'd told him of her planned stop through Nairobi on the way to Washington, DC. They would overlap, he said. They'd see each other. They'd have one night together.

Nothing lasts forever, though, and as the first donkey of the evening brayed plaintively, somewhere near the UNHAS airstrip, the connection had begun to fade. They'd both been on enough bad Skype calls to know to squeeze in their last "I love you" and "good-bye, darling/*ma cherie*" before the line went dead and all Mary-Anne had in her headset was silence.

* * *

The USAID partners meeting on the Horn of Africa had gone every bit as well as Jillian could have ever hoped. There would be additional funding coming through USAID and the State Department, and both were looking for additional and/or new partners. All of which meant that the game was far from over for Jillian and for WAC.

She'd been able to get one carefully planned question onto the floor at exactly the right moment. "Good question," the director, chairing the meeting, had congratulated her. The principals from CARE and Mercy Corps on the other side of the table had nodded copiously and then whispered together while glancing in Jillian's direction. *Good.* She was getting good attention. WAC was slowly easing on to everyone's radar.

In the mill-around-and-say-important-sounding-things session which invariably follows USAID briefings, Jillian had managed to nail down the principals from CARE and Mercy Corps for drinks at the DuPont Circle Bistro immediately following. She was, in fact, feeling quite pleased with herself as she began to move to toward the elevators when the USAID Horn of Africa desk officer approached her.

"Ms. Scott, I just heard from my colleague Rick, in Addis, that WAC will be submitting a proposal for the current round of OFDA funding in Dolo Ado."

Jillian nodded. "Yes, my team in Ethiopia is working on the proposal now. I understand they've vetted the concept through the mission, through Rick."

The desk officer wrinkled her brow worriedly and Jillian felt her confidence begin to wane, but she soldiered on. "My star player from the Ethiopia team, my chief of party, in fact, will be here for the Horn of Africa roundtable next week."

"Yes, I see." The desk officer still looked worried.

"Anything wrong?" Jillian asked.

"I'm sure WAC's proposal will be very good. Rick normally has good instincts on these things. However because you're a very new partner, I just wanted to throw out there that we're looking very carefully and favorably at applicants who propose good partnerships and who bring match to the table." She adjusted her gaudy spectacles before continuing. "Obviously match is not a requirement for OFDA grants, but we're looking for evidence of collaboration and synergy."

The desk officer's mouth kept opening and closing, but Jillian's mind was already racing ahead.

There it was—"collaboration and synergy." That partnership with Oxfam America would be vital. Mary-Anne was turning into one of the best investments in the whole WAC response.

* * *

Mercy turned away from the screen and rubbed her eyes with the backs of her hands.

It couldn't be.

She scrolled to the top left corner of the spreadsheet, and began—for the third time—to go through the columns, checking every calculated cell and every embedded link. Twenty minutes later she sat back in her chair.

It couldn't be, but it was.

Someone *was* stealing from WAC and now she knew *who*.

Chapter 25

Mary-Anne could see that a storm of some kind was brewing over Somalia. *Odd for this time of year*, she thought to herself.

It had only been three days since her last visit to Kobe Camp, and to Mary-Anne, it felt like returning to the scene of a crime. She felt heavy with secret guilt as she walked from T-shelter to T-shelter, going through the questionnaire one last time, using her practiced lines with the women she'd begun to think of as friends without even knowing their names. By now, she'd adjusted flawlessly the cadence of Tekflu's translation of the questions and answers with.

Normally she would have welcomed another chance to get out into the field, but today even calling Kobe Camp "the field" felt self-important and dishonest, as if Dolo Ado was the center of the universe and anything away from it was just an outpost in a bad movie remake of a Joseph Conrad novel. Maybe it was the weather, strangely overcast, gray and ominous, casting a pall of melancholy over her mood. Suddenly Mary-Anne felt overwhelmed with the feeling that her career in the humanitarian world had thus far been built on so much self-important dishonesty.

Yes, a storm was brewing. Probably an hour, maybe two, out, Mary-Anne estimated. Time enough to finish up. As they walked back toward the intersection of Sector C-3 and C-5, Mary-Anne was startled to see an Oxfam-branded Land Cruiser parked near the small market where Somali women sold camel milk from dusty calabashes or smuggled pasta and scrawny vegetables on low wooden tables. She could see a figure sitting in the front passenger seat. Although they were still some distance away Mary-Anne knew immediately that it was Jon Langstrom.

She found herself fighting the urge to run the remaining fifty meters between them and throw her arms around his neck as he stepped out from around the front and gave her his signature casual grin.

"Mary-Anne, I'd owe you more beer than you can possibly drink in one night if you'd give me and one of my team a lift back to Dolo Ado."

And suddenly Mary-Anne's day seemed infinitely better.

*

Several hours later, as she lay on her cot listening to the desert wind rippling softly through the fabric of her small tent, Mary-Anne replayed the events of the ride from Kobe in the IMAX cinema of her mind.

He'd been in Kobe Camp with a driver and two Ethiopian staff. There'd been an engine issue on the way there, and the driver along with one of his team would stay in Kobe to sort out the repair. Jon and an Oxfam program officer—a young woman with large hoop earrings and too-red lipstick—needed a ride back to Dolo Ado that night. Mary-Anne felt a twinge of guilt as she "approved" for non-WAC staff to ride in a company vehicle.

Tekflu took the front passenger seat, and because she was the foreign woman, Mary-Anne found herself in the middle of the backseat, her overstuffed rucksack on her lap, squished between Jon Langstrom and the young Ethiopian program officer. Mesfin put in the Amharic music mix tape and chatted with Tekflu. The Ethiopian program officer slouched in her seat and promptly fell asleep, her head bouncing against the headrest.

Mary-Anne anticipated talking with Jon for the three-hour ride back, but as the WAC Land Cruiser bounced down the gravel road, she found herself strangely uninterested in conversation. Jon, too, seemed content to mostly stare out the road at the hypnotically monotonous, khaki-colored landscape. For the first half hour or so, they both made the point of obviously bracing themselves against the jolting and bouncing of the road, arms extended to the seat ahead, or Jon gripping the "Oh, crap!" handles over the door. Then Mesfin dropped the front right tire into a deep pothole and the Land Cruiser veered and swayed violently. The Ethiopian program officer jolted awake, and Jon leaned heavily into Mary-Anne. Then she leaned heavily into him as the wheel came up out of the hole and the vehicle swayed the other way.

The soft, warm weight of Jon's arm against hers felt good and comforting, and when the Land Cruiser stabilized, she didn't pull away. Nor had he. By the time Mesfin hit the next pothole, Mary-Anne was sitting relaxed, neither making any effort to counteract the rocking motion of the Land Cruiser as the two of them bounced against each other.

She felt vaguely guilty. Jon was married. She was "with" Jean-Philippe. And she remembered something she'd once read about breaking the "contact barrier," and how once that happened there was little telling where things might go. But then the Land Cruiser jostled again and she felt herself lean into Jon and it all felt secure and safe. She couldn't say who initiated the breaking of the contact barrier, but she kept her gaze focused on the road ahead, her hands around the rucksack on her lap. What was there to feel guilty about, really? Bumping shoulders and elbows with the person next to her in a crowded car on a pot hole-ridden road? Hardly something to make a point of confessing.

About 15 kilometers before the turnoff point for Bur Amina Camp, Mesfin pointed out the ominous clouds, now visibly rolling toward them from the direction of Somalia. The few trees along the road were starting to whip and blow in the wind, and Mary-Anne could feel the WAC Land Cruiser sway even more. Jon had been the one to point out the wall of reddish-brown blown sand moving toward them, small at first, almost imperceptible on the horizon, but rapidly looming—blocking out what little late afternoon light still made it through the thick cover of angry gray clouds. Mesfin began talking animatedly to Tekflu, who nodded solemnly, then turned toward the backseat and said only, "Sand storm."

Mary-Anne had been through sand storms before, but this one was by far the worst. Within moments, the entire landscape was bathed in a dim, eerie red light. She could hear the soft sounds of grains of sand pelting the windows, a little like rain, but somehow different. Mesfin slowed the car to walking speed to make up for the poor visibility. Occasionally, a truck or car, its lights struggling against the thick, dark air, would fade slowly into view out of the gloom—indistinct at first, then clearer as it came closer and passed. She thought she saw a camel huddled by the side of the road, then a person walking, but it was hard to be sure. Tekflu turned down the Amharic music mix tape, Mesfin gripped the wheel and peered through the windshield at the road ahead. The Ethiopian program officer pulled a colorful shawl over her head before falling back to sleep.

Now, in near total darkness, the Land Cruiser inching ahead at a snail's pace, there was no pretense of bracing or adjusting as Mary-Anne and Jon leaned heavily into each other. Mary-Anne began to feel a warm tingle, deep in her belly, akin to, but still different from the tight, hot, ache she'd felt in Haiti as Jean-Philippe had taken her in his arms. It was, rather, like the early onset of giardiasis or amebic dysentery: not entirely uncomfortable, but letting her know that an undignified episode might be in store. A small bump jostled her arm into the crook of his, another and her hand slipped down her rucksack to the point that their wrists touched lightly with the motion of the road. By then, a small bur of guilt began to nag at the back of Mary-Anne's conscience, but she consciously, intentionally batted it away.

The wind outside intensified and Mesfin slowed further, then pulled off the road and came to a dead stop. "I'm sorry, Madame." She couldn't see his face, but she knew he was talking to her. "I think we stop here until the storm goes away. Very dangerous, driving, Madame."

"It's no problem, Mesfin," she replied. "Let me call Rolf and tell him we'll arrive late. This storm can't last all night." Then, as she turned on her VHF handset to check in with Rolf, almost without even thinking she deftly threaded her arm through Jon's and laid her hand deliberately on his in the darkness as she made the call. Rolf promised to inform the Oxfam security manager and Mary-Anne turned her head instinctively toward Jonathon. It was hard to tell for sure, but in the faint light of the illuminated LCD dial on her radio, Mary-Anne could make out his eyes, intense, quizzical, and comforting, and oddly with a hint of the same sadness she'd seen that evening, before, at Billy-Bob's.

She could tell that everyone was asleep. Mesfin and Tekflu, both asleep and breathing heavily in the front seat, the Ethiopian program officer almost snoring in the darkness to her right. Only she and Jon were awake. And although they said not a single word as the Amharic music mix tape replayed again.

It took an hour for the storm to dissipate enough for Mesfin to start up the WAC Land Cruiser and continue the journey back to Dolo Ado. It was almost pitch black as he carefully negotiated the terrible road toward Dolo Ado, and even as the shapes of town faded into view, the only light came from the instrument panel and the occasional car coming toward them. Jon Langstrom's hand had been warm and comfortable, and in total darkness, it never strayed or wandered. The sensation of it, *of him* close enough to feel the muscles in his arm ripple in response to the sway of the road, to hear his breathing low and soft, all melded together into a spark, then a smolder, then a small blaze deep in Mary-Anne's loins that grew and spread and intensified. The Land Cruiser finally ground to a halt outside the gate to the Oxfam compound and Jon whispered a soft "good night." He was so close she could feel his breath on her cheek, and she felt flushed and damp, despite the cool dryness of the night.

And now, as she lay, dead tired but unable to sleep, every nerve ending sensitized, Mary-Anne felt her first true guilt. She pondered how far she'd come since she'd been engaged to marry the son of the pastor.

There were the obvious things. The physical, moral boundaries she'd blurred, then crossed, then broken altogether. She'd gone to Haiti utterly innocent, clueless even, in the ways of love and of the world. And then there'd been Jean-Philippe and a night of intense, carnal passion which changed everything forever. There were the behavioral things, too. A single bottle of Bud Light during the Super Bowl back home had turned into a beer a day in the field. Or a rum sour. Or just plain rum. *Every* day. And now she was downing more than she could specifically remember for more days than she could specifically remember. Or the *deployment smoking.*

These were the obvious things that anyone could see if they could see her living her life the way she did. There was, Mary-Anne reflected, something about being in "the field" that made it seem as if the way she lived her life didn't matter as much as it all did "back home." Or as if no one was looking.

Three days out of five, the work she did could almost as easily be done from a cubicle in DC, or from a coffee shop with Wi-Fi, or even at home in her pajamas while watching daytime television. But what set the field apart was the distance between it and home, and between those who knew her as the Mary-Anne they'd always known and those who knew her from coordination meetings or technical working groups or expat hangouts like Billy-Bob's. Despite the emails, the Skype video chats, the radio checks, and the reporting and accountability, and just the hyper-connectivity of it all, she still felt as if it was possible to be anonymous in "the field." In "the field" it felt as if no one was really watching what she did in her personal life. Mary-Anne suddenly realized that she was essentially living two lives. At that moment, she understood for the first time that for her, for all of its nobility and altruism and very often even genuine good, aid work had created a space where she could be someone she wasn't, or wouldn't normally be.

And not necessarily for the better.

But it wasn't the drinking or the smoking or what Mamma would, if she knew, have called "living in sin" with Jean-Philippe that nagged at her now. It wasn't even that she'd just engaged in extra-marital interdigitation with a married man. What now prodded at Mary-Anne's stream of consciousness and kept her from sleeping was the slow, terrible realization that she was compromising within her personal life the very humanitarian impulses that had motivated her to take up the life of an aid worker in the first place. She winced at the memory of the women's faces—resigned, knowing, anxious—as she'd told the focus group the

DANIDA project was ending. Then, the sight of a much too thin child, limp in her mother's arms, her life ebbing. Then—Mary-Anne stifled a spontaneous, uncontrollable sob—the memory of a young mother, huddled in the gloom of a UNHCR tent, telling in a soft, low voice of the death of her child.

No, a Land Cruiser cuddle during a sandstorm with Jon Langstrom wasn't exactly what Mary-Anne had envisioned for herself as she sat on the front porch in Kentucky four years ago. But the thought that she held people's livelihoods, and even lives, in her hand, even if only a little, and even if only temporarily, and then that she'd let them down in service to some twisted notion of an even greater good: *this* was the thought that kept Mary-Anne from sleeping.

Then, as if by magic or divine spell, sleep was upon her. Her last thoughts that night were of the warmth of Jon Langstrom's hand holding hers. But then, also, through the fog of fading consciousness, as a donkey brayed loudly just outside the WAC compound, Tekflu's voice resounded in her brain, his words this time felt openly mocking.

"You are a good person."

And as wakefulness faded into sleep, Mary-Anne was overcome by the notion that she might perhaps be many things, but among them all, *not* a good person.

Chapter 26

Jon Langstrom squinted and held up a pillow to shield his eyes against the radiant morning sun slanting in through the small window. A large fly buzzed loudly against the inside of the flimsy screen before circling around the room and settling comfortably on the bristles of Jon's toothbrush lying upturned on the small night table.

He'd swirl it in mouthwash before using it, he thought to himself. Not like it mattered all that much, anyway. Within a few days, he'd be back in Boston, presumably in time for Chloe's all-important dance recital. If he got sick, he'd get treated in America. *Easy.*

His mind wandered back to the previous evening, the ride back from Kobe, the sandstorm, and Mary-Anne. *What were you thinking?* He chided himself. *Why would you lead someone on, or allow someone to be lead on, or allow your*self *to be led on*? Bumping shoulders or thighs in the crowded darkness of the WAC Land Cruiser would have been one thing. *That* would have been easy enough to play off, to dismiss as the not un-enjoyable but innocent natural outcome of being squished together on a bumpy road. But holding hands crossed a line, even if he couldn't put into words where or what that line was.

In their twenty-something years of marriage and almost as many of being routinely thrust into high-stress, often dangerous environments, frequently bunking in co-ed teamhouses in an industry where the preponderant demographic was 30-something single women, Jon had never seriously contemplated the possibility of being unfaithful to Angie. Sure, there were some aid women—colleagues or aid workers with other organizations—who he'd found immensely attractive. Sure, there were some with whom he'd become very close and to whom he felt deeply connected. And sure, there were even one or two who, he knew deep down, had the potential to be more than just friends, had circumstances been different.

But circumstances were what they were. While it was one thing, in the privacy of one's own thoughts, to spin Whitesnake-fueled fantasies about what one might do if given the opportunity, it was something altogether different to have been given the chance and taken it, even if only a little. And while there was nothing, really, to confess—he hadn't slept with her, they hadn't even kissed, not even *talked*—he couldn't quite shake the feeling that he'd done something *wrong*.

And yet there was something about Mary-Anne that unsettled him.

She was beautiful, of course, but it wasn't that. In some thirty years of humanitarian work, Jon still had not been to a country or worked in a disaster zone that lacked beautiful women. But with Mary-Anne, there was something he hadn't felt in a very long time: *a sense of connection*. And for a career humanitarian worker, weeks or months or years on the road, in-person friendships, by definition short-term, any few enduring relationships relegated to Skype and social media, few things are more seductive or more frequently mistaken for love, than a sense of connection.

* * *

There wasn't much point in going to the airstrip early. Mary-Anne slept in a little (7:30), lingered over a second mocha in the outdoor WAC dining room, and checked her email. Jillian wanted Mary-Anne to email her with information she could have easily found on the OCHA website; someone in the marketing department "urgently" needed a photograph of a donkey, purchased by a "very important" donor from the gift catalogue; someone in corporate relations "urgently" needed field approval to accept a donation of new, high-tech material for building T-shelters; and Rick from USAID in Addis Ababa confirmed their meeting for later that day.

Mary-Anne sighed as she dutifully responded to Jillian. She then forwarded the goat and T-shelter emails to Andy, and sent two sentences to Rick confirming that *yes*, she'd be at the U.S. Embassy that afternoon.

She was just checking Skype (everyone but Jean-Philippe was online, lighting up her window with flashing orange pleas for attention) when she heard the UNHAS Dash-8 circle overhead. Everyone in the Dolo Ado humanitarian community knew that when the UN plane buzzed the town, it was time to head to the packed, red clay river bed that served as Dolo Ado's airport.

An hour later, she'd completed security formalities (a circle of white rocks in the red dust where WFP ground staff checked the aid workers' bags) and settled aboard. By the time the pilot pushed the throttle forward, she'd retreated into her Shania Twain playlist, and by the time she was through the first verse of "That Don't Impress Me Much," Dolo Ado was little more than a tiny bit of distant texture on the horizon of an otherwise monochromatic landscape.

She'd meet with Rick at USAID, spend one night in the relative luxury of Hotel Kaleb, and by tomorrow would see Jean-Philippe.

A week ago, Mary-Anne would have been excited, almost giddy, at the news that they'd have a night together in Nairobi. Now, as much as she truly wanted to see him and to *be* with him, the thought of him caused her stomach to tighten in knots. A wave of guilt washed over her, made all the worse by Shania's sweet voice crooning, "*You're still the one*" in her earbuds.

It was two hours, more or less, to Addis, and as Mary-Anne tilted her seat back as far as it would go and then turned her iPod up as loud as it would go in the hopes that Shania Twain might drown out the noise of the engines, she suddenly couldn't decide what it was *she* longed for more:

Was it to be with Jonathon Langstrom? Or to be with Jean-Philippe? To take back her decision to pour WAC's resources in a new camp at Bur Amina instead of Kobe? To somehow undo driving away from a tired mother holding a dying child?

Or was it simply to sit down at the bar at Beer Garden Inn and have a beer that *wasn't* St. George?

Chapter 27

Rick shook his head in annoyance.

The concept papers were crappier than usual. They were just the same old players proposing the same tired strategies in the same jargon-laden language. None—not a single one—of the papers in the pile on his desk "sparkled." USAID, DCHA, and the State Department were all breathing down his neck to fund somebody, and quickly. Everyone from Congress to the President to the Administrator needed to show new American dollars being spent on the ground in the Horn of Africa. But spending down by itself wasn't enough. There needed to be "innovations" and "outside the box thinking" and "novel approaches." And everything the NGOs were suggesting plain sucked.

The only concept paper he'd not received yet was the one he expected from World Aid Corps. His friend Brandon had flaked out—okay, had an understandable in-context "complication" —but pressure was pressure.

Mary-Anne, Brandon's replacement, would be meeting with him in an hour. He hoped she'd propose something that he could conscionably put U.S. taxpayer dollars behind.

* * *

Chloe Langstrom knew she wasn't allowed to ride in Tyler's car, but she didn't care. Who would ever know? And what was the big deal, anyway? Angie—her mother—didn't like the fact that Tyler was sixteen. She thought he was "too old" for her.

She did a meticulously rehearsed teenaged girl eye-roll.

She knew that Tyler's "bad boy" reputation bothered her mom, too. He'd been arrested once or twice, and had even done a few hours of juvenile court-ordered community service. But Chloe knew he was good and gentle deep down. He'd told her so himself. He was better when he was with her, he'd said. Sure he still liked to get a little crazy, but it was all harmless fun. Nothing bad would happen to Chloe so long she stayed close to him. The transition from middle school to high school could be tough for girls, but Tyler was two years ahead (he had to repeat seventh grade) and knew the ropes. He'd promised to look after her.

Chloe tossed her backpack in the backseat of Tyler's battered Jetta with the Insane Clown Posse bumper sticker and then slid into the front seat. "I'm starving. You mind stopping by Taco Bell with me on the way home? It'll only take a few minutes. Your mom won't even know you're gone," Tyler said as he casually laid his hand on Chloe's left knee. As he eased the Jetta into late afternoon Boston traffic, Chloe thought she caught the faint smell of beer on his breath.

* * *

Jon knew that he and Mary-Anne should probably talk about their evening together in the WAC Land Cruiser. It was uncomfortable and awkward, and the fact that he felt as if they should talk about it made it seem all the more so. With almost anyone else he would have just let it lie, and carried on down life's pathway as if nothing had ever happened. Maybe it was the fact that he actually did think of her as a "friend," albeit one he'd not known for too long. He also found it increasingly difficult to ignore reality that he also found her attractive as something more than a friend.

He muttered under his breath at this thought. He was what, ten, maybe twelve years, too old for her? But then, *she'd* been the one to initiate it all.

Or, maybe it was the fact that their two organizations were about to embark on an operational partnership in Bur Amina. Oxfam America and World Aid Corps would work directly together, collaborate. He would have to work directly with Mary-Anne. It would be a textbook case of "conflict of interest."

In his head, Jon Langstrom cursed Mark and Mulu Alem and ARRA and Ethiopia. It would have been so much easier to just work in Kobe where Oxfam already had a presence. Bur Amina was turning into a huge liability, professionally as well as personally. He needed less complexity rather than more. If for no reason other than simply keeping his job and his family intact, Jon needed to do all he could to minimize any residual drama that might result from the moment of lonely weakness when he'd allowed Mary-Anne to reach for his hand in the dark.

He dialed Mary-Anne's cell number. No answer. When he dialed the WAC landline, the European accent on the other end informed him that

Mary-Anne had left on the first UNHAS flight to Addis. After Addis, she'd go to Washington, DC for meetings. They expected to see Mary-Anne back in Dolo Ado in about ten days.

Jon would have preferred to talk with her in person over lukewarm St. George at Billy-Bob's. He could try calling her that evening in Addis. Or they could connect by phone once he got to America in another three days. Worst case, they'd have the talk once they were both back.

* * *

The meeting with Rick at USAID went well. He'd skimmed the WAC concept paper quickly in front of Mary-Anne, nodded approvingly several different times and made a small note in the margin on page two that she couldn't see. He'd asked only a few easy questions about the budget and then about the nature of the partnership between WAC and Oxfam America. After that, there'd been a few moments of small talk—comparing notes on people they both knew. Rick shared his favorite story about being in the Peace Corps with Brandon back in Sri Lanka, and then the meeting was over and Mary-Anne was done for the day.

She'd meant to have a "Blonde" at the Beer Garden Inn, but it was packed and loud, and she left after a few minutes without ordering. Back in her room at Hotel Kaleb, she'd checked her email quickly before collapsing onto her bed in a sudden fit of fatigue.

The only new message had been from Mercy, who'd attached a spreadsheet detailing the amount of money one of the staff was stealing from WAC. It was not a huge amount but it was still significant, and Mary-Anne knew she'd have to deal with the issue directly as soon as she got back. Mercy's message had gone on to explain:

Ma'am,

I am almost certain I know who is taking money. By the time you come back, I'll have confirmed it (or not).

Talk then,
Mercy

Mary-Anne sighed in the darkness. There were no donkeys braying in Addis Ababa. Only the general faint buzz of traffic nine floors below.

Tomorrow would be an early flight to Nairobi. Tomorrow she would see Jean-Philippe. She needed to rest.

Chapter 28

Angie Langstrom was beside herself as she maneuvered the family RAV4 through what remained of Boston rush hour traffic.

The call from the police had been precise enough but lacked detail. Any *usable* detail, that is. There'd been an accident. Chloe had been in the car. She'd been taken, along with the driver—that Tyler boy—to the trauma and emergency care center at Boston Medical, but no details of any consequence could be given over the phone. Chloe was alive, but other than that her condition was unknown.

Angie blared on her horn impatiently at the battered pickup ahead of her, checked her rearview mirror, and pressed the accelerator toward the floor. 9:22 p.m. on a school night, Chloe—*their daughter* —involved in a car accident and now at a trauma center with God-only-knew-what broken or impaled or dismembered. And as usual, Jon was off in another country, probably drunk or hungover at this moment, all in the name of "helping the downtrodden."

She stepped hard on the brake pedal to avoid running a red light. Angie gripped the wheel bitterly. *Forget about the stupid dance recital.* This was real life. *Their* life. And Jon was conspicuously absent. *As usual.*

And right there in a Boston intersection, without her wanting or willing it, fifteen years' worth of pent-up anger, loneliness, and frustration swept over Angie Langstrom like a heavy, dark wave. She couldn't have cared that he'd missed Valentine's Day or even Thanksgiving. No, it was the smaller, yet at the same time bigger events—the first steps, the first day of school, the skinned knees. The light turned green and she pressed on the accelerator again. Boston Medical was only two minutes away.

No, Jon had missed the small moments, the ups and downs, the daily drama that made a family a family. And today as Chloe was lying in an emergency room with who-knew-what wrong, Jon was gone. She needed him. No, the *family* needed him, and he was gone.

Again. As usual.

She turned angrily into the parking garage at Boston Medical. Angie didn't give a *damn* about the dance recital, just two days away. But Jon had damn well better be back in time for it.

* * *

Mary-Anne woke with a start, her heart pounding.

The images had been a blurry collage: her, racing through the streets of Cite Soleil, the sounds of an angry mob but steps behind, her breath coming in ragged, hot bursts; magical lighting and soft music in a beach-side restaurant at Playa Punta Cana; a too-thin mother with skin the color of expensive chocolate holding a dying child; Jean-Philippe's lean body next to hers, the faint, comforting aroma of the field—tobacco mixed with desert dust and sweat—lingering about him.

She lay back, panting on her pillow, as the room, dimly lit by pre-dawn trickling through crudely wrought thief bars, came slowly into focus. Jean-Philippe was still asleep, his chest rising and falling with rhythmic regularity, his face peaceful. Her heart slowly stopped pounding, as she nestled into him, and as pre-dawn faded into actual dawn, her mind wandered first backward over the previous evening.

She'd arrived on the last flight of the day from Addis to Nairobi. Her entry forms were filled out before the Ethiopian Airlines Airbus rolled to a stop at the gate. Although she'd been seated in the middle of the cabin, she quickly skirted past the gaggles of tourists clogging the jetway, and cleared immigration while the matching T-shirt "Youth Music Ministry" volunteers were still clustered around the forms kiosk (brows furrowed, rummaging through overstuffed backpacks for proof of yellow fever vaccination). Only minutes later, she was striding purposefully through the customs area toward the waiting line of taxis outside while the sky was still fading from dark purple velvet to black. An hour later, she was fumbling in her backpack for the key to her (and Jean-Philippe's) flat in Westlands.

It was surreal being back.

After nearly five months away, the little apartment that she and Jean-Philippe had argued over—first the flat itself, then the décor—seemed at once familiar and also strange. The tiny kitchen, the coffee maker, the futon in the bedroom—*their* bedroom. He wasn't home, and Mary-Anne was almost relieved at the opportunity to shower quickly, unpack a little, and relax for a few minutes on the worn sofa with a glass of the only wine in the flat (a four-year-old South African Merlot) before Jean-Philippe's key rattled in the door.

Seeing him again after so much time apart had been surreal, too. Maybe even a little awkward at first. She leaped into his arms, of course, but their conversation had been slow, strained. The nagging guilt of having broken the physical contact barrier with Jon Langstrom threatened to engulf her. But before long, the Merlot set in and she was leaning on him. Then they were holding hands. Then his hand caressed her dirty-blond hair, and her lips sought his. They made love slowly, passionately, then held each other and talked. Then made love again. Then again.

Jean-Philippe told her about the consultancies in Mogadishu and Kinshasa, the life-saving conference in Dakar where he'd argued with the entire IASC about something important sounding, and upcoming travel to Paris for a family reunion. He'd missed her terribly, passionately. He wanted to be with her. Maybe it was the security of having stayed together these many months, or maybe it was belief borne of guilt for her almost transgressions with Jon Langstrom, but when Jean-Philippe said that he'd been true and that he only wanted her, Mary-Anne believed him.

She told him about Dolo Ado, too, and about how hard it was, but not because of rebels with guns or the possibility of an infectious disease. No, Dolo Ado wasn't hard because of the harsh conditions (whichwere rustic, for sure, but not so harsh for expats) or the danger of beneficiaries rioting at a distribution site. Mary-Anne went on to explain that Dolo Ado was hard because of the monotony and the isolation and the *loneliness*. Dolo Ado was hard because you went to work every day, booted up the same computer, answered the same emails from the same people, drove the same roads to refugee camps and beneficiaries that all looked the same, where you asked the same questions, and invariably got the same answers. All with no perceptible change, and no perceptible *possibility* of change.

Dolo Ado was hard because you could work your ass off for months on end and not feel as if you'd made even a tiny dent in the towering wall of need that loomed in front of you *every day*.

Jean-Philippe remained quiet as Mary-Anne spilled her feelings and cried on his shoulder. And he only sighed deeply, sadly, as she explained that Dolo Ado was hard because, somehow, something about the place or the work or the impossibility of it all caused her to be a person that she didn't want to be. She could tell from the way that he grew quiet that while perhaps he didn't know—didn't need to know—details, he'd been in the same space himself. Jean-Philippe didn't pry, but instead just held her closer as consciousness faded into unconsciousness.

And now, as her brain lingered in that scathingly honest liminal space between asleep and awake, Mary-Anne was conscious of two things: For the first time in months there were no lone donkeys, braying plaintively in the quasi-darkness, off in the general direction of Somalia. Second, no matter what might happen with Jean-Philippe and Jonathon Langstrom or Jillian Scott or Bur Amina, everything would be okay.

*

Dawn had broken. Jean-Philippe stirred.

"Mary-Anne (*Mehhreeeee-ahhhhn*)... you didn't sleep, *ma cherie*. You will be too tired on your flight to DC, *non*?"

Mary-Anne had been through more departure lounges than she could specifically remember. She knew fluently the routine of what identification to show, where, or when to remove her combat boots. But for the first time she felt the departure anxiety that every professional aid worker in a relationship feels before every deployment or mission: *Simply walking out the front door is the hardest part.*

Chapter 29

Jon Langstrom looked at the printout of his e-ticket again.

Addis to Frankfurt / Frankfurt to LaGuardia / LaGuardia to Boston

Simple. Straightforward. *Easy.*

All he had to do was make the flight from Addis to Frankfurt. From there, it would be an easy run. Long layovers every step of the way. Have a few beers in Frankfurt. Log back into the grid from LaGuardia. Land in Boston in the morning. Go to Chloe's (damned) dance recital in the evening. Angie off his back until the next "urgent" family event. *Easy.*

Maybe.

The pretty young Ethiopian gate attendant was calling for "Boarding Group 2" to board. Jon Langstrom scanned his e-ticket once more.

Next stop, Frankfurt.

* * *

The conference room on the fourth floor of the Ronald Reagan Building was crowded, the air stale. By the time Mary-Anne had gone through security, signed in, received a VISITOR badge, and actually found the room, there were only one or two seats open, back in the corner. She chided herself for being late to the USAID Horn of Africa partners' roundtable.

Just getting there had been a disaster. When she'd booked the ticket, three weeks ago, it had all seemed straightforward enough. Addis to Nairobi, Nairobi to London, London to DC. All straight shots with easy layovers. She'd arrive in DC late in the afternoon, stay a night in what would feel like pure opulence at The Liaison, then have a leisurely breakfast at a decent hour before heading for a late morning meeting. But the flight from London to DC had been delayed for reasons unknown. Then the airline had lost her luggage. And then there'd been a mix-up with her reservation at The Liaison, and by the time it all got sorted out and she was finally able to collapse onto the king-sized pillow-top mattress, it was early morning rather than late afternoon. Not only was Mary-Anne late to the partners' roundtable, she was wearing the same worn cargo pants, faded black V-neck T-shirt, and dusty hiking boots she'd worn as she headed for the plane in Nairobi, now some thirty-six hours prior.

Just as she sat down, Mary-Anne caught sight of Jillian across the room, seated next to the deputy administrator, motioning frantically for Mary-Anne to join her. *No scooting by under the radar this time*, she thought to herself as she pushed and stumbled her way past rows of impatient NGO workers to get to the seat next to Jillian, nearly front and center, and now impossibly conspicuous.

There were basically two agenda points for the meeting today: General coordination—who was doing what, where with USAID money? And, what was almost certain to be a more pointed conversation, what the issues were with this new camp being opened by ARRA at Bur Amina.

She could coast for the first part. WAC wasn't doing anything with USAID money in Dolo Ado. At least not yet. So while the predictable array of habitual Washington, DC meeting attenders in turn gave their organization's elevator speech on Dolo Ado, Mary-Anne allowed her mind to wander.

The night in Nairobi had both reassured and rattled her, emotionally. She was as sure now as she had ever been that Jean-Philippe was the love of her life, her soul mate. There had always been an intense physical, sexual chemistry between them, but that night in Nairobi, she had suddenly felt an equally intense emotional connection, too. Maybe it was that they'd gone so long without seeing each other that suddenly being together again had helped it all gel and solidify. Or not. *Who knew?* But what Mary-Anne did unequivocally know was that she belonged with Jean-Philippe. As the guy from Human Rights Watch wound his update to a close and the moderator nodded to the young woman from UNICEF, Mary-Anne suddenly found herself resolving to find a way to be with Jean-Philippe. *Permanently.*

But resolve immediately gave way once again to nagging guilt. Jon Langstrom's face loomed, almost ominous in her mind's eye. How could she have been so foolish? What had ever possessed her? Yet, even as she chided herself, Mary-Anne also savored the memory of her hand in his as the darkness of an Ethiopian night softly engulfed the WAC Land Cruiser. There was a connection there, too. Jon made her laugh. Jon made her feel like everything would be alright, like whatever problems the aid world had thrown at her were totally resolvable. Jon exuded quiet, calm confidence and when she was with him, it seemed that all would be well.

In an odd way, she even loved him, she realized. Not like *that*—not the way that she loved Jean-Philippe—but loved him nonetheless. Suddenly the weight of what she'd potentially communicated by her touch that dark night fell heavily on her, and as she'd resolved to be with Jean-Philippe, Mary-Anne also felt herself resolve to not let things remain unspoken between her and Jon Langstrom. She needed to see him.

Updates were finished and the moderator was moving on to the discussion of Bur Amina. Jillian nudged Mary-Anne's arm, and then whispered, "Now's your time. Let them know that we're in the game for *real*."

* * *

Ali pushed a final round into the battered magazine, checked it once more to be sure it was completely full, and then clicked it into position. His rifle felt heavier now. More solid, more secure.

Ali, Hamid, and the other young men from the village had run three raids, now. It was almost too easy, taking vehicles from the foreigners. One car—a battered Mercedes-Benz—had tried to run, but Ali had easily shot out the tires. Not even as hard as hitting a Coca-Cola bottle from fifty paces. The driver, an Eritrean businessman, had begged for his life. After a brief consultation with Hamid, Ali had let him go, but not before relieving the driver of his cell phone and his watch.

When the Arab came back, he'd been pleased, too. Three vehicles. *Well done.* The *jihad* was going well. Ali just needed to keep doing what he was doing—watching the roads going to and from the border of Ethiopia. Those foreign humanitarians drove unarmed. Taking their vehicles would be easy. *Too easy.*

The sun was almost down. He looked over at Hamid.

"Ready, brother?"

"Ready."

Chapter 30

She knew it was pointless to keep calling. Jon was in the air now, and almost certainly unable to check messages, let alone take calls. But Angie Langstrom had already left at least five messages on his phone ranging from "Honey, we really need to talk. Please call me." to "Jon, I know you're in the air. Call me as soon as you get this." to simply two or three seconds of silence before hanging up.

The ER nurses had tried to be reassuring. Chloe would live, that much was certain. But she'd received a bad concussion in the collision and the doctor wanted to hospitalize her overnight for observation. All pretty standard, but none of it made Angie feel any better. It was yet another family drama, another situation that she would have to deal with on her own. Jon was off saving the world, having his deep, gender-sensitive, ethnically inclusive, more-ethical-than-thou experiences interacting with the world's needy and down-trodden, while yet again she would be left with the daily work of washing dishes or paying bills. Or going to the emergency room to sit with their daughter who'd just been in a head-on collision in the car of a teenaged boy she'd probably never even be interested in if her own father were around more.

Jon had better make it back in time for the dance recital that, by this point, was very obviously not going to happen, at least not for Chloe.

* * *

Frankfurt's international airport is among the most uninteresting and inconvenient in the developed world. The number of security checkpoints and border crossings between concourses and terminals borders on the ridiculous.

But "ridiculous" was not exactly the word in Jonathon Langstrom's mind as he shuffled impatiently in the X-ray line. A large, aging woman of apparent South Asian extraction with five large pieces of carry-on luggage and no perceptible command of either English or German was making her third pass through the metal detector. The young woman running the checkpoint had been cheerful and gracious at first, but was now becoming visibly frustrated. The growing crowd behind Jon began to murmur its disapproval.

Jon glanced at his watch again. The tenth time in as many minutes.

Damn. Gate B-67 was at least a kilometer away, and boarding for LaGuardia would close in twelve minutes.

The metal detector beeped loudly. The young woman running the checkpoint began to flush in pre-anger. Jon rested his carry-on knapsack on the floor. Angie was *so* going to kill him.

* * *

Neither Mary-Anne nor Jillian could have anticipated the outcome of the USAID Horn of Africa partners' roundtable. It is one thing to make a splash in a room full of DC NGO cubicle farmers, and it is something altogether different to influence the world's largest aid donor: USAID. But apparently Mary-Anne had accomplished both.

Before they were even out of the Ronald Reagan Building, Jillian's iPhone 5 began to chime "Shake Your Groove Thing."

Would she be able to have coffee with the director of OFDA next week to discuss innovation and PPP? Yes, and by the way, you have a verbal Pre-Award Letter (PAL) for ten percent of the budget of the recent proposal. We're sure that Rick in Addis will be supportive. We may come back to you with a few questions, but final approval is pretty much a formality at this point.

We expect to release a request for applications for sustainable resilience programming in the Sahel sometime soon, and we hope to see a proposal from World Aid Corps.

Jillian's head was spinning. She'd taken World Aid Corps from being a no-name upstart to a serious competitor in one of the largest, most visible complex humanitarian emergencies currently ongoing. Sure enough she'd had her reservations at first, but that little Mary-Anne was turning out to be one of the best investments she'd ever made. Grungy aid workers who could sit on the border between Ethiopia and Somalia and fill in blanks on donor reporting forms were a dime a dozen. But Mary-Anne had held the room just now. Mary-Anne was young and pretty and had just the right mix of passion and actual knowledge. Mary-Anne was good at this. Jillian needed someone like her *here*, in DC, at WAC HQ.

A cab pulled to a stop, the two got in, and Jillian gave the driver the address.

"Mary-Anne, what's next for you?" An idea was suddenly taking shape in Jillian's mind.

"Not sure," Mary-Anne replied. "Get through the day, head back to the hotel and make an early night of it. I'm not up for a long evening."

"No, no—I mean, what's next for you career-wise?"

"I don't know, really…," Mary-Anne's voice trailed off. "I'll stick it out in Dolo Ado a bit longer, I expect. You know, see things through with this new grant and the transition to Bur Amina."

"I could really use someone like you here." Jillian was intentional now. "Think about it. And let's discuss further when you're not so tired."

Mary-Anne didn't know what to say, exactly. Until that moment she'd never really thought about taking a job at HQ. From what she could see in barely three years as an aid worker, the culture of camaraderie in the field revolved around three things: drinking, sex, and bitching about HQ. And as surely as all the beer would be perpetually drunk from the Oxfam team house, or as surely as one could count on plenty of shagging in the MSF team houses, no topic of discussion evoked nearly as much vitriol or disdain, whether in the office, in the Land Cruiser *en route* to the next distribution point, or over the third St. George at Billy-Bob's, as "HQ." Even contemplating the possibility of taking a job at HQ felt to Mary-Anne like an infidelity. And yet, in that moment, the thought of a "normal" life with an apartment and neighbors and a routine—she could join a reading club or take a spinning class—sounded incredibly appealing.

She thought, too, of an evening just a few weeks before, listening to Jon Langstrom wax eloquent under the benevolent gaze of Billy-Bob the goat. "Recognize this opportunity for what it is…" Mary-Anne couldn't help but wonder whether this was one of those opportunities that needed to be recognized, or a deathtrap, away from which she should run like hell.

"Yes, sure. I'd like to discuss it. I'd like to hear a bit more about what you have in mind."

The DC sky was turning grey. It was barely 1:00 p.m. They'd missed lunch, but Mary-Anne was not hungry, and just then it occurred to her that she was very, very tired.

"Jillian, would you mind terribly if I went back to the hotel? I'm afraid I won't be worth much this afternoon even if I did come to the office."

"Sure, Mary-Anne. Go back and rest. We're almost to DuPont Circle. If we let you off here, you can take the Metro back to Union Station."

As Mary-Anne stepped from the taxi to the sidewalk she heard Jillian's voice.

"Think about it. Think about what it would take to entice you to HQ, and we'll continue this conversation tomorrow."

Chapter 31

Jon knew it would be bad when he got home.

Thanks to an impossibly tight connection, he'd missed his flight from Frankfurt to LaGuardia, and the domino effect of taking the available re-route added up to him arriving at 3:00 a.m., not 3:00 p.m. He'd heard all six of Angie's voicemail messages in Frankfurt, and, from what she did say, managed to surmise that the dance recital was off. He'd texted her back and tried to call from his first port of entry (Chicago on his re-route itinerary) to let her know what was happening. He'd be home later than expected, later than promised, and it would mean he'd miss whatever was going on now to replace the dance recital in Angie's personal hierarchy of family needs. It was obviously not his fault, but as he fumbled in the darkness with the front door to their quaint Boston townhouse, he knew it would make no difference.

At least the key still worked.

Angie was awake when he crept into the tiny, darkened master bedroom, but he only heard her voice, soft, low, and intense: "I don't want you sleeping in here tonight, Jon." This was the first time he'd ever heard Angie talk like this. In all their years of marriage, no matter how bad things might have been, they'd always slept in the same bed. He caught his breath. Angie continued.

"Sleep downstairs on the couch or roll out the guest mattress pad and try to get some sleep. We have to pick up Chloe at Boston Medical at 8:30."

"*What happened to Chloe?* Why is she at Boston Medical?" Jon suddenly felt a cold hand of fear gripping his heart.

"She's okay, just a concussion. They're keeping her for the night for observation."

"How did she get a concussion?!" Jon was suddenly intense.

"She was in a car accident. A collision. She was riding home with Tyler. You wouldn't know him. He's a boy from school she's been hanging around with. Anyway, she's fine. It was scary, but our daughter will be fine."

Jon heard Angie roll over in the darkness, her voice now laden with tired finality. "Get some sleep, Jon. We can talk about things in the morning, maybe."

* * *

The Big Hunt was unusually empty and quiet that evening as Mary-Anne sat down and ordered her first round of Guinness. She'd been dead tired as she stepped from the cab hardly fifteen minutes ago, but the walk toward the DuPont Circle metro station had had a livening effect. As she passed the awning and bay window of the pub, Mary-Anne suddenly felt hungry. The DuPont Circle area is jammed with trendy bistros and delis of the very sort that she'd spent the past six months daydreaming about while eating greasy goat meat and bland carbs in Dolo Ado. But for reasons that she couldn't quite explain even to herself, what she wanted at that moment was a dingy pub with greasy fish tacos on the menu and graffiti on the bathroom walls. Thus, The Big Hunt.

Jillian's offer of employment at WAC HQ still rang in Mary-Anne's ears. She'd go into the office tomorrow, of course, and talk specifics. But for now the opportunity by itself seemed to rock her. She longed to nestle into Jean-Philippe, to hear the thud of his heartbeat, to feel his arms around her and to share a moment of celebration for having been offered a second promotion in as many months. The warm glow of having been tangibly recognized for her contribution and capability was still a warm glow, regardless of whether or not she eventually accepted the position.

At almost the same moment, she suddenly wanted to share the moment with Jon Langstrom, too. She could almost picture him in the fading light at Billy-Bob's, a small smile tugging at the corner of his mouth, and saying something affirming like, "Good for you!" or, "Take this opportunity and run with it!" She sincerely wanted his advice. Jean-Philippe, it occurred to her, could philosophize at length about the Humanitarian Imperative or the impossibility of remaining simultaneously true to the principles of neutrality and impartiality and also adhering to The Code of Conduct. His depth and casually articulate manner during these intense discussions was almost erotic, and even just thinking about it there at the bar inside The Big Hunt made Mary-Anne's neck grow hot.

But Jon Langstrom understood the mechanics of the aid system in a very real and practical way. Sure, he had his deep, reflective moments, too. But she was suddenly keenly aware of the fact that out of all of the great people, friends and acquaintances alike that she'd met and worked with since becoming an aid worker, there was no one she trusted more to give her good advice than Jon.

Mary-Anne checked the calendar on her smartphone. Jon should be in the US now.

And then, as the effects of the first pint of Guinness began to comingle with emotional overload and general exhaustion, Mary-Anne picked up her phone and began composing a text message to Jon Langstrom.

Chapter 32

The visit to Boston Medical to retrieve Chloe had gone as smoothly as Jon could have hoped under the circumstances.

"Daddy!" She'd thrown her arms around him and hugged his neck from the hospital bed. As she tearfully apologized for riding in Tyler's car without permission, Jon found himself fighting to his own tears.

"It's okay," he almost whispered into her hair. "*You're* okay, and *that's* the most important thing."

Angie had been silent and physically reserved at first. But as Jon held his daughter he could see her softening out of the corner of his eye. First a step closer. Then a hand on Chloe's shoulder. Then a hand on his shoulder. And for the first time in a very long time, he felt as they were a family. In his heart —maybe it was the jet lag, or maybe a sense of generalized, compounded guilt for years of having been partially absent—Jon Langstrom resolved to "be there," whatever that might mean for his career or life. He'd take a desk job, play the NGO political game at Oxfam America or wherever, make nice with Mark, take the meetings and the conferences seriously. He'd travel less and help with homework and class projects more. After years of vowing to walk into live fire for Angie and Chloe if need be, the sudden realization that what his wife and daughter really needed was simply for him to walk through the front door of their little townhouse burned his heart like a firebrand.

Just get through the next couple of months, he told himself. *Have the awkward conversation and sort out any residual loose ends with Mary-Anne, get the new project/partnership with WAC up and running in Bur Amina, then slide over and let one of the bright-eyed, eager young program officers take the wheel.* After that, who knew, exactly? He'd work on his relationship with Angie, take the family on vacations in Nicaragua or Turkey or maybe Florida, read novels, quit smoking…

Just get past Bur Amina.

*

The attending physician confirmed that Chloe's concussion had gone down and that it was safe to take her home. They'd need to watch her for the next few days and keep her away from anything physically strenuous, but she'd be fine.

* * *

Mark could hear Doris on the phone making arrangements for a coffee cart and pastry platter. The board meeting was in just two days, and if Mark had his way, it would be the beginning of the end for Jon Langstrom in Oxfam America.

"Doris, can you give Jon a quick call to confirm that he's actually in the U.S. and that he'll be at the board meeting?"

* * *

The news that OFDA had issued a pre-approval for their relief proposal for Bur Amina was reason to leave work a few minutes early and take the entire WAC Dolo Ado ops team to Billy-Bob's for a few celebratory rounds of St. George. Andy had called the Oxfam compound—Oxfam was to be a partner. An *important* partner—but Aengus the site manager was the only one who could make it. Aengus wasn't exactly thrilled that the mighty Oxfam would for all practical purposes be the accompanying partner to a small, no-name American NGO. Even worse, that although no U.S. Government money would touch Oxfam's books or operations, Oxfam in Dolo Ado—*his operation*—would essentially be subbing on a USAID grant.

That all as may be, Aengus was still a man of principle and if Andy and WAC were buying, he was definitely in. Beer was beer, regardless of which logo might be on the name badge of the person doing the paying. Besides, the new WAC Chief of Party—Mary-something—was pretty hot. Getting to know her a little better couldn't be *all* bad.

*

As he walked through the dingy restaurant into the open courtyard at Billy-Bob's, Andy ran mentally through the tasks he'd need to start first thing in the morning, now that they had pre-approval from OFDA. It would be a few days before Mary-Anne got back to Ethiopia, but there was a lot that he needed to get rolling on now:

- *Start procurement of office furniture and equipment.*
- *Get the logs team going on the NFI supply chain.*
- *Have Mercy set up the accounting and banking.*
- *Design the baseline assessment.*
- *Inform ARRA.*
- *Reconnaissance visits to Bur Amina.*
- *Chair the next NFIs cluster meeting.*

Andy heard the WAC table before he spotted it in the unusually crowded courtyard, back in the corner beneath Billy-Bob's tree. Rolf's heavy East German accent and Aengus' broad Irish enthusiastically toasting each other carried easily above the din of the UNHAS pilots, the WFP logisticians, and a large miscellaneous collection of INGO expats. Andy thought he caught the whiff of clove cigarettes. It was a sweet, nostalgic smell that reminded him of his first relief job ever—Indonesia.

He smiled to himself as he wound his way back to the small gaggle of exuberant WAC staff (plus Oxfam Aengus). They'd get cracking on the startup of a new OFDA grant first thing in the morning. This was what aid work was all about. Tonight was time to celebrate.

Chapter 33

"How's the jet lag?" Jillian was using her concerned face and her mothering voice.

"Better for now, thanks." Mary-Anne sipped her coffee. A Starbucks *Grande* Americano. Her first week in Dolo Ado, the dark, thick, sweetened coffee that Tekflu called "mocha" was exotically delicious, and she'd sworn she'd never again drink Starbucks with a straight face. But somehow today, the warm light, and saturated tones of an American coffee chain, the sounds of over-produced world music coming through discreetly placed speakers, and the ritual of ordering (not "large," not "big," but *Grande*) all merged into a strong sense of familiar strangeness. Or strange familiarity. After almost a year away, and no matter how much she still loved Ethiopian "mocha," Starbucks felt strangely like home. As artificial as she knew that particular sensation was, Mary-Anne found herself not wanting to leave. But the office was opening soon, and she had an important conversation scheduled with Jillian.

She sipped her coffee again. It tasted strong and earthy and good. Trying her best to sound congenial and conversational, Mary-Anne continued. "You know how it is. The second day's the worst. Yesterday I was dying…"

"Yesterday you were on fire!" Jillian interjected. "Your brand of no-nonsense, know-your-shit-cold is exactly what I'm looking for."

Jillian studied Mary-Anne intently for a moment before continuing. "I wasn't just making small talk in the taxi yesterday. You know Eric, right? He's just announced his retirement. The Director of Programs position will be open in two months, more or less, and while of course we'd have to go through the motions of you applying and maybe being interviewed, I'm telling you now that if you want the job, it's yours." She paused to let her words sink in before going on.

"Obviously there are limits. This is the aid world after all. But name a salary within the range of comparable positions with other NGOs headquartered here in DC, and you've got it. You'll find our relocation package is very adequate." Jillian had hunched forward as she spoke, but leaned back now. *Let Mary-Anne talk.*

Mary-Anne shifted in her chair. A million questions flooded her mind. In the forefront, very simply, should she do it? What would happen to the program in Dolo Ado? What of Jean-Philippe? Could they, *would* they, stay together if she took a job in the United States? Would taking an HQ job be selling out? Director of Programs at the global headquarters of an NGO was an important position. It was a far cry from just three years ago as a program officer in Haiti, a far cry from just three months ago as senior programs officer in Dolo Ado. She remembered something she'd read, or maybe heard—she couldn't quite place where—a bit of advice for young up-and-coming stars in the aid world: *Beware the meteoric rise.*

Then Mary-Anne heard her own voice, as if of its own accord—cool, confidant, and assured—speaking to Jillian. "I'm definitely interested. Tell me more. What does a WAC Director of Programs actually *do*, day to day?" She sipped her *Grande* Americano from Starbucks with affected nonchalance. "And what's your drop-dead deadline for a decision?"

* * *

They'd come back from Boston Medical by late morning, and after Chloe had taken a leisurely teenaged girl shower and put on fresh clothes, gone out for lunch. A nice lunch. At a nice restaurant.

Chloe told her dad all about school, her dance class, and her friend Tyler, and while Jon of course didn't really approve of Tyler (based on what Angie had told him), he didn't scold or lecture, but simply listened attentively. Chloe was a good girl, the normal adolescent mishaps notwithstanding. Jon smiled with obvious pride when she told him about how well she was doing in school. The smile of approval grew even larger and more obvious when Chloe told him about the colleges she was already considering. Although he couldn't be completely certain, Jon thought he saw Angie also smiling in approval at them, and perhaps—just perhaps—the look of defensive reserve in her eyes soften ever so slightly.

By mid-afternoon, the jet-lag began to set in and Jon began to fade, and Angie insisted that they go home. He secretly wondered if he might be allowed to sleep in their bed that night—Angie had held his gaze once or twice over the dinner table as they ate lunch and even smiled slightly, once. Then later as they walked to the car, his arm had brushed hers and she'd not pulled away. There was obviously still a great deal of relationship work and fatherhood penance ahead of him, but Jon had begun to feel optimistic again that things would be okay.

*

Somehow, between the time differences, attempts to connect to some seven different networks in some four different countries in the past seventy-two hours, and the mysterious, magical inner workings of the interwebs, unintelligible to mere mortals, a week's worth of text messages suddenly descended on Jon Langstrom's phone in the space of a few minutes.

*

He was in the shower when a week's worth of text messages suddenly landed on his phone in a nearly continuous stream of dinging and buzzing. Jon and Angie had the same model and color of iPhone, and it just happened that both of their phones were lying next to each other on the small, carved wooden table from Malawi that they used as a night stand. And it just happened that Angie was nearby when all the dinging and buzzing commenced. She, quite innocently and without any intention of snooping or spying, picked up *his* phone, mistaking it for her own, to see what all the dinging and buzzing was about. Out of all the automated airline updates about flights being cancelled or delayed, out of all the innocuous messages from Aengus reminding him to bring a bottle of Jack Daniels back to Dolo Ado, and the needy texts from Mark reminding him that tomorrow was a mandatory board meeting, the message displayed on the screen when Angie picked up Jon's phone was from a contact labeled simply as "Mary-Anne." The Guinness-laden text read:

"*I really, really need to talk to you. Miss you. Call me.*"

Angie's heart froze in a way that it never had before. Something about the "*miss you*" plus the "*call me*" seemed at once too devoid of context to really decipher, but felt at the same time threatening. Who *was* this Mary-Anne? And why did she need Jon to call her? And why would she be missing him?

The water stopped, and a moment later, Jon came out of the bathroom wearing only a towel around his waist like a sarong. He was about to ask Angie if she'd like to rent a movie for the evening—the perfect, familial end to a good-ish first day back, when he saw her face. It slowly registered that she was holding *his* phone, looking at him with a look he'd never seen before. Jon didn't know what she knew or thought, exactly, but his heart began to freeze as well. Then Angie spoke in a voice he'd never heard before, intense and accusing, her eyes wide. As if in a slow, bad dream her words sank in. *"Who is this Mary-Anne?"*

And Jon Langstrom knew that no matter what he might say, no matter what explanation he might try to give, he would be sleeping on the couch again that night.

Chapter 34

Mary-Anne wrestled her oversized duffel bag into the back of the WAC Land Cruiser, slammed the door shut, and climbed into the front passenger seat. *It was good to be back.*

"Madame, are you tired? They're waiting for you now." Mesfin was his usual cheerful self.

"I'm okay. Let's go. We've got a lot to do!" Mary-Anne tried to sound energetic, but the truth was that she was exhausted. After her meeting with Jillian, she'd spent another full day at WAC HQ in DC before heading to Kentucky for one of the most awkward weekends home ever. Mamma had never really understood Mary-Anne's love of humanitarian work. If she'd been skeptical when Mary-Anne went off to Haiti "on a childish whim," she flat disapproved of Dolo Ado.

"Surely there are people here *in America* who need help, too," Mamma had said more than once as Mary-Anne tried to explain what she did and why it was important to her. In the end, Mary-Anne just resigned herself to small talk about the weather or local sports or church gossip, and steered clear of anything that might lead the conversation back to humanitarian work or Dolo Ado or Jean-Philippe.

She tried not to act too excited as her parents drove her to the tiny local airport, and she breathed a sigh of secret relief as the small commuter plane took to the air and rural Kentucky dissolved into a collage of green patchwork before disappearing altogether. The series of layovers and connections back to the packed red mud river bed that served as Dolo Ado's airport had been intensely tiring. But as Mary-Anne buckled her seat belt and Mesfin ground the transmission into first, the smell of dust and cow dung and the heat waves shimmering up off the ground under a breathtakingly bright mid-morning sun suddenly all felt very much like "home."

Mary-Anne reached over and turned up the Amharic mix tape that Mesfin always had in the tape deck. She couldn't understand a single word of what was being sung, but it felt like "home", too.

There was work to do. *A lot* of work to do. Not a moment to waste.

* * *

Jon knew that Mark was annoyed with him, but he genuinely didn't understand until that morning just how bad things were.

Everyone in the programs unit was openly glad to see him. Before he'd even made it to Mark's office on the third floor he had more invitations to "grab a coffee" or "hit a happy hour before you leave town again" than he could possibly accept. But as he came around the corner toward Mark's office, he couldn't help but notice that Doris, Mark's admin, usually jovial and outgoing, was strangely reserved. He sat and waited in increasingly awkward silence outside Mark's closed door while Doris avoided his eyes and pretended to be busy on her computer.

When the door finally opened and Mark appeared, Jon knew immediately that it would be a difficult meeting. He'd dealt with enough corrupt local officials and belligerent cluster leads to know an adversarial demeanor when he saw it. And Mark was clearly adversarial that day.

"C'mon in, Langstrom. Let's get started." Mark's tone was clipped, his face expressionless. The door swung closed behind them and Jon sat down facing Mark across the large, impressive wooden desk.

"So look, let's dispense with the pleasantries. I'm glad you made it back safely and all of that. I'm sure you're not interested in my golf game or discussing politics." Jon had never seen his boss like this before.

"Cutting to the chase, I know you don't like what I sent you to do in Ethiopia any more than you don't like the fact that I sent you to do it," Mark scoffed. "Langstrom, I know what you think of me, and to be honest, I really don't care." He casually tossed his pen onto his desk for effect. "But it does concern me that you went out there and spent two months *not* doing what I very clearly told you to do."

Jon shifted uncomfortably in his chair and Mark continued. "You'll be presenting to the board of directors on our Horn of Africa portfolio in an hour or two, and we both know that you'll wow them. You'll do your thing… you're smart and articulate, and they see you as some kind of aid worker silverback cowboy." Mark scoffed again and shrugged dismissively.

"I'm sure that no matter what hard questions they might throw at you, you'll have a ready answer." He leaned across the desk toward Jon, his face dark. "But again, you and I both know that I sent you to Ethiopia to plant a flag and instead you signed us up to be Jillian Scott's handmaiden." Mark was turning red, his voice getting louder. "We had the budget to actually *do* something. Five hundred grand is not chump change, my friend."

The veins in Mark's forehead were bulging out now, and his pupils were dilated. He took a breath, sat back and continued in an almost sneer. "But *you* thought the best course of action would be to ride the coattails of World Aid Corps. What are you smoking out there?" Mark glared at Jon across the desk. "What in the hell is your problem, Langstrom?"

Jon returned Mark's gaze without glaring and answered in the most even voice he could muster. "Just so that I understand you now, in a few hours I'll brief the board, they'll love it, and they'll basically congratulate you for having had the good sense to send me out to do what I just did." He paused to let to words settle. "And you're pissed off at me for that. Is that about right?"

"Enough, Langstrom!" The veins in Mark's forehead were protruding again, but his voice was low and menacing. "In a few minutes, HR is going to come through that door, sit down next to you, and begin to walk you through the process for disciplinary probation. Don't worry. My ducks are in a row on this one. I've got the documentation. I've got the blessing of the CEO. It's a done deal."

"But—" Jon wanted to say something, anything, but the words wouldn't come.

"No buts, Langstrom. This *is* happening. Be glad I'm not firing you, but be advised that you are very close."

"*What?!*" Jon's mind was awash in disbelief.

"Don't play dumb with me." Mark was sneering again. "I know how you are, constantly undermining me, endless passive-aggressive pushback. I've fired others for far less. Look, a lot of people in this organization respect and look up to you. I get that. But that doesn't give you *carte blanche* to do whatever you want, and it certainly doesn't give you a free pass to go against a directive from executive leadership."

Mark paused again, then continued. "A bit of candid advice, Langstrom. You're always rambling about your network of contacts in 'the humanitarian sector' as if you're some sort of guru. I strongly suggest that you work your network. The laws of the land require me to follow a process here, but make no mistake about it: I want you gone. In the meantime, if you want to stay employed here, you *will* follow directives. I trust that's sufficiently clear?"

Jon nodded dumbly, deflated.

"Take two or three days. Spend some time with the fam. No need to come to the office. Then get your ass back out to Dolo Ado. I don't know what planet you were on when you hatched this thing with WAC, but we're in it now. So get back there and get it done, and I don't want to see you in this office again until it *is* done."

Chapter 35

Between jet lag on top of jet lag, operations and a new OFDA grant to start up simultaneously in Bur Amina, and a small mountain of admin work to catch up on, it was almost a week before Mary-Anne had either time or energy to contemplate an evening bottle (or maybe two) of St. George at Billy-Bob's.

But that afternoon as the sun began to dip toward the horizon and she felt more awake and less tired than she had in what felt like weeks, she decided to go. The urgent tasks had all been done, and while there was always more to do, there was nothing left on her desk or in her inbox that couldn't wait until tomorrow. Mary-Anne released Mesfin for the evening, took the keys to one of WAC's white Land Cruisers, changed into an unbranded black V-neck T-shirt, and drove the three pothole-ridden kilometers to Dolo Ado's primary expat watering hole.

It was an average crowd for an average night. The Serbian WFP warehouse manager was holding forth in a slurring eastern European accent about the awesomeness of his last trip to Bangkok to a rapt audience of IOM, Save the Children, and Concern Worldwide staff. The uptight NRC Director of Programmes from the coordination meeting on Bur Amina was sitting alone chain smoking and fiddling with his phone. The pretty young program officer from CARE was engrossed in earnest conversation with a well-groomed and (Mary-Anne couldn't help but notice) exceptionally handsome Ethiopian man she'd not seen before.

She was pleased to see that her and Jon's table—the one under the tree back in the corner—was empty. While she wasn't *not* in the mood for conversation, Mary-Anne knew she was also equally uninterested in stories of Bangkok carousing, as well as earnest conversation on anything. She called for a bottle of St. George and then seated herself on the small plastic chair at the low, grimy table. As she extended her hand for the obligatory greeting head-butt by Billy-Bob the goat, Mary-Anne became acutely aware that it was the first time since—she couldn't remember when, exactly—she'd last come to Billy-Bob's and not drank St. George and deployment smoked and talked with Jon Langstrom.

Although the St. George tasted as good and, in an ironic way, as much like "home" as the *Grande* Americano had just a few days ago in a DC Starbucks, the whole moment suddenly seemed, well, lacking, and perhaps a little sad.

Suddenly Mary-Anne wasn't all that thirsty. In a moment that would have made mamma cringe and Brandon thump her boisterously on the back, she drained half the bottle of St. George in a single pull. She motioned for the swarthy young man serving tables, and when he came over, she handed him the birr equivalent of one bottle plus a little bit.

Strange as it seemed to say, it felt *good* to back in Dolo Ado. Tomorrow was a new day with a lot to get done. Sure, there were some unknowns, some big decisions, some issues to work through. There would absolutely be challenges, that much was certain. But Mary-Anne knew that she could take whatever might come, and more importantly, she was up to whatever tasks Jillian or OFDA or Dolo Ado might throw her way.

At that moment, as if in cosmic affirmation, the first donkey of the evening brayed in the darkness somewhere in the general direction of Somalia.

* * *

Mulu Alem checked his phone for messages. Nothing. *Where was Aster?* He hadn't heard from her in almost five weeks. No phone calls, no emails, no text messages. Nothing.

He sighed deeply and turned back to the coarse, limp papers in front of him. There was a sealed envelope with the ARRA logo on it, and inside a message that made him do a double-take: The refugee response in Dolo Ado was expanding, thanks to his deciding vote on Bur Amina. Ethiopia was looking great in the international community. Well done. After Bur Amina, who knew? Maybe there'd even be another camp. And maybe even another after that. He'd need to hire more staff.

The silence from Aster was momentarily forgotten. But Bur Amina. Bur Amina might just have been the *best thing to have ever happened.*

* * *

Rolf's cheap Nokia local SIM card cell phone buzzed.
Another automated security update from the UN.

He shook his head in annoyance. *The worst security analyses ever.* The message read:

Be advised: Increase in random armed banditry around Dolo, Somalia and the Ethiopian border.

He shoved the phone into his pocket and turned back to a vehicle movement tracking spreadsheet. Whatever.

* * *

Jon Langstrom walked tiredly toward the arrivals hall at Addis Ababa Bole International Airport. He'd not slept much during the series of long, tedious flights and equally tedious layovers between Boston and Addis. Most of the way, he'd mentally replayed the last, fraught conversations between himself and Angie, inventing alternate endings with better outcomes almost subconsciously as he'd grown more sleepy. The remainder of the way, he'd mentally replayed his last conversation with Mark.

Neither scenario was particularly positive, but as much as Jon tried to put it all out of his mind and focus on the tasks of the weeks ahead—a coping technique he'd grown adept at using during the past two and a half decades—this time, he could not. Like so many other aid workers who'd gone before or would come after, Jon Langstrom had built up an impressive level of tolerance to ambient toxicity, whether in the workplace or in his own personal life. But by the same token, when things in either sphere progressed beyond the point of "ambient toxicity" and began to approach "imminent system failure," he, like so many others, found it increasingly impossible to mentally push those issues to the side. It was all or nothing: either general denial or obsessive focus. And right now, Jon Langstrom was in an obsessive focus phase.

The idea that Mark might actually fire him—not just "might," but actually wanted to—was scary, of course. After thirty or so years of what anyone might call distinguished service, being fired from a senior role in a prestigious organization like Oxfam America would be difficult thing rebound from. There would be the inevitable awkward and impossible-to-answer-well questions at every interview for every new job. And if he did land something new, a termination would still follow him. Sure, he could go it on his own as a consultant, but that game would be altogether different. He'd be competing directly with new graduates, half his age, fresh out of Tufts or Harvard or the LSE, CVs full of publications in peer-reviewed journals, spouting the latest theories and jargon, all while simultaneously updating Twitter, Tumblr, Facebook and Pinterest from their Macbooks. It would require a hard scramble, and while Jon knew he had a lot of fight left, a lot still to do and a lot to offer, he wasn't sure he was up for the hard scramble at this point in his life.

No, better to eat humble pie, and let Mark score a "win," and all of that, Jon thought to himself. He'd kowtowed to more uneducated, iodine-deficient, snaggle-toothed, low-ranking officials trying to demonstrate their power to the foreigner (him) than he could specifically recall in as many third world backwater districts, all for the sake of causes far less noble in retrospect than his own livelihood. *He could do this*. It wouldn't be fun, but he could do it.

The prospect of Angie leaving him, of losing his family for real, was the one which scared him the most. In two decades of marriage, no matter how harshly he and Angie might have disagreed or fought, neither of them had ever even alluded to the possibility of divorce. But although they'd both remained calm, almost cordial, during his last two days in the U.S. before heading back to the Horn of Africa, Angie had made it pointedly clear that divorce was absolutely among the options she was seriously contemplating. She hadn't totally made up her mind, and she supposed, for the sake of argument, that he might be able to turn things around, depending on how well it all went with his plan to change his career trajectory post-Dolo Ado. But there were no givens, and probation was closing. He'd better act soon if he wanted a shot at changing what was currently the most likely outcome. Jon cursed himself for having let things get this bad, and even more for not recognizing that things were this bad.

There was, Angie said hesitantly, another event at which Jon's in-the-flesh presence would mean a lot. Chloe's final parent-teacher conference was in about three weeks. This conference would mark the end of her middle school career and the beginning of her life as a high school student. Of course they'd have the usual private conference with her home room teacher, but there would also be a lengthy presentation by Chloe herself. It was a highly scripted event around which hype had been built for months already. When Jon actually asked Chloe how she would feel if he was able to be there for it, she'd welled up and hugged him tightly and in a small voice said, "Yes, please come, Daddy." Right then, Jon Langstrom knew that regardless of what might happen between he and Angie—whether or not this gesture would change her mind—or no matter what the status of the Dolo Ado operation might be, and no matter what Mark might say or do if he took a week of leave and flew home at his own expense, *he would be there in person for his daughter's final middle school conference.*

Jon sighed as he hefted his battered roll-along suitcase from the luggage belt and headed for the "Nothing to Declare" lane. 11:15 p.m. Time for a few hours of sleep at Hotel Kaleb before catching the UNHAS Caravan, or—if he was extra lucky—a Dash-8, out to Dolo Ado first thing in the morning.

Chapter 36

"*Ma cherie*, you must do what you feel. You must follow your heart..." Jean-Philippe's words still rang in her ears. She had been almost afraid, at first, to tell him about the offer from Jillian. But even across the interwebs he had put her immediately at ease.

"*Oui. Directeur d'programmes*. It is a senior position for you, *non?*" The Skype connection had been unusually stable and strong, and they'd been able to video chat. Mary-Anne could see that Jean-Philippe was talking to her from the flat—their flat—sitting at the small table in the tiny kitchen, sipping casually from a glass of what looked like chardonnay. The afternoon light accentuated the piercing greenness of his eyes, and the poor quality of the built-in camera on his computer making his hair appear darker than in real life. *God*, she wanted to have this conversation in person.

He'd been profoundly supportive as she talked through her uncertainty, her indecision about moving to Washington, DC and taking a HQ job. When she worried aloud how such a move might affect her credibility with aid workers in the field, he simply mouth-farted (*pfffffff...*) and said, "Mary-Anne (*Mehrrrreee-Ahhhn*), you must do what makes you happy (*'appEEEee*)... you are not in some website about the things that the foreign aid workers are liking. You are a *real aid worker*, no matter in which seat you sit to do your job and no matter how far you must travel to come to 'the field.'" And when she shared her fear of what such a move might mean for *them*, he became almost strident: "No! When you went to Nairobi, I also went here. If I think you will stay one more year in Dolo Ado, then I will come there. And if you go to DC, then I can go there, too.

"We belong together, *ma cherie*. I can work from anyplace which has Internet, good wine and a nearby airport. And DC is something a little bit like Paris (*Pahhhrrreee*), *non?* If you take this job there, we will still live together." Mary-Anne breathed easier at that moment, knowing that no matter what hard choices she might yet be called on to make, on *this* one, at least, Jean-Philippe would be her constant.

* * *

The morning sun blazed down on the Oxfam Land Cruiser as it ground its way toward Bur Amina. Jon Langstrom yawned. His head hurt and he desperately wanted to sleep. He'd been back in Dolo Ado less than ten hours—not even enough time for a proper beer at Billy-Bob's—and already he was on his way out to 'the field.'

As the Land Cruiser turned left, off the main road, through a small cluster—it wasn't a town, really—of low, nondescript buildings toward Bur Amina Camp, his thoughts were still on Angie and Chloe, and their problems. Which in part stemmed back to Mary-Anne. He needed to talk to her. *They* needed to talk.

Maybe she'll be at Billy-Bob's tonight.

* * *

Mary-Anne's brow was furrowed in concentration as she read down through the list on the screen in front of her.

"I'm thinking we put all of warehouse team B onto new ops in Bur Amina. They can start out one hundred percent to OFDA, and then as we get additional funding we pro-rate their time and warehouse rent accordingly." It was Andy, hovering over her shoulder. Mary-Anne nodded. It made sense. Starting up new operations to support a new grant at Bur Amina would require dedicated staff. And with the in-progress closing out of projects and generally scaling down at Kobe, WAC would have many of the staff they needed already. For many of the admin support and operations positions it would be a simple matter of reassigning, and in a few cases sitting down with HR and the staff person in question to discuss changes in roles, possibly promotions.

For the loggies, sweating it out in the warehouses there would be no perceptible change. Relief NFIs and shelter kits were about the same regardless of who the donor was. For the admin and finance departments, it would be a matter of using a few different forms, changing reporting schedules, and maybe slapping a few "From the American People" stickers on furniture or computers purchased with project funds. Procurement would be busy at the beginning—maybe they'd need a little temp help. Mary-Anne would personally negotiate rental permits with ARRA, and then under the watchful eye of Rolf, lead the search for the space WAC would need on-site at Bur Amina. But otherwise, with a little savvy rearrangement and some creative reworking of a few people's contracts, she had what she needed to lay the operational foundation for a new OFDA grant.

That left the programs side largely empty. They'd budgeted a program officer and an M&E specialist. Andy would probably insist on taking on the PO role himself, at least at first, and Leila (WAC/Dolo Ado senior M&E advisor) would probably just assign one of her staff to the grant. The more difficult challenge would be to quickly build a community mobilization team. They'd need to recruit and hire twelve local mobilizers, but that would take time. It would also require someone who knew the context, the culture and the language to help with recruitment, and then eventually lead the team. They needed a local community mobilization team leader.

Mary-Anne squinted again at the list of local programs staff on her screen. Ismael was talented and energetic, but too young to be taken seriously by the refugees. Helena was vibrant, fun and had rock solid community mobilization skills, but her husband was already calling from Addis every day to complain that she wasn't home looking after the house. No telling how long Helena would be able to stay in Dolo Ado. Ibrahim? No, that would be a bad idea.

"What about Tekflu?" Mary-Anne asked without looking up.

"Sure," Andy was casual. "There's not enough going on in Kobe to really justify keeping him there any longer. That'd work."

Mary-Anne looked across the table at her finance officer. "What do you think? Should I put Tekflu in charge of the mobilization team in Bur Amina?"

Mercy's face was expressionless. "Ma'am, may I speak with you privately?"

Chapter 37

Mary-Anne's head was swimming. "I can't believe Tekflu would steal from us."

Mercy's voice was calm and assured. "Ma'am, I've been over and over the evidence. I wish it wasn't true. Believe me, I don't enjoy accusing a colleague of embezzlement." She paused and deftly placed a manila folder with what looked like twenty pages worth of documents inside on the table between them. "Here, see for yourself."

*

An hour later, Mary-Anne was convinced. Mercy had everything in order. The evidence was damning and, as far as she could see, conclusive. There was no question. Tekflu was embezzling from WAC.

But what tormented Mary-Anne was the "why?" Why would Tekflu steal? He was stable, had a respectable career behind and also ahead of him. *Why?* The amounts he'd taken—as Mercy had meticulously documented—were pathetically small. Sure, he was pulling a local salary in a country where local salaries, even in the NGO sector, were low compared to what went to internationals. But
Tekflu had been embezzling, skimming, *stealing*, or whatever, the birr equivalent of five, ten, maximum twenty US dollars, maybe every two weeks. Day to day it amounted to a cup of coffee here, a meal at a moderately nice restaurant there, perhaps the cost of topping up the minutes on a local SIM card. Although she couldn't have approved, she felt she could have at least understood stealing to make ends meet. But Tekflu was stealing piddling amounts. It wasn't like he needed the money.

She'd fought for his promotion to site coordinator at Kobe. She'd advocated for extended leave so that he could attend to pressing family matters in Addis last fall. She'd fought both Brandon and Mercy to keep Tekflu on staff last spring, before the DANIDA grant had been won and money for salaries had been tighter than at any time prior. He'd always been a solid employee who never missed deadlines and always followed through on tasks, and he'd never been sullen or disrespectful or insubordinate.

Mary-Anne thought too of the innumerable hours they'd spent in the WAC Land Cruiser or in focus groups. Tekflu had been more than an employee: He'd been her coach, her confidante, her translator, and her main source of explanation for things she didn't grasp about the local culture or context. Staff who actually added value, whether local or expat, were not easy to find. But Tekflu clearly added value. It suddenly dawned on her that he was her friend, too. She knew the names of his children and where they were in their respective university careers. He knew of her struggles as a humanitarian, of her relationship with Jean-Philippe, and her apprehensions about her own promotions within WAC. All of this made his embezzlement from WAC, no matter how inconsequential the amount, feel like a personal betrayal, like a slap in the face.

"What will you do, ma'am?" Mercy's voice jerked Mary-Anne back to the reality of the moment. "I don't think we can put Tekflu as mobilization team leader at Bur Amina."

"I know." Mary-Anne nodded dumbly. "Please work with Andy to post the vacancy announcement as soon as possible. We need a qualified local. I've heard that OCHA is downsizing over in Assosa. Maybe we can poach one of their bright stars."

They'd find a good candidate for the community mobilization team leader role, Mary-Anne knew. It wouldn't necessarily be easy, but it could be done. Operationally, this was more of an inconvenience than anything else. What had her stomach suddenly tied in knots, though, was the prospect of having to fire someone she'd not only worked closely with, but also valued—highl— as an otherwise excellent employee *and* as a personal friend.

But the WAC global employment policy was crystal clear and left very little room for either interpretation or alternative action. Sure, there were famous, possibly apocryphal exceptions in WAC's short past; examples of early senior staff who'd been personally pardoned by Jillian Scott herself after having committed the aid world equivalents of organizational treason or adultery. But Tekflu wasn't senior, and the periodic executive updates from Jillian to WAC managers around the world seemed to increasingly paint a picture of low-to-zero tolerance in situations like this. Mary-Anne knew that she'd very likely have no choice but to fire Tekflu. Further, as chief of party for the organization in Ethiopia she would almost certainly have to do it herself.

Mercy was still looking at her.

"And," Mary-Anne was suddenly strong again. She knew what had to happen. "I'll deal with Tekflu."

* * *

Jon Langstrom shook his head in annoyance. He normally liked Aengus, but today he found the pudgy, outspoken Dubliner incredibly annoying.

"Look, mate," Aengus was saying. "Are you the relief director for Oxfam America or aren't you? You can't just sit here and manage one little project in Bur Amina."

He knew Aengus was right. But somehow, the combination of jet lag, general exhaustion, specific exhaustion from having just finished a day of difficult reconnaissance under a blazing sun in Bur Amina, and lingering anger at Mark (and by extension all of Oxfam), made him want to be argumentative. Vitriol rose in his throat, but he resolutely pushed it back down before speaking. "Okay, right. Sure. Let's talk about what portfolio you want me to cover." Take whatever. Just get through the meeting. No need to tell Aengus anything about the plan to change jobs once the WAC partnership was up and running.

Aengus softened ever so slightly. "So obviously you're the man for this thing in Bur Amina with WAC. That's a given. Hilaweyn needs help and Kobe has issues. And now it seems we're supposed to do something with MSF in Dolo Somalia. Here, take a look." He pushed the printout of an email message across the desk toward Jon. "If you'd take on full ownership of one of these special needs sites in addition to Bur Amina, that'd be great."

Jon skimmed the message. It was from the Oxfam GB chief of staff to the MSF head of mission in Mogadishu, full of the usual platitudes and expressions of solidarity and commitment to a common mission in support of the world's most vulnerable. There were no real specifics in terms of actual resources being committed, from where to where, or for what, other than that Oxfam would "support MSF operational presence" in Dolo Somalia. So, apparently Oxfam would do something and MSF would do something and maybe they'd share space or give each other rides around the desert in company vehicles. Specifically vague. Go in, figure something out, do something. And suddenly it occurred to Jon that this might be exactly the assignment he needed right then. Suddenly Aengus was his new best friend.

"What kind of budget are we looking at on the Oxfam side?" Jon squinted at Aengus over the top of the paper in his hand.

"Uhhhhh… Hard to say. You thinking you might want to take on the Somalia piece?" Aengus was suddenly cheerful. Jon nodded. Aengus paused for a moment and then went on, parsing his words carefully. "I can give you a vehicle for your exclusive use, a bit of per diem for nights you spend inside Somalia, and—ooooh—say, thirty, let's make that thirty-*five* thousand USD for 'programs' or 'operations,' whichever term you prefer. You'd be on your own. Security will have a cow, but I'll help you work around that. We can't spare any of our existing staff. You'd need to hire a translator, get yourself to Dolo, link up with whomever MSF sends, do some kind of need assessment and just figure it out."

Jon paused for effect before answering. "Okay, I can live with that. You deal with the 'special needs' sites, by which I specifically mean Kobe and Hilaweyn, and I'll take on the startup sites which as of now are Bur Amina and Dolo Somalia. That sound about right?" It was like haggling for a camel.

The Irishman grinned and thrust a stubby hand across the desk toward Jon. "Done. And remind me to never again say anything bad about working with you Yanks!" Jon took Aengus' hand and grinned back. "Done." Somalia was as close as it got to the Wild West these days. If Jon was headed for a life of cubicle farming after this, he might as well make his last hurrah as memorable as possible.

Aengus gave Jon a knowing smile. "And how many of those young wannabes would donate vital organs to science for this kind of assignment, *eh?*"

Chapter 38

Jillian Scott felt like a new woman. A win from OFDA was invigorating. The award letter had come yesterday, and while of course she needed to allow WAC legal counsel the time to comb through the legalese there was *no way* she wasn't signing. Then the promise of new opportunities in West Africa or southern Asia had her head spinning with possibilities. In just a few short months her dream for WAC had begun coming together even better than she could have imagined. World Aid Corps would be a major industry player and she would be recognized as the architect of it all.

Now she *really* needed a star player as her new director of programs.

She glanced at her watch and ran the time differences in her head. 9:30 a.m. on the border of Somalia, give or take. Mary-Anne should be up and at it by now. She needed an answer. The operation in Dolo Ado was important, of course, but not that deep. There was a bigger picture. There were broader issues and larger pieces in motion, and Jillian needed Mary-Anne to make up her mind sooner rather than later.

* * *

Jon Langstrom turned up Foreigner and jammed the battered Land Cruiser into second gear. The road from Dolo Ado town to the border of Somalia passed directly through the town dump—a large open area littered with piles of trash among which feral dogs fought with abnormally large buzzards over the rotting remains of what appeared to be goats. He remembered what Aengus had told him about the cloud of circling buzzards being a landmark visible for miles. The stench of it all hung heavily in the already stifling morning air and Jon was thankful he didn't have to walk the last two or so kilometers to the border.

Less than half an hour later he was handing his passport over for inspection by an Ethiopian border guard wearing jungle camouflage fatigues and a DKNY flat hat. The guard flipped through Jon's passport, looked casually through the back window (nothing inside), and in surprisingly clear and oddly un-ironic English said, "Have fun in Somalia."

As Jon drove across the bridge he found himself thinking two things. First, this job was "way below his pay grade," but even so it was the first time he'd actually looked forward to getting up and going to work since… Sri Lanka? Those two months in Jalalabad, maybe? He couldn't remember exactly. But something about setting out across the desolate hinterlands of western Somalia in a battered Land cruiser to just sort of "figure something out" somehow felt almost primal. His pulse quickened and he turned up Foreigner ("Feels Like the First Time") even louder.

Second, he'd not seen Mary-Anne in almost three weeks. Putting aside talk of their organizationally mandated partnership, or discussion of any field-based weirdness which may or may not have ensued between them, he really, really wanted to sit and just catch up with her over a few lukewarm bottles of St. George. Strange as it seemed to say, he missed her.

*

"Ma'am, are you ready?" Mercy's voice pulled Mary-Anne forcefully out of the virtual world of Facebook and into the tangible world of Dolo Ado.

"Is the first one here?" She answered Mercy's question with a question as she locked her computer, then picked up a small notebook and pen from her desk. It was the first interview with the first local candidate for the community mobilization team leader position at Bur Amina. They'd narrowed the list of applicants down to five on paper, and now it was time to start meeting them in person.

"Yes, she's in the board room now."

Mary-Anne's mind wandered as she walked the fifty meters from her container office to the small brick building that housed WAC's multipurpose community space—lunch room, meeting room, television and entertainment center after hours. One of the Ethiopian staff had lovingly dubbed it "the board room" back when WAC had first rented the compound, and the name stuck.

She wondered what Jean-Philippe was doing. He'd be in Nairobi now, probably over at the UNHCR office. He was doing a lot with them lately. Mary-Anne smiled subconsciously with pride. He was good at it. Between his keen ethical and philosophical mind, his casually articulate way of presenting, and his dreamy French accent, she knew those UNHCR staffers didn't stand a chance. Whatever it was Jean-Philippe wanted from UNHCR, he'd almost certainly get it.

There was Jon Langstrom, too. They hadn't talked in a couple of weeks, and she missed him. Mary-Anne openly admitted this to herself in as many words. While there was much about their relationship and her feelings for Jon that she couldn't put into words, she did know that she missed him. She'd heard via the aid worker grapevine that he was just back from America and that he'd been assigned to support some kind of startup op in Dolo Somalia, but they'd not had a chance to talk. They needed to talk. There was work–WAC and Oxfam America were partners now. WAC was contractually obligated to the United States government to deliver on that partnership, so they had a real work reason to talk. And then there was their "incident" which seemed smaller and of less consequence the further it faded into the past, but which Mary-Anne felt a lingering inexplicable need to address. They needed to have "the talk."

But beyond work and sorting out anything that might be hanging between them, Mary-Anne just wanted to see him, to hear his voice telling her wise things about how the aid industry worked. She wanted to sit under the tree at Billy-Bob's, drink St. George, and listen to him give her sound advice, just being real and nonjudgmental with nothing to prove and no reason to bullshit her.

She and Mercy were at the door of "the board room" now. Time to get back to the moment. But there was one more thing nagging at her. Under other circumstances, the most obviously logical move *would* have been to simply transition Tekflu to the new Bur Amina team as community mobilization team leader. Yet here she was, interviewing external candidates for a role everyone assumed would have just gone to him. Although she hadn't heard anything yet, she assumed that staff were talking, which would invariably mean gossiping. And if staff members were talking, it was safe to assume that Tekflu knew, too, and would be wondering what was going on.

No point in trying to hide from the fact that it just had to be done.

Chapter 39

Angie Langstrom's pointer hovered momentarily over the "send" button. She hesitated, reread the message, and then clicked "save as draft." She needed to give Jon space. For all of her pent-up anger from the past many years, having spilled it all out to him had suddenly made her feel—well—better. Or less angry, which was kind of the same thing.

Part of her desperately wanted to beg him to change, to come back, to be a real part of the family. And another part resolutely clung to her anger and dared him to slip up, to justify what in Angie's mind was already all but *fait accompli*.

A mysterious text message from a woman who very obviously thought a great deal of her husband had not been the cause of anything, but rather the icing on the cake, the cherry on top of the sundae. It was simply apparent confirmation of something she'd assumed for many years but until now had no tangible reason to suspect. Jon was never home. Jon wasn't getting any from her (not that she'd have been into it even if he'd showed interest). *Ergo*, he was getting some from someone else, somewhere else. It all seemed straightforward enough.

No, she wouldn't fill Jon's inbox. He was a big boy. He'd made his own choices knowing full well what was at stake. He knew what to do if he wanted to turn things around. Not that she was ready to change her mind, but she was certainly ready to have Jon try.

Angie shut down her computer and stood up. 11:35 p.m. Shiraz? Or bed? She was leaning toward the Shiraz.

* * *

Mary-Anne's pulse suddenly quickened as she saw Jon Langstrom walk through the low, grimy doorway into the courtyard at Billy-Bob's. She'd come alone, expecting to drink alone (the experts say to never do that), but the sight of Jon walking toward her table was an unexpected, welcome surprise.

"May I sit here?" he asked as he always did, and it was all she could do to keep from jumping up and hugging him right there. Instead she just beamed and said, almost shyly, "Of course! It's *sooo* good to see you!" and then waved for the young man waiting on tables to bring them a few more rounds of St. George.

Bottles magically appeared. As Jon seated himself the awkwardness of their encounter, now almost a month ago, in a Land Cruiser during a sandstorm weighed heavily on Mary-Anne. She desperately wanted to talk, to listen, but she had to clear the air first. "Jon, we need to talk—"

*

"Yes, we do," he'd almost interrupted. His voice was more emphatic than she was used to hearing from him, but his eyes were warm. Seated now, he casually lifted a bottle of St. George toward hers in an aid worker toast. "Cheers." Their bottles clinked and then both drank. Then Jon went on, "And why do you think we need to talk, Mary-Anne?" His eyes were probing now, and she found herself wanting to avoid his gaze. She fought the urge to stand up and run.

"Jon, we need to talk about that evening in the Land Cruiser on the way back from Bur Amina. I… I…" Her voice faltered. "I'm sorry, Jon, if I led you on or made you think that I thought that I wanted…" She'd rehearsed this moment a thousand times in her head, but now that he was there, next to her, in the flesh, she struggled to find the words.

"No need, Mary-Anne." Jon's voice was warm and reassuring. "It was one of those things that happens. It was my fault, too, and I apologize if I acted inappropriately or offended you in any way." She started to protest, but he rolled on. "Mary-Anne, I'm married, and while there's plenty wrong at home and I'm far from a good, let alone ideal, husband, believe it or not, I do take that seriously. It was wrong of me to allow…" he hesitated as if searching for the right word, "to allow what happened to happen. I misrepresented myself to you. It amounted to dishonesty, and for that I do apologize."

He took a long pull on the bottle of St. George, took a deep breath, and then finished. "I think highly of you, Mary-Anne. I respect you. Not to be weird, but I see a lot of myself as a younger man in you." He was openly smiling now, the serious moment over. "Don't misunderstand. If I was single and, like, fifteen years younger…" His eyes twinkled and he chuckled softly as if to himself. "Well, you get the point." Jon set the near empty bottle of St. George on the table, put a cigarette between his lips and began fumbling in his pocket for a lighter.

Mary-Anne breathed an involuntary sigh of relief. It was as if a weight had been lifted from her shoulders. And at the same time, Jon Langstrom seemed even more attractive than ever.

"No, Jon. I'm the one who owes *you* an apology. I started it all. I don't know what got into me." She could feel her eyes begin to well up. "I don't know... it's just so hard... and you're such a good friend, and..."

"Okay, okay." Jon was smiling broadly now. "You're forgiven. I think we've established what good friends we are." He'd found the lighter and as he lit up he held the remnants of the pack toward her.

"Deployment smoke?"

Mary-Anne nodded, reassured. "Deployment smoker in the house."

"So, what's been going on with you the last few weeks?" Jon was looking intently at her now, intentionally moving the conversation along. "You obviously won the OFDA grant for Bur Amina. That's got to be good for your résumé..."

Chapter 40

Mary-Anne took a long drag on her cigarette, and then exhaled slowly before speaking. It wasn't that she liked it so much, but smoking was social, kinesthetic. Smoking was something to do while doing nothing or just talking, or when she wasn't sure what to do or what to say. The taste, the aroma of the tobacco brought back memories, some bad, some painful, but mostly good.

She'd *never* smoke at home. But in the field, on a relief op, whether at a party in the MSF team house in Port-au-Prince, or here, at Billy-Bob's in Dolo Ado, smoking was the natural thing to do. And for the first time she really got what Jon Langstrom meant when he used the term "deployment smoker."

Jon's voice pulled her back to the moment. "So, besides winning loads of OFDA cash, what's new?"

What was new? Where to start? "Well, I guess the big news is that I've been offered a job at the head office, back in DC." *Might as well just get it out there.*

"Wow!" Jon sounded impressed. "That *is* big. You gonna go for it?"

Mary-Anne hesitated. "Well, I guess I'm leaning that way, but not sure. I keep going back and forth." Another long pull of St. George, another long drag, another exaggeratedly slow exhale. Jon's eyes never left hers.

"I guess I'm seriously considering it. It's a good job, I guess. I dunno. It's an attractive offer. But every time I'm about to send the email saying I accept, I have all these reservations and just can't make myself do it." She turned and searched his eyes for a moment. In daylight, Jon's eyes were just plain brown. But in the fading twilight of Billy-Bob's and a glowing almost-done cigarette, they took on an almost three-dimensional quality, and were deep and warm. "Jon, I could really use your perspective. What would *you* do?"

Jon chuckled softly. "Well, the bad news is that there's no right decision here. No matter what you decide, you'll look back on this exact moment in a few months and wonder what the hell you were thinking!" He drained the bottle of St. George and waved to the waiter. "One more?" Mary-Anne nodded, and Jon continued.

"But then, the good news is that there's no *wrong* decision here either. Stay on in Dolo Ado for the life of another grant, or maybe two or three. Know this response and this place inside and out. Some would question the value of the specific knowledge you gain here. They'll say you spent all this time in the Horn of Africa, so how could you possibly work effectively in, say, Southeast Asia or the Middle East? It's little more than aid world provincialism, basically." He shrugged dismissively and snuffed out his cigarette before going on.

"On the other hand, no hiring manager—and let's be honest, that's who you care about most, after yourself, of course, in all of this—will fault your CV for having eighteen months or thirty-six months on one response, rather than just six. A series of six-month bounces makes you look flighty, unable to commit. Two-year stints make you someone worth investing in a little more. They make you someone to consider for more senior slots."

Jon fumbled with the soft Marlboro pack, fished out one more cigarette and lit up. The sun had almost completely set now, and she could see only the last hint of color in his eyes in the light of the flame as he went on. "But a move to HQ, eh? Unless I miss my guess, you're worried about the loss of field cred, the loss of connection with the field, whatever that even means. Maybe you're afraid that you'll somehow be less of an aid worker in your office in DC, than you would be in a stinky tent in Dolo Ado. That about right?"

Mary-Anne nodded. It was like Jon Langstrom was reading her thoughts. "So why would anyone ever work at HQ?"

Jon chuckled ruefully. "There's more than one kind of 'field cred' in this industry, and anyway, there are things more important than field cred." He exhaled sharply, a cloud of gray smoke toward the now black sky overhead, before continuing. "You need to take care of yourself. You need to have a life."

Mary-Anne nodded, thinking. "A life" sure sounded good, although she wasn't entirely sure what Jon meant by it. "Go on."

"You need to understand that this industry—the *aid industry*—will take everything you have to offer, and it will give you nothing back, if you let. It will not necessarily treat you unfairly. But there will be no medallion on your grave. You will not get anything more than token recognition for the times when you work eighteen-hour days in the field while your HQ counterparts head for happy hour at 4:00 p.m. You will, or may be, passed over for promotions or jobs that you've rightfully 'earned' in favor of colleagues who are less qualified than you, or who have done less for the organization than you, or who have pulled fewer hardship deployments or all-nighters, or had giardia, or been shot at by armed militants fewer times, or brought in fewer grant dollars than you. It is important for you to understand that the aid industry is just like any other. Which is to say that it is cold, calculated, political."

Mary-Anne took a long pull on the bottle of St. George as Jon's word sank in. "Got another cigarette?" Jon held out the pack nonchalantly and Mary-Anne took the second to the last one. Jon cupped his hand around the flame as she lit up, and then continued his monologue.

"All of which means that you need to hedge your bets. I see so many young aid workers who think that their sacrifice or suffering somehow translates into them being more effective." Another long drag. "But that's misguided thinking." He was more serious now. "You need to take care of *you*. No matter what you do, someone will criticize you or feel empowered to share the opinion that you should have done the other. But you have to let that stuff slide off. And you sure as hell can't retire on simply the number of years you've lived in the field under harsh conditions, far from family, with low salary and no retirement. Aid world field cred won't keep you warm at night or pay your mortgage or cover your health insurance."

"These are things that you need to take care of on your own. Manage your relationships. Take care of your health, whether it's physical or emotional. The aid industry is big enough and diverse enough that you don't *have* to pull hardship postings. You can still do good work and make a difference and all of that, and still be a whole person with meaning outside of the industry." Now Jon was very serious.

"I figured this out much too late, and now I'm afraid it's cost more than I ever thought it would." In the flicker of his lighter, flaring up for the last time, Mary-Anne could hardly see Jon's face. But it looked as if he might actually cry. His voice was almost a whisper. "Commit to the work, to the cause, or whatever. But take care of yourself, too. They're not mutually exclusive, and if that means moving to DC, then so be it. For heaven's sake, *have a life*."

"Okay, fine. *I get that*." Mary-Anne felt a twinge of impatience. Jon was brilliant, but not exactly helpful in a concrete sense. "Have a life. *Right*. I have an iPhone and a Kindle Fire with more books than I can possibly finish during this deployment. If I ever get around to taking R&R it'll be someplace like southern France or maybe Bali. I do things that my thousand-plus Facebook friends envy. I have a life that some of my friends from college would envy, and that others cannot possibly imagine. But I'm no closer to knowing what to do about this job offer."

Jon chuckled softly. "You'll be alright, Mary-Anne. Like I said, there's no wrong decision. Either one— staying on here, or moving back to DC can be the next step in a great career. And either one can become your crash and burn." He shook out the last cigarette, crumpled the empty pack, lit up, and exhaled slowly before continuing.

"What's important is that you do not just sort of slide into whatever is next. Have a longer plan, know what comes next. Or at least have some idea."

"But that's just the problem! I don't know what's next, or even what I want." Mary-Anne felt at once very old and also very naïve. "I'm not one of those twenty-something prodigies who has a Fortune 500 company, a million dollars in the bank, and a plan to retire by forty."

Jon took a long drag. "Like I said, you'll be fine. It's okay to change the plan. Just have a plan. Go to DC and be a director of programs, but have a plan for what comes after. Say you'll stay four years and then look for a promotion. Or say you'll stay two years and then move back to the field. And if you change your mind mid-stream, it's okay. Things happen, *life* happens and sometimes you have to adjust. But if you don't think now about what comes after, trust me, you will end up like those guys—you know who I mean—who spend fifteen years in the same cubicle, managing the same spreadsheets, and telling the same tired stories about Mauritania in 1989 or that one time, on the Hurricane Mitch response. All the while, they're being passed over for promotion time and time again by people half their age, and wondering how, exactly, they got there."

He paused. "Or, if you stay here, that's fine, too. But say to yourself that your plan is to stay one more year, and then it'll be time to go. If something happens in that year which changes your mind, fine. Plans can change. But be intentional. Think through the trade-offs now. Because if you don't, three years from now you'll still be drinking St. George at Billy-Bob's every night, listening to donkeys calling for love in the desert. And fif*teen* years from now, you'll wake up one morning having been nowhere but a series of stinky towns where maternal mortality and assault-rifles-per-capita are both far too high, nothing at all to show for it, and no clear idea of what's next."

Jon stubbed out his cigarette and sat back. "Sorry, I'm rambling. One more thing, and then I'll shut up." He picked up the bottle of St.

George and studied it exaggeratedly in the darkness. "Here it is: It's equally okay to like the cubicles in DC, or the stinky border towns with too many guns. To each her own. There's nothing wrong with liking where you are and what you're doing, and it doesn't have to be about climbing the ladder and becoming VP or president. But I'll say it once again: be intentional."

Mary-Anne sipped her own St. George. Once more it tasted homey, like the *Grande* Americano had a just a few weeks ago. She'd miss it. But then, she knew she could probably find St. George somewhere in DC. *If she decided to take Jillian's offer.*

Chapter 41

Mary-Anne looked at her watch. Almost 6:45, but there was more she wanted to talk about.

"I may have to fire someone on my team."

"Oh?" Jon sounded piqued. "What's the issue?"

Mary-Anne sighed. "The issue is that he's been stealing. Up to now he's been an excellent employee, a friend, even. I work with him almost every day. He's been invaluable."

"Local staff?" It was hard to see his expression in the gathering darkness.

"Yeah, local guy. From Addis." Mary-Anne took another long drag. *Deployment smoker*. "Anyway, we're close. Almost like friends. He's been great. Always reliable, never late, great translator. And the amount we're talking about, here—the amount that he's stealing—it's minimal. It's less than our monthly variance due to currency exchange rate gain and loss." She stared into space.

"And our policy is clear. I have to fire him. There's no option, really, under the circumstances, of offering suspension or even demotion. I get it. I really do. What he's done is against policy, clearly, and it's *wrong*, too." She suddenly felt very tired. The weight of the past weeks felt heavier in that moment than she'd ever imagined it could. "I know what has to happen, but for some reason, with this, I just can't seem to gather the strength to do it." *There, it was out.*

*

Mary-Anne sat in contemplative silence as she finished the last centimeter of the smoldering Marlboro. Any pretense of adhering to WAC's curfew was now totally abandoned. She was here for the duration of the conversation, however long it might take. Rolf would be grumpy, but he'd get over it. She was chief of party. It wasn't like she'd been out on the town. And in Dolo Ado, even in the dead of night a lone white woman could walk safely from Billy-Bob's to the INGO neighborhood.

As she crushed out the last three millimeters of her cigarette, it occurred to Mary-Anne that Jon was right. It didn't make her choices or tasks easier. But it was somehow comforting to know she was not the first to struggle with them, and even someone of Jon Langstrom's experience found them confounding. One way or the other she knew she was up to the challenges of Dolo Ado and WAC. There was one more thing she wanted to ask him. The St. George (was it the third or the fourth?) was lukewarm and flat.

"So what's this I hear about you doing some cross-border stuff in Somalia?"

"Yeah. Things aren't going so well at home. I need to make a few changes on the job front and I fear this'll be my last deployment for a while. Might as well go for the gusto."

In the near total darkness of Billy-Bob's outdoor courtyard, Mary-Anne could just tell that Jon was grinning roguishly to himself.

"Just be careful, Jon." She sounded more earnest, even to herself, than she'd intended. "Things are a bit random across the border right now."

* * *

Jon wasn't sure quite what to think. He knew that Angie was mad and fed up. He knew that she'd been holding in her anger for years now, and he cursed himself for missing the signs.

But he'd gone two weeks without even one email message. Not even a single sentence fragment like, "get home now." It was unprecedented. While the other extreme was certainly annoying—the terse daily reminders of all the home and family related events he'd been absent for and, by extension what a horrible father he was—he found Angie's virtual online silent treatment intensely nerve-wracking. The silence in his inbox screamed at him each time he checked. She'd not even acknowledged his email confirming flight details which would bring him home well in advance of Chloe's final parent-teacher conference and presentation, even taking into account the inevitable delays due to flight cancellations. This was uncharted territory, and his gut told him that this was the worst that things had been yet. More troubling still, he was uncertain that he—that *they*—would come through on the other side as a complete family unit. For all the years of annoyance at the seemingly endless email nagging from Angie while he was busy in the field, wherever that might have been, dealing with logframes and pipeline analyses and NFI distributions, the thought of being without it all suddenly terrified him.

Jon refreshed his inbox once more. *Still nothing.*

His marriage to Angie might be all but over, but there was still time to salvage fatherhood. A few mouse clicks more and he was looking at his calendar. Chloe's final parent-teacher conference was in eleven days, which meant he needed to be home in ten days at the absolute latest. Which meant that he needed to be on the morning flight out of Dolo Ado in eight days, maximum. Seven days would be better, just in case there were delays (there almost always were) and he missed a leg along the way.

He checked his notebook. There were a few life-saving meetings and a visit to Bur Amina over the next three days. Then a run across the border to Dolo Somalia that would take at least three days: one day in, one day of work on the ground with MSF, and one day back. *Inshallah,* he'd get it all done, be back in Dolo Ado for a few rounds at Billy-Bob's before catching the next morning UNHAS flight to Addis, and end up back in Boston in time for Chloe's conference.

No need to tell Mark. Mark could kiss his ass. This run back home would be at Jon's own expense. Maybe it was a token gesture. Maybe Chloe would forget about it all in six months and hate him for something else. But he'd missed too much already. No matter what fraught drama the future might hold, Jon was resolved that there was no way he was letting his daughter down *this* time.

Chapter 42

Mark adjusted his tie one last time and studied his reflection in the large mirror. He cleaned up well. It wasn't quite a white tie event, but the gala and silent auction was important—and hoity-toity—nonetheless. Boston's elite would all be there, raising paddles, silently vying for the opportunity to part with their millions (*thousands* was probably closer to the actual truth) to make life better for a small cadre of handpicked and lavishly photographed women entrepreneurs in various developing countries.

Oxfam America had a detailed manual for hosting fundraising events like this one, including a carefully scripted liturgy of how everything should flow for the evening and even a detailed sample floor plan of who should sit where. But Mark had intentionally left all of that to the "major donor" fundraising team and their interns. *He* was going to simply be present as the resident expert on "how those who worked hard for their money think." He'd look good in his suit, be reserved at first but mingle casually later, and utter pithy, enigmatic nuggets of wisdom about the simple nobility and strength of the women served by Oxfam America.

This was totally his kind of thing.

Mark checked his iPhone, more out of habit than actual necessity. There were the usual daily revenue updates, summaries of Oxfam America media coverage for the day, and an InterAction list-serve that he couldn't figure out how to unsubscribe from. He made a mental note to have his intern unsubscribe him tomorrow. There was also a Google Alert notification. His name had appeared online once in the past twenty-four hours (someone with a tulane.edu URL had posted a listing of US PVO senior staff, including him). Nothing urgent.

But the last message caught Mark's attention. He'd been copied, along with about thirty other people, on a long chain of communication between Oxfam GB and the Dolo Ado team. Apparently a Jonathon Langstrom had agreed to take on some cross-border responsibility on Somalia, in addition to his operational role in Bur Amina. Mark grunted in annoyance. Any mention of Jon Langstrom—any mention at all—made him grumpy. But then, as he checked his reflection in the mirror and adjusted his tie one last time, it occurred to him that this was a good thing.

He was about to walk into a room full of wealthy donors, and could tell them that Oxfam America had a senior staff member working on the front lines of one of the worst and probably more dangerous places on the planet. They'd eat it up. He snorted.

Jon, you crazy bastard. Maybe I'll get something worthwhile out of you yet.

* * *

It had been three days since their late evening conversation at Billy-Bob's. She'd been appropriately contrite with Rolf, and she'd made up work-wise for a morning lost to what she called "a stomach bug" but what anyone else would have called "hangover." She had two weeks still before she had to give an answer to Jillian about the position at WAC HQ. But there was one thing still hanging over her head. There was no getting out of it or putting it off any longer.

She had to fire Tekflu.

For the past few days Mary-Anne had found herself avoiding Mercy. In those instances where avoidance was simply not possible, she felt Mercy's eyes boring right through her. She'd been through enough with Mercy to know what she was thinking without asking: The longer she put it off, knowing the truth, but not dealing with Tekflu and his embezzlement, the more it was as if she condoned it. Mercy saw things in black and white, Mary-Anne understood, and while she'd always known Mercy to be a warm, kind person, she was also utterly uncompromising when it came to policy and truthfulness and the management of WAC's money. All good, Mary-Anne knew. Having someone like Mercy on one's senior team didn't necessarily make things easier, but it certainly helped to keep one honest.

Andy knew, too, and while she didn't sense the same kind of accusation from him, it was still obvious that he expected her to take action. And it wasn't just Andy. Now everyone knew. She could tell by the way they looked at her.

Even so, Mary-Anne was conflicted. She'd informed Jillian about the situation with Tekflu by email, and then called a few days later at Jillian's suggestion. "You're the chief of party, so ultimately it's your call. There is enough wiggle room in our global personnel policy to give you some breathing room if you want to keep him," she'd said. "These things are always more complicated than they appear at first blush, and while of course I have my opinion based on what you've told me, you're the one who's there. It's your team. You know the context. It's your decision. I just recommend that you decide soon and then let people know."

While Jillian's confidence and support were good to have, this also did not make Mary-Anne's decision easier. If she chose to forgive Tekflu and keep him on, she would almost certainly alienate her senior team. Giving Tekflu a pass would immediately end any friendship, trust or professional deference she currently enjoyed with Mercy, and probably Andy, too. The local staff would all hear eventually. Some would feel emboldened to maybe steal or break other rules themselves. All would respect her less. In raw accounting terms, the benefit of going through the policy and leadership contortions needed to keep an embezzling site coordinator around was too far below the cost of losing the respect of her team.

But on the other hand, Tekflu was not just an embezzling site coordinator. He was good, one of her best. Worse, and the part that made Mary-Anne wince, was the reality that they worked so closely for months now. He'd been her translator, her cultural guide, her confidante. She'd been able to be as successful as she'd been—success which had resulted in one promotion already, and a second promotion offered—because of Tekflu's solid performance as an employee and colleague. One could make the case that he'd been a vital element, instrumental even, in her recently new and improved career trajectory. It seemed at least crass and possibly immoral to discard Tekflu for a single lapse in judgment.

*

Mary-Anne sighed heavily and picked up the folder of evidence Mercy had prepared. She knew it by heart, but found herself leafing through the papers once more. Last-minute procrastination. It was all there, iron-clad. He'd been blatantly stealing. No dispute, open and shut.

The early afternoon sun was high as Mary-Anne walked the fifty meters from her container office to the admin container. Conversation ceased mid-sentence into awkward silence as Mary-Anne stepped through the door. All eyes were on her.

"Where's Tekflu? Is he out in the field today?"

"He's just back, aa'am. In the warehouse, maybe. Or in the Internet kiosk." It was Sundra, the receptionist.

"Please find him and tell him I need to talk to him. I'll be in my office."

Chapter 43

A donkey brayed loudly in the darkness. It sounded as if it was just outside her tent, but Mary-Anne knew objectively that it had to be at least a hundred meters away. In reality, it was probably farther. The dry, night desert air carried sound efficiently and made sounds seem closer than they were in fact. But the effect was the same, and Mary-Anne struggled to find sleep.

Billy-Bob's had been deserted that night. A Canadian WFP pilot, a visiting humanitarian officer from OCHA in Addis, and a few apparently local men. But no Jon. She'd texted him to see where he was and whether he was coming, but he'd not responded. After one cigarette and half a bottle of St. George, she'd simply come back to the WAC compound where she spent a melancholy hour or two checking email, arranging spreadsheets, and trolling Skype.

Now she lay in bed unable to sleep, replaying the events of the afternoon on an endless loop in her head.

Tekflu had come in as his usual warm, understated self. She'd tried to act normal through a few minutes of general pleasantries until, to her dismay, he'd read her eyes or maybe the strain in her voice and simply asked, "Madame, what is going on?"

At that Mary-Anne had simply laid out the evidence, piece by piece on the faux cherry finish locally produced desk between them. He'd taken it all in silently, stone-faced until she'd finished. She remembered looking him in the eye and saying, "Tekflu, I'm sorry but you know I'll have to fire you. World Aid Corps global personnel policy is clear. Stealing money is one of the few things that actually gets you dismissed outright, but that's where we are."

And then, "Why did you do it? Did you need the money? Do you feel that WAC owes you money? What's going on?"

Tekflu had stared at the papers on the desk for a brief moment before looking up and fixing his gaze on Mary-Anne. It was a look that she'd never seen before. Severe, stern, intense. "*You* accuse *me* of stealing…"

She'd nodded, returning his unsmiling gaze as he'd gone on.

"You come here, you and your foreign friends. You spend hundreds of thousands of dollars to instruct refugees about drinking enough water or where they should shit every day." He snorted derisively. "These people were mapping the stars and perfecting mathematics while your ancestors were painting themselves blue and dancing naked around fires in the forest."

He sat back, confident now, his voice still soft but gathering intensity. "You *children* come here to patiently explain to Ethiopians about accountability and honesty. You think we need you to help us know right from wrong. Yet you come here to 'supervise' people old enough to be your parents. My youngest daughter is your age. And you pay us the wages of common laborers, which we accept because we want to help. But you take your salary and spend it on beer and cigarettes, you get your expense-paid R&R back to America, but we don't even get bus fare back to Addis to take care of our sick parents…"

Tekflu's eyes were flashing now, and his voice had grown louder. "You close down programs at Kobe. Programs that make life better. A program whose total budget is not even equal to the salary and benefits of two expats. You take WAC's small change for yourself, and leave women and children without options because it is inconvenient for you. And *you* accuse *me* of stealing?!" He'd been leaning forward toward Mary-Anne over the desk, but suddenly he'd sat back.

Mary-Anne had looked at him, holding his gaze but feeling her confidence ebb. Incoherent, babbling thoughts filled her mind. She wanted to speak, to tell him off, but words wouldn't form. It was Tekflu who broke the silence, his voice once again soft and now eerily calm.

"You think your job is telling us how to build Sphere standard latrines or report to donors. But you don't do your real job. The job that we actually need you to do. We need you to fight for resources for projects like DANIDA in Kobe." Tekflu's tone was now pedantic, lecturing.

"You come here, you live your foreign life, you have your adventure. You work for a charitable NGO, you think you do good…"

*

The air inside the tent was stifling and the darkness felt as if it would close in and swallow her. The last donkey of the night had brayed his last hours ago. Mary-Anne could not even discern the sound of desert wind through the mesh in her tent.

And in the total silence of a desert night on the border of Somalia,

Mary-Anne heard Tekflu's final accusatory words again and again in her head, each time burning her to the core.

"You think you do good. But I see how you are and how you treat others. Maybe you *do* do some good things. But I can see that *you are not a good person.*"

Chapter 44

It had been a hard day.

After everything else, and despite what he'd objectively done, Mary-Anne felt guilty for having fired Tekflu. She'd avoided the other WAC staff that morning as she quickly—*too* quickly—ate her greasy eggs and *injera*, and slurped down a single mocha without lingering. They'd given her space, too, but she felt their sideways looks and heard their conversations grow awkwardly silent when she walked past. Simply walking into her container office had felt like returning to the scene of a crime.

But she'd made it through. The admin staff had been sober and silent at first, but by the end of the day seemed to be back to their ordinary selves, at least around Mary-Anne. Andy was out in the field with Rolf, checking out possible distribution sites in Bur Amina. There'd been a slew of allegedly urgent emails from WAC DC, each one crying out for attention, or at the very least acknowledgement of receipt. It hadn't been fun, but she'd hunkered down and muscled through. It was a good day to hide away in her office and plow through some of the admin work on her desk.

Late in the afternoon, Mercy had come by under the pretense of a preliminary quarterly statement that needed review. "You did the right thing, ma'am." Mercy's eyes were soft, her voice calm and assured. "I had nothing against Tekflu personally, but he'd been stealing, and the rules are the rules. I'm sure he can get another job elsewhere."

Mary-Anne had only nodded miserably. Mercy was right, but it didn't make her *feel* right. All she could think about were Tekflu's final words: *"You are not a good person."*

As she closed down her laptop computer for the evening, and then changed out of her WAC branded T-shirt into a plain, unbranded, black T-shirt, she was struck with the irony of it all.

When she'd left a malnourished little girl to die in the arms of her refugee mother, it had been Tekflu who'd reassured her that it was okay, this one mistake maybe wasn't really a mistake, that she was a good person. But then, when faced with objective evidence of Tekflu's misdeeds and after having taken the only viable course of action—a course of action that *Tekflu himself* knew perfectly well she could not avoid taking—he'd accused her of not being a good person, of herself being guilty of stealing by virtue of how she lived her life.

As Mary-Anne climbed into the WAC Land cruiser and navigated over the red, pothole-ridden road to Billy-Bob's, she hoped with all her heart that Jon Langstrom would be there that evening.

*

She heard Jon sigh and then take another drag. The cigarette glowed bright red, then dimmed again before he spoke. "Yeah, it's never easy."

She'd told him everything. Spilled it. Told him all about firing Tekflu before the first St. George was drunk or the first Marlboro smoked. She'd seen him, alone at the corner table—their table—beneath the tree, and after a hasty palm to Billy-Bob's forehead, she'd sat down without even asking if the seat was free.

Jon had smiled and quietly ordered more St. George as she talked. And then the story was out and he was talking. Just the sound of his voice was reassuring.

"It's never easy. We often naïvely assume that it's all black and white, good versus evil, and that we and 'our' beneficiaries and 'our' local staff are on the good side."

Mary-Anne felt herself nodding. Jon was right. She heard his voice continue. "We all blur the professional boundaries. We think that because we're here to work with 'the community' or something that we have to be friends with everybody. We're lulled, maybe by our naïveté, into thinking that being friends with our local staff somehow both makes us more effective as humanitarians and also puts us on some kind of moral higher ground. How many aid workers have you known who thought they were better than others because they had more local friends? And then it comes back to bite us. We're unprepared when they turn out to be… you know, as *human* as everyone else."

"Truth is, we're all on a continuum. We're all as capable of dishonesty or graft or evil as anyone else. What's even sadder is that there are times when the industry itself brings this out in us."

"How do you mean?" Mary-Anne's brow furrowed as she struggled to wrap her head around the idea.

"Somewhere I read—can't remember where, exactly. Anyway, it

was a description of aid workers as missionaries, mercenaries, mystics, and misfits. And the longer I stick around, the more I see it." Jon looked around for the waiter, and then motioned for two more bottles of St. George. Mary-Anne could already tell that she'd probably miss curfew. Again.

"The problem is that when people use that phrase, they're usually describing where we've come from. They mean it's what we were before we accidentally found our way into humanitarian work. But I think they're wrong. I think it's about what we *become*. It's a description of states of being toward which humanitarians gravitate."

Mary-Anne was suddenly on the edge of her chair, hanging on every word.

Jon Langstrom's tone was matter-of-fact. "We all start out with these altruistic intentions. We're going to save the world, or at least a little corner of it. We're going to do everything properly, we're on the 'right' side of all the issues all the time. We're self-styled warriors for truth and light. That's the 'missionaries' part."

Two more bottles of St. George appeared and Jon held one out to her. Mary-Anne took it although somewhere in the back of her head she knew she'd probably regret doing so. But for now she was in the mood to drink a bit more and listen to Jon Langstrom bequeath his wisdom. She took a sip and said, "Go on."

Jon took a sip himself and nodded.

"So, we're all on the side of right and light, warriors for the poor, and all of that. *Then* we get into it a little way and we see that it works by calculus, not math. We see what goes into the sausage. We see that for all of our dialogic, participatory, multi-stakeholder, community-led, bottom-up, embrace-and-empower-everything-local ideals and maybe even practice, that the decisions that truly matter are made elsewhere and on the basis of other things entirely. We come to understand that we have to play hardball. If we stick around long enough, we usually get to the place where we're willing to fight for a program or strategy we think is the best one, even when it means throwing a colleague under the bus. There are times and places in this industry where, for all of our professed love of all humanity, a win-win is just not possible. We choose this poor community rather than that one because the donor wants this one, not because the needs are greater. We sacrifice little bits of who we are and what we believe in the service of some alleged bigger picture. Then the little bits get bigger. We become extreme. We're willing to execute more tactical bad in the name of an increasingly elusive and vague strategic 'greater good.' For some, it becomes an 'ends justify means' thing. But one way or the other, we become *mercenary*."

He exhaled sharply. It was almost totally dark in the courtyard at Billy-Bob's now. Without waiting for a response from Mary-Anne, Jon continued.

"That altruism, or what we took as altruism that drove us to this line of work isn't a bad thing. We want the world to be better. We can envision a more just or a less *un*just world. Some of us become hyper cause-oriented. We delve into the theory or maybe the technical nuts and bolts of practice in a particular sector. And in that sense some of us become mystics."

"But as in everything else, there are trade-offs. There is always the danger of spending so long immersed in the language and culture of humanitarian aid that anything outside feels incomprehensible. We spend so long focused on a particular way of thinking about issues, like reproductive health or third world hunger, that we lose our ability to engage with those who see the issues differently. Or, and this is the even greater danger, we lose the ability to really engage with those who simply haven't thought about them at all: the ordinary people in our families and social circles."

"It's a paradox, but we can spend so long out here that we begin to treat home like we treat 'the field.' Which is to say that we become perpetual temporary interlopers who embrace our 'not from here' status as an excuse to see everything clinically and still always have a way out. Our visa is about to expire and we have to go home or to the next mission. Or we have another mission and have to leave home…"

Jon stopped mid-sentence and paused, as if weighing his words.

"We become misfits."

Chapter 45

"No way, man!" Jon Langstrom gesticulated stridently. "There's no way I can stay on."

He'd been in Somalia for two days now. The rental agreement for the field office was done, the office itself was mostly cleaned, and the first staff hired. By next week, the place would be repainted and there'd be V-SAT. With any luck, the furniture would be there by this weekend. Now they were at a remote clinic site about seventy kilometers farther inside south-central Somali. He wanted—had—to leave *now*, but Henri, the MSF site manager, was just being needy.

"We need someone to manage the distributions," he was saying. "Sure, I have doctors, but I need someone who knows field ops." But Jon knew he could not stay another night. Even at this hour he was pushing it. It was getting late and he needed to hit the road. Forget those last few rounds of St. George at Billy-Bob's tonight. At this point, all he cared about was catching the UNHAS Dash-8 to Addis in the morning. If he accomplished anything at all this month, it would be getting back to Boston in time for his daughter's parent-teacher conference.

"Look, Henri, I've given you the field manual for distributions. It's not rocket science. You can train your local staff. I'll send you the .pdf when I get back to Dolo Ado. But I *have* to get back to Ethiopia today— *tonight*." Jon looked at the sun. Still an hour, maybe an hour and a half of daylight left. It was clearly against organizational policy to drive alone in Somalia. And at this hour... Aengus was going to have a cow. But Aengus would get over it eventually, whereas Angie would not. More to the point, there was no way he could let his daughter down again.. If he left now he could make it before the border closed.

*

An hour later, to his great annoyance, Jon was just pouring a jerry-can worth of gasoline into the battered Oxfam Land Cruiser that Aengus had assigned to him. *Still in the middle of nowhere*. He'd have to put the pedal down. Henri was grumpy but that would just have to be.

Grumpy never killed anyone, so far as Jon knew. He climbed into the driver's seat and turned the key in the ignition.

* * *

"Ali!" It was Hamid. "Are you coming tonight? The Arab says we need to take more vehicles for the *jihad*."

Ali looked at the sun. One more hour and it would be dark. He looked over at his brother Ismael. *Ismael could watch the goats.* He ran quickly to the large rock where they'd laid their jackets, a few pieces of bread, and Ali's precious AK-47. The weapon felt heavy and good in his hands.

"All right, let's go!"

* * *

Jon looked at his watch for the third time in ten minutes. The scrubby, rocky terrain of Somalia flew past the window as Foreigner ("Worlds Apart") blared through the small speakers over the road noise. The border would close in less than one hour, and if he missed crossing tonight, he'd almost certainly miss the morning UNHAS flight. And if he missed the morning UNHAS flight, there was no guarantee that he'd be able to catch the afternoon UNHAS flight. And if *that* happened… Jon shook his head instinctively.

Missing the morning UNHAS flight was simply not an option. He *had* to cross over into Ethiopia tonight. He scanned the horizon ahead looking for the telltale cloud of buzzards over the Dolo Ado dump, signaling his approach to the border. Nothing. The border was still kilometers away.

The mostly flat, mostly open rocky desert had slowly given way to a few gentle hills. Up ahead, in the distance, Jon could see that the road curved sharply and then descended into a low draw with high bushes on one side and large rocks on the other. Somehow, somewhere in the back of his mind, a red alarm light went off, but there was no way around. He had to continue on this road.

He slowed to take the curve, and as he drove carefully down the incline he thought he saw movement in the bushes off to his right. But it was twilight now, and he couldn't be sure. Maybe just a stray camel or donkey.

A loud *bang!* confirmed that what he'd seen wasn't just a stray camel. Another *bang*, and he heard the *thunk* of a bullet against the side of camel. Another *bang*, and he heard the *thunk* of a bullet against the side of the car, toward the rear on the right side. Up ahead, Jon saw indistinct movement, then suddenly the outline of a person, a man, standing in the road pointing a rifle at him, maybe one hundred meters ahead. There were flashes and the sound of bullets hitting the Land Cruiser, riddling the windshield.

More bangs. *Rapid fire.*

Jon could only see one person—looked like a teenager—firing at him, but it sounded like there were more, and he could hear rounds striking the back of the Land Cruiser, too.

He'd been through the usual Red-R hostile environment survival trainings and taken the online courses. But in the brief instant it took Jonathon Langstrom to comprehend what was happening, another three rounds had hit the already tired Land Cruiser. Almost without thinking, he flipped the headlight into "high beam," spun the wheel so that the Land Cruiser was on a course for collision with the figure in the road, and pushed the accelerator forcefully against the floor.

Over the years Jon had said many times to Angie and to others that he'd walk into live fire for his family. And while he'd been dead serious, he had never believed that it would actually be necessary. Or that it would go down quite like this. But in his mind, he repeated the words again, subconsciously, involuntarily, ritualistically as he gripped the wheel and stood with all his weight on the gas pedal. There was no way he was going to miss Chloe's conference.

He was almost upon the person firing. It *was* a teenager. Or a young man. A thin, black Somali dressed for the desert, pointing an automatic weapon at him. Jon could see the muzzle flashing and a shower of spent shell casings ejecting from the breech.

A bullet smashed through the windscreen and whizzed past his head. Another loud bang, then a hot, piercing pain in his shoulder. *Then another*. A wild series of images flashed through Jon's mind in a nanosecond: a tree-lined street in the heartland, Laos, Kosovo…his wedding day, Angie walking down the aisle toward him, a tiny baby—Chloe—in a wooden crib, Ampara after the tsunami, a high, red, billowing cloud of dust, blocking out the sun, Mark's angry face, Mary-Anne in the flickering light of Billy-Bob's courtyard…

Then darkness.

Chapter 46

-- FOR EXTERNAL RELEASE --

Oxfam America mourns the loss of Mr. Jonathon Langstrom. Mr. Langstrom was killed by armed bandits inside Somalia near the Ethiopian border town of Dolo Ado, late yesterday. He was on assignment as part of the Oxfam Federated Network's response to the growing crisis in the Horn of Africa.

Local Somali authorities confirm the attack on Mr. Langstrom was carried out by local bandits and was not ideologically motivated. No other Oxfam personnel were involved or injured in the incident.

At the time of his death Mr. Langstrom was serving in the role of relief director for Oxfam America, a position he held for nearly ten years.

Our thoughts and condolences go out to the family of Jonathon Langstrom at this difficult time.

-- ENDS --

* * *

187 aid workers were injured, kidnapped, or killed in 2012.

Source: Humanitarian Outcomes 2012, *Aid Worker Security Database*, https://aidworkersecurity.org/

Chapter 47

Mulu Alem smiled to himself. This was turning out better than he could ever have imagined.

Instead of throwing his career into the toilet as he'd anticipated, opening Bur Amina was turning everything he touched into pure gold. He was hosting visiting dignitaries from the government and receiving briefings from senior UN staff. His team was being expanded, and they were giving him more budget to work with.

He looked down at the résumé in his hands. It looked good. The candidate had all the right skills and qualifications. He had the right education from the right mix of foreign and Ethiopian institutions, and he'd spent over a year working for a respected INGO right here in Dolo Ado. Best of all, Mulu Alem couldn't help but notice, the candidate also happened to be his very own brother-in-law.

There was a soft knock on the door.

"Come in." Mulu Alem smiled broadly as the door opened, then stood to his feet, his hand extended in greeting.

"Tekflu, my brother! Come. Sit down. I heard you'd left World Aid Corps. Good, good. It's time for you to come back over to ARRA."

Tekflu smiled as he sat down.

Chapter 48

The mid-morning sun cast warm dusty rays on the scuffed wooden floor. Mary-Anne sighed, set down a peach box full of books, or maybe it was shoes, and pushed a stray strand of dirty-blond hair back from her forehead. Not even noon and she was already tired.

Her mind wandered back over the past weeks. The frenetic startup at Bur Amina, the traumatic climax somewhere in the desert between Dolo Somalia and Dolo Ado—she felt a tear well up—and the pain and then numbness that followed. The news of Jon Langstrom's death had shaken the entire NGO community in Dolo Ado, but Mary-Anne (not surprisingly) had taken it the hardest. She'd been physically ill, unable to leave her tent for two full days. After that, even though physically at work, in the office, she'd been distracted and unable to focus for weeks.

Jon's tragic death had broken something in her. The decision to accept (or not) Jillian Scott's offer had tortured her before. But after, it had seemed like the only option. There was no way she'd ever stay on in Dolo Ado after Jon... after Somalia. She'd finally accepted Jillian's offer almost casually, days before the deadline via text message despite having three fastidiously crafted emails in her DRAFTS folder.

Those very last days in Dolo Ado seemed like a blur now. Last field visits, an awkward courtesy exit meeting with Mulu Alem at ARRA, brief farewells with acquaintances in the INGO and UN community. Her main internal handover meeting was less about physically handing over boxes of documents and more about brain-dumping to her poor, clueless incoming replacement about how to manage particular personalities, and then taking him on a tour of the NGO neighborhood and introducing him to Billy-Bob's. He was an energetic young man, fresh out of his MA in international development studies. By Mary-Anne's estimation, he was far too green to know how far in over his head he really was, all the while trading far too heavily on six months in The Gambia as a Peace Corps volunteer and another six in Rome as an intern in the communication department of WFP. She wondered how long he'd last before washing out, getting fired, or simply being killed by one of his own colleagues for starting one too many stories with, "Back when I was with Peace Corps in The Gambia…"

Her very last day had been anti-climactically bland. There'd been a small party the night before, and the WAC team had dutifully turned up, bought her rounds of St. George and wished her well. Even Aengus had come over, given her a European kiss on the cheek and congratulated her on the new job.

Then that last morning, it was business as usual for everyone but her as she crammed the last pair of dusty cargo pants into her tattered duffel before tossing it in the back of the WAC Hilux. Rolf had hugged her stiffly after logging back into inventory her WAC local SIM card phone and radio and confirming when, exactly, she'd be out of Ethiopia (and therefore technically no longer his "jurisdiction"). She'd not even seen Andy that morning—he'd left early to go to Bur Amina. And she'd received only a quick hug and 'good-bye' from Mercy ("So sorry, Mary-Anne… I'm soooo busy… budgets, spreadsheets… you know. Mesfin will take you to the airstrip. See you on Skype! 'Friend' me on Facebook?").

Odd, she thought, that for as frequently as aid workers bemoan the fragmented and disconnected nature of their personal lives, at the same time, they so often treat as casually inconsequential those rare in-person relationships. For as close as she might have grown to Mercy, Andy, Mesfin, Aasiya, and even Tekflu, she'd left Dolo Ado in much the same way as she'd come: a managed detail on a logs form, anonymous and unsung. Just another dusty aid worker, skin tanned and clothes faded by the desert sun, clustered along with the others around a UNHAS Dash-8 parked on a parched, red riverbed.

There'd been a series of flights, followed by a few days off. Followed by another few days of frantically sifting through a small storage unit in Louisville, throwing into a rented truck the books, the shoes, the random lamps and cushions and knick-knacks she hadn't even touched since before Haiti. She'd couch-surfed with friends in DC for almost a week before finding a small row house on Capitol Hill that she and Jean-Philippe could afford.

Back to the present.

Tomorrow she'd be at work by 8:00 a.m, 8:30 at the latest. Jillian was expecting her. It would be the start of a long week at the head of a long month of orientation. There would be the usual forms to sit and fill out, process to go through with HR and building security. Then there would be a string of meetings upon meetings, in which she'd meet what would feel like an endless stream of new colleagues, some of whom, she knew, would eventually schmooze her, and some of whom would become close friends for real. Others would resent her—the new face, fresh in from "the field," taking a job they'd thought should be theirs—and others still would turn out to be sworn enemies over some difference of opinion or perceived slight as yet uncommitted. But of course in the "meet and greet" sessions, they'd all be cordial and smiling and positively *thrilled* to welcome someone of her background and experience into such an important role.

Just last night she'd attended an informal happy hour at Birch & Barley at the invitation of several new colleagues-to-be. It hadn't been un-fun *per se*, but she felt like she didn't belong, standing there at the crowded bar, sipping over-priced Stella Artois, and straining to follow conversation shouted over the ambient din. She'd caught herself feigning interest in discussions about college basketball, or the new World Bank study, or office gossip just to be nice. Everyone was friendly, just as she knew they'd all be in the office come tomorrow, but even so she'd found herself struggling not just to find things to say to them, but struggling to want to find things to say to them. She'd begged off before 9:30 p.m. on the pretext of being "tired from moving."

Through the open window, she could see that the trees were beginning to bud. Spring time in Washington, DC. In a few days, the city would be wreathed in lovely pink cherry blossoms. She could hear the sounds of children laughing on the sidewalk outside.

For all of his promises about going where she went, Jean-Philippe was at least two months out. He had a consultancy in Bujumbura, then a few weeks of writing in Chiang Rai. After that, he'd planned to visit his family in France, and after *that* climb the Matterhorn with a friend from university. But Mary-Anne didn't mind too much. After the drama of the past few months, the prospect of again being an anonymous new face in a new place felt strangely appealing. She looked forward to properly decorating the lovely Capitol Hill row house with him. He *was* coming and she truly looked forward to his arrival, to being with him. But for now she also welcomed the chance to ease into the next phase for a few weeks. Alone.

She climbed the narrow stairs to the small master bedroom, walked through and then out onto the small balcony. As she leaned on the low, wrought-iron fence around the balcony, Mary-Anne suddenly found herself craving a cigarette. She never smoked in the U.S., but for this morning, for reasons she couldn't yet describe, she felt like it. Mary-

Anne sighed deeply. The rituals of being a guest, of renting a house, of riding the DC Metro, or even of simply going to happy hour with her new colleagues all felt strange and foreign. She could read every word, understand every conversation, but still she felt out of place and foreign. On one hand it was hard. Fitting in, "belonging," took energy and was wearing.

But on the other hand, and perhaps more to the point, she also found herself not really caring. Not caring what people might think, not caring that her points of cultural reference were two years old, and therefore all but obsolete in fast-paced North America. Not caring that in but a few short months in Dolo Ado, she'd managed to embody each of the four humanitarian states of being that Jon had described, the last time she'd ever seen him.

Missionary. Mercenary. Mystic. *And now misfit.*

As Mary-Anne fumbled with her lighter and the last Marlboro in the battered pack, she remembered what Jon had once said about his job at HQ being the toughest deployment he'd ever done.

She exhaled heavily into the morning air. In an intensely mystical moment, the light of a warm spring sun in the tree branches suddenly evoked Billy-Bob's. She missed Jon. She missed Dolo Ado. It must have been a car honking, but if she hadn't known better, Mary-Anne would have sworn she heard a donkey bray mournfully in the general direction of Union Station. She took a long drag instinctively. And as she exhaled again, in a brief moment of complete lucidity, it occurred to Mary-Anne that in an odd way, the universe had suddenly aligned itself.

Deployment smoker.

TO BE CONTINUED…

The Usual Disclaimers & Caveats

Missionary, Mercenary, Mystic, Misfit is a work of fiction. All characters and situations portrayed in this story are fictitious. Any similarity between any of the characters in this story and real-life people, or between situations in this story and real-life situations, is purely coincidental and entirely unintended.

While of course the setting for this story (an interagency refugee response in the refugee camp complex of Dolo Ado) is real, the story itself is not. For the sake of authenticity, I have tried to recreate the feel of the place, made references to real events, and incorporated references to real NGOs and local agencies. Fortunately, there really is a Billy-Bob's Restaurant with a goat who greets the guests (although I hear lately that the name may have changed to "The Dolo Ado Sheraton"). And the main contextual event in the plot, the opening of a new camp at Bur Amina, has obviously happened for real.

This said, the actions and interactions described in this story are fictionalized. So far as I am aware, there is no real-life NGO by the name of "World Aid Corps" (WAC). As far as I know, there was never a coordination meeting in Bur Amina at which the representatives from GOAL and NRC got mad at each other. And, of course, almost no INGO would allow its staff to drive alone it inside Somalia near the border of Ethiopia.

The characters are similarly made up. Mary-Anne, Jonathon Langstrom, Jillian Scott, Mark, Mulu Alem, Mercy, Mesfin, Tekflu, Aasiya, Andy, Brandon, Rolf the security manager, and of course the dreamy, piercing-green-eyed Jean-Philippe are all composites. Any and all similarities between any of the characters in this book and real people, whether in the Dolo Ado refugee response or elsewhere, are entirely coincidental and not intentional. I've been around the aid world for quite some time, I know a lot of people, and I've seen a lot go down. Tempting as it might be to believe otherwise, trust me: this story is not about *you*.

About The Author

J. is a full-time professional humanitarian worker with more than twenty years of experience in the aid industry. He currently holds a real aid world day job at a real humanitarian organization. He writes about humanitarian work in his spare time with a personal computer because he enjoys it and because he believes that there is not nearly enough popular culture out there specifically for aid workers.

Many have asked how J. *can ever find the time*? (Most aid workers take great pride in reminding as many people as possible that *they* are much *too busy* for such endeavors so frivolous as writing fiction). His response is that everyone, even aid workers, finds the time for what's important to them. Some play fantasy football, some get good at yoga, and some put cute pictures of kittens on Twitter. J. writes humanitarian fiction.

In a previous blogosphere life, J. wrote a blog about aid work called *Tales From the Hood*. These days he is half-owner/blogger of the uber-awesome *Stuff Expat Aid Workers Like* (stuffexpataidworkerslike.com) and one-third owner of *AidSource: The Humanitarian Social Network* (aidsource.ning.com).

Follow the author on twitter: @talesfromthhood
Follow the author on Facebook: https://www.facebook.com/Tales-FrometheHood

"Like" *Missionary, Mercenary, Mystic, Misfit* on Facebook: https://www.facebook.com/MisMercMysMis

J.'s first foray into high-stakes world of humanitarian fiction was the aid world cult classic, *Disastrous Passion: A Humanitarian Romance Novel*.

Missionary, Mercenary, Mystic, Misfit is his second book.

Read J.'s latest book, the non-fiction, non-memoir, *Letters Left Unsent*

Made in the USA
Lexington, KY
07 August 2017